New York Times & *USA Today* Bestselling Author

CYNTHIA
EDEN

CHAPTER ONE

"I want to know everything about her." Dexter "Dex" Ryan put his hands on his hips and stared at the computer screen. Or rather, at the woman on the screen. "What she eats for breakfast. How she likes her coffee. Her favorite color. What makes her laugh. What makes her cry. What she fears—"

"Uh, Dex?" Antony Kyle paused with his hands curled over the keyboard. "Is this...personal? Because, I mean, I don't know if we should really be using agency time to spy on your new girlfriend."

Dex smiled and clamped a hand around Antony's shoulder. A very hard clamp. Then he leaned in close to the other man's ear. "Have you forgotten?" he murmured. "I am the agency. So if I say that I want you to investigate someone, if I say I want to know every single thing she does and every secret she has...then, obviously, it's agency business."

"Obviously," Antony replied, but his voice said he was far, far from convinced. "And you wanted *me* to do this job for you instead of one of your normal techs because...?"

"Because I trust you. One hundred percent." He did. There were only a handful of people in this world that he truly trusted, and Antony was one of those select few. A top operative, Antony's tech skills had come in handy more times than Dex could count. By day, the man ran a huge, billion-dollar gaming business. But by night...

He works for me. "Now come on, man, stop dicking around. I know you can get the job done for me."

Antony's shoulders stiffened. "Well, of course, I can." His fingers flew. "It's *me*. But I just wanted to state—on the record—that I wasn't down with helping you stalk your new girlfriend."

"I am not stalking..." He stopped and sucked in a deep breath. "Someone is feeling pissy tonight."

"Someone was pulled away from a date to handle your shit, so yep, pissy. Right here." The light from the screen reflected off Antony's glasses as he leaned forward.

Dex lifted his hand from Antony's shoulder even as his gaze tracked to the screen Antony viewed. Hell, the room was full of computer screens. After all, this location was the best surveillance and data collection center on the East Coast. Completely off the books. Completely contained.

Completely his.

"Lacey Amari is an operative for Wilde." Now Antony was pulling up data left and right. "She's worked there for approximately eight months."

Dex already knew all about her involvement with the security and protection firm—that involvement was what had brought her onto his radar in the first place.

"Parents are deceased." Another box opened on the screen nearest Antony. "Jason and Elora Amari died four years ago but..." He frowned. Tapped more. A new box popped up on the screen. "Jason Amari wasn't listed on Lacey's birth certificate. No father's name was listed."

Dex's arms crossed over his chest. "You haven't said anything to surprise me yet, Antony." Frustration rolled in his voice. "I wanted more from you. Why do I pay you the big bucks if you can't impress me?"

"You *don't* pay me the big bucks. I make that on my own." Antony glanced back at him. "I've had like...two minutes to work. Two minutes. You can't expect miracles."

His eyebrows shot up. "Of course, I can. They are the only thing I expect."

Antony's lips parted. He didn't speak. Just stared. Then, finally... "Do you have any idea how hard it is for me to work when you are breathing down my neck? Like, literally, *breathing* on me."

A long sigh broke from Dex. "Fine. Don't appreciate me."

"I do not. Especially when I'm trying to stalk—I mean, research—your new girlfriend."

"Not fucking stalking," he growled. It wasn't. It was intel gathering. A normal tactical routine. Antony knew this crap. "You have an hour. Get me good intel. Then dig even deeper and get me *better* intel." He inclined his head toward the screens. "But before I go, I want to know exactly where Lacey Amari is."

"But...but how am I supposed—"

Dex rattled off her phone number. "Get her location from that. We both know you can." Seriously? Was Antony going to play amateur on him?

Looking disgruntled, Antony quickly obtained her location. He even did a step better and hacked into the security feed at the club where Lacey was dancing.

When the feed appeared, Dex's body tensed. Lacey was dancing way too close to some jackass who had his hands clamped on her hips. What. The. Hell?

"She likes to dance," Antony noted dryly. "So I discovered something else about your target. She appears to be a, um, very good dancer. She's limber. Flexible. Look at how she can undulate her hips and—"

"Fuck off, Antony."

"Yes, consider me fucking off."

Dex's gaze narrowed on the security feed. Lacey's dark hair was loose and tumbling over her shoulders. Her jeans fit her legs like a second skin, and the sexy, white top she wore slid off one shoulder. The dick dancing with her had his hands way too close to Lacey's pert ass.

I will be breaking those hands.

He forced his back teeth to unclench. "In an hour, I expect you to have intel I can use."

"Uh...if you could be more specific—"

"I already have been specific." There was no audio with the feed, just a visual but the music in the club had obviously changed. The couple started gliding together slowly. Unacceptable. "I want to know everything about her. Good, bad, and all the secret parts in between." He turned on his heel. "Now excuse me, but I have to make sure that bastard gets his hands off my fiancée."

"Oh, sweet hell." Antony's shocked voice followed behind him. "That poor woman is engaged to you?"

He paused at the door and looked back. Antony's horrified stare was on him. Dex tossed the guy a grin. "Not yet, but before the night is over, she will be."

***

"Another dance?"

Lacey Amari forced a smile to her lips. She loved dancing. It was the perfect way to let off steam after a long day, and her day had been *killer*. Emphasis on the killer part. She'd ended her protection detail for a Broadway actress by stopping the stalker who wanted to attack the woman. The takedown had been textbook, but facing off with someone who had a gun aimed at her had left Lacey battling the aftereffects of a vicious adrenaline rush.

Dancing usually helped her with the rush.

But the fellow before her—Aidan something— was getting a little too close. She could tell by the look in his eyes—and the expression on his face— that he thought the night was going to end with more than just dancing.

He was wrong. She didn't pick up strangers in bars. With her line of work, she knew exactly how dangerous the world could be. No, when it came to lovers, she was very, very selective.

And that was probably why she was in the middle of a dry streak.

Aidan's fingers trailed over her side. "The band is about to play something slow and romantic. I'd sure love to have you in my arms again while we—"

"First, stop touching her." The voice was low, hard, and coming from right behind Aidan.

Lacey couldn't help but gasp because that voice—oh, no. It was familiar to her. And not in a good way. More in the please-God-let-me-be-wrong kind of way.

"Second, you're wasting your time. She's not sleeping with you. You're playing a million miles out of your league, and you just need to be grateful for the time that she spent with you. Call that a win and drag your ass over to someone else."

Lacey knew she wasn't wrong about the voice. It was definitely familiar. The kind of voice that would haunt your nightmares.

Aidan had stiffened. His gaze was on her face as the speaker delivered his flat announcement. Aidan's hold tightened on her.

"So, you're still touching her, and I did warn you about that. It was my *first* point—"

Aidan spun to face the other man. "Who the hell are you?"

"I'm the guy telling you to get lost." A shrug. "And you're the guy who needs to listen."

Aidan puffed up his chest in that annoying way men could do as he headed—with his chest out—forward. "Like I need to listen to anything you say!"

"Um, Aidan," she began. This wouldn't end well. Aidan was completely outmatched, and he didn't even realize it.

Because he was facing off against Dexter Ryan. She'd been right about the unforgettable voice, and now that she could see his face...

Hello, Dex.

Tall, broad shouldered. Carrying a relaxed air of power. With kind of a...screw-the-world attitude clinging to him. He wore battered jeans and a faded t-shirt. He didn't look at all like the type of man who managed one of the world's biggest spy operations.

But he was.

"Your hair is darker," she blurted. It was. She was sure it had been a bit blonder the last time—

"You know me, sweetheart," Dex murmured without looking her way. His focus was on Aidan. "I am a chameleon."

Yes, because the super spy looked just like all the other guys in that club. He didn't look like the most dangerous man in the room, even though she knew with utter certainty that he was. She was sure that Dex could have Aidan crying on the floor in less time than it would take for her to blink.

"Sweetheart?" Aidan fired a glance back at her. "You involved with this jerk?"

Involved? Ha. "Not in a million years." Her answer was automatic. She stayed away from trouble. She didn't get into a relationship with it.

Dex smiled at her.

His smile made her stomach feel a little odd. It was a sweet smile. Almost tender.

Then Dex winked at Lacey. "Don't make promises that you don't intend to keep."

She hadn't made a promise. She'd flatly said "not in a million years" because it was a true statement and—

"You're still here." Dex waved vaguely toward Aidan. The band had started to play another of their slow, romantic tunes. "This is getting old," Dex added. "You're between me and my lady, and I need to talk to her so...I'll ask nicely just one more time. Ahem. Get the fuck out of my way."

That was asking nicely? Lacey could only shake her head. What would it sound like when he *wasn't* being nice?

A snarl escaped Aidan. He jabbed his index finger into Dex's chest. "Listen, asshole...."

Uh, oh. "Um, Aidan, you don't need to—"

Too late. Dex had grabbed him—or rather, he'd grabbed the finger that Aidan had shoved into his chest. Dex did a quick twist, applied what she knew had to be wicked pressure, and had Aidan on his knees, with his hand locked behind his back in seemingly the next second. "Didn't your parents ever tell you," Dex asked in his cold, emotionless voice, "that you don't put your hands on other people?"

"*Dex!*" Lacey surged forward. "Let him go. Now."

Dex looked up at her. Smiled once more. And kept right on holding Aidan's hand behind his back. "You look lovely tonight. Is that a new top?"

He wasn't serious. But, yes, it was new. "Let go of his hand before you break the man's fingers."

Dex actually pouted. His lips curled down as he said, "Am I the kind of fellow that would do something like that?"

"You are exactly the kind of bastard that would do something like that."

He shook his head. "You wound me. I was simply defending myself."

She rolled her eyes. "Let him go."

"L-let go..." Aidan gasped.

"Fine." Dex immediately freed him and stepped back.

Aidan rose slowly, a bit shakily, and glared at Lacey.

Hold up. Why is he glaring at me? She'd defended him! If it hadn't been for her, he would have still been trapped by Dex.

"Your ex is an asshole!" Aidan spat. He fisted his fingers. "And you are not worth my time."

Her jaw dropped.

Aidan began to storm away.

Dex casually stepped into his path. "Hello."

Aidan flinched.

"If you will remember, I was counting points with you earlier. I think I started with my first point, then my second, and I feel I must end our conversation with our third point." He smiled. "A very important point that you should never, ever forget."

Uh, oh. She knew his smiles were dangerous things.

"Third..." Dex tilted his head and let his gray gaze sweep over Aidan. "She is worth far, far more than you are ever capable of giving. That's why she was out of your league from the beginning.

She just wanted to dance, not to fuck, and if you ever give her attitude like that again—if you ever look at her with that much rage in your eyes again—you'll be sorry. You want to fight someone, come at me. Only me."

But Aidan wasn't in the mood to fight. He was in the mood to get out of there, fast. He shouldered his way through the crowd and didn't look back.

"You have terrible taste in men." Dex watched Aidan leave. "I mean absolutely horrible. What in the world were you thinking?"

She tapped her right foot.

His gaze slowly swung back to her. His smile came again and lit his eyes. "Want to dance?"

"You are not serious."

He waved toward the dance floor and all the cuddled-up-close couples. "This is my speed, and I'd love to dance with you."

Unbelievable. She shook her head and marched past him. She hadn't seen Dex in weeks—a situation she was very grateful for—and now he'd just popped back up to ruin her night for shits and giggles—

His hand wrapped around her wrist. His touch seemed to send a surge of pure heat all the way through her body. She sucked in a sharp breath as her heart lurched. *What in the heck?*

Lacey swung toward him.

"I'm a pretty good dancer. Maybe you should see my moves before you reject me."

"Unnecessary." She yanked her hand from his grip. He'd been very careful with her, touching her gently, but she swore that she could still feel the imprint of his fingers on her skin. "I can reject you just fine without seeing or knowing anything else. Now, good night."

With that, she turned on her high heel and stomped for the door. It had been a long day, a tiring night, and the adrenaline would be plunging from her system soon. Once she got home, she'd want to crash. Maybe she'd enjoy some ice cream, then a long night in bed while cozied up in her favorite jammies.

The bouncer gave her a wave as she exited, and, once outside, Lacey turned to the left. Cabs lined the street, but she wasn't going to take one. No sense in doing that, not when her apartment was just a few blocks away. Her spine stayed straight and her gaze darted around to scan the area as she—

Lacey stilled. Huffed out a breath. "Do you enjoy following women?"

The faint rustle of a footstep reached her ears. "I was merely making sure you arrived home safely."

She whirled to confront him. "I'm more than capable of looking after myself, Dex. I can handle any trouble that comes my way."

He studied her as he closed in, and she couldn't help but feel a wee bit like a bug who'd just been caught in a spider's sticky web. "You can handle trouble," he agreed. "That's one of the many things I like about you."

Her head tilted back as she stared up at him. Her mother had been a dancer, and Lacey had gotten her slight build and petite height. She'd always been envious of her taller friends, but she'd clocked out at five-foot-two, and she'd learned to deal with being perceived as fragile. Delicate. At first, she'd hated the way others viewed her. Then she'd decided that if they underestimated her, that was their problem.

And her advantage.

"In fact," Dex continued in his rumbling voice, "your ability to handle trouble is the reason I sought you out tonight."

"And here I thought you just liked to dance the night away." No, she hadn't thought that. Not even for a second. When he'd appeared behind Aidan, she'd known that Dex had come to the club for her. An unnerving realization. "Are you planning to follow me all the way home?"

"I told you, I want to make sure you're safe—"

A couple hurried past them, and Dex stopped talking. Secretive Dex. Of course, he wouldn't want to talk with others around. Lacey shook her head. "Look, I'm not interested."

"You don't even know why I'm here."

"You're trouble, Dex."

The streetlamp fell on his face and let her see the half-smile that slipped over his lips. "Thank you for noticing."

"That wasn't a compliment."

"I think it was."

He thought—Her lips thinned. "How did you know I was at that club?"

He leaned toward her, and his scent—rich, masculine, and...oddly yummy to her—teased her nose. "Want to know a secret?"

He was so close that onlookers would probably think they were about to kiss. They weren't. Absolutely were not. But... "Yes." She wanted to know his secrets.

"I can find you," he told her quietly. "Anywhere. Anytime."

Her eyes narrowed. "That sounds like some serious abuse of power. Better be careful, or someone will report you to your bosses at the CIA."

He laughed, and the sound sent a shiver over her. Not a bad kind of shiver. It should have been bad. But no...It was the *good* kind of shiver. The kind that told her she liked his laughter.

The kind that told Lacey her dry spell must have lasted way, way too long. Especially if she was now starting to think anything about Dex was sexy.

"I don't have bosses at the CIA. I am the boss." Spoken with utter confidence.

She wasn't so sure she bought that line. "You're in charge? Then how come I don't ever see you out there with the press or talking to senators in clips on the evening news?"

"You won't ever see me in scenes like that. I'm too busy doing the dirty work. The bloody shit that keeps everyone safe." His voice had hardened.

This time, the bad kind of shiver slid over her.

"You're cold." His hands reached out and curled around her. He tugged her closer to him and began to rub her arms.

"I do not understand you, Dex."

"I'm trying to make you warm. Sorry, I don't have a coat to offer but—"

"I'm not cold." If anything, standing this close to him, having his hands on her...she was feeling pretty hot. "Let go."

He did, but Dex didn't back away. "I want five minutes of your time."

"I'm pretty sure I've already spoken with you for five minutes."

"Let me be more specific. I want five minutes, in your home, alone with you. I want you to hear me out, and then, I want you to accept my offer."

A surprised laugh burst from her. "That is *not* going to happen." *Arrogant much?*

He shoved his hands into his pockets. "Then you have nothing to fear. Give me those five minutes, and I'll get out of your way."

Her lips pressed together. "I don't trust you."

"That hurts."

"No, it doesn't." Like she was going to believe anything she said would have the power to hurt him.

He shrugged. "Do I get my five minutes?"

She spun on her heel. "Yes, fine. But only because I don't want you pulling some crazy stunt like hanging out in my hallway all night long. Or showing up at my work tomorrow—or...whatever. I'll give you five minutes, and then you leave me alone."

"If that's what you want."

She cast a suspicious glance back over her shoulder. Alarm bells were blaring in her head. He'd just sounded entirely too satisfied.

And a satisfied Dexter Ryan was a scary thing.

***

"Talk to me, Antony." He was in her home. A good start. But he was far from sealing the deal. Dex cast a quick glance down the hallway. She'd disappeared into her bedroom, and he had to be ready before she came back. His hold tightened on the phone. "Don't exactly have time to waste here."

"She doesn't drink coffee. When she goes to the coffee shop on the corner, she just orders hot chocolate, even in the summer."

Dex pinched the bridge of his nose. "Not helping."

"She loves horror movies. I checked her streaming history, and I think she must be addicted to the B movies, you know the really crazy ones where—"

"The ones where the dumbass techie gets his ass kicked because he can't give me anything I can use?" Dex snarled.

Silence. Then... "You seem stressed."

Yeah, understatement. Antony didn't understand the stakes in this particular game. "You could say that."

He heard the tap of keystrokes in the background. Then Antony revealed, "I think Santana is her favorite band. She plays *Black Magic Woman* over and over—"

The bedroom door squeaked open.

"I need more," Dex urged. "Come on, buddy. Do not let me down here."

More keystrokes.

Dex turned so he could have a clear view of the hallway. Lacey had just left the bedroom. She'd ditched the heels but still wore her jeans and the sexy top. She was headed straight toward him, and her delicate jaw was hard with determination.

"Wait...wait! I just found a record of a payment that she sent to a PI. Oh, that guy is a sleaze. I've heard about him before. Total loser."

She was closing in.

Talk faster, Antony.

"Accessing his records now. The man has like, zero security on his system. Anybody can just hack right in. Like, seriously, I bet some eleven-year-old kid could—

"Hello, Lacey," Dex said clearly. She'd stopped right in front of him.

Her head tilted back. Her scent—a light, quick breath of roses—drifted to him.

"She's there? Of course, she's there." Antony's voice was tight. "Shit. Shit. *Motherload.* That's what I've hit. As in, her mother. Lacey went to the PI because she wanted him to investigate the death of her mom and dad. Their car crash looked like an accident, but she wanted proof and he couldn't deliver so—"

"I have to go now," Dex interrupted him. "Someone very important is here."

"You're not even going to thank me, are you? That is rude. So rude."

"Thanks for updating me," he forced the words out.

"Aw, you're welcome, bro—"

"Keep working on the assignment. I have faith in you. You'll deliver everything else I need to know."

"That means I can't go home yet, doesn't it?" A long sigh.

"Damn straight." Dex hung up the phone. Smiled at Lacey. "I like the toenail polish."

She automatically peered down at her feet. So did he. How about that? Lacey Amari had cute feet. Small feet and dainty toes—toes with a deep purple polish on them. And she even wore a toe ring on the second toe of her right foot.

Okay, that was kinda sexy.

"You are not here to talk about my feet." Her head tilted back up. He'd shoved his phone into his pocket when she looked down. "Your five minutes are ticking down, and so far, I have not heard anything that—"

"Your boss at Wilde gave approval for you to join me on a case."

"What? When?"

He opened his mouth to reply—

"No." Lacey shook her head. "He wouldn't do that. Eric knows you piss me off."

"I do? Hmm. Unusual. Most people find me charming."

"I don't think that they do." As if imparting a secret, she added, "You don't have the best people skills."

He would *not* smile again. "I am fantastic with people. I can always get them to do exactly what I want."

"Yeah, that doesn't mean you have good people skills." She turned away. Moved to sit on the overstuffed and extremely comfortable-looking couch in the corner. "It just means you probably threaten folks far too much."

She wasn't necessarily wrong. She wasn't necessarily right, either. Regardless, time to get down to business. "I spoke with Eric Wilde and told him that you would be very useful on a case that I'm working. He agreed with me."

A furrow appeared between her brows. "Eric didn't mention this to me."

"Didn't he? Odd. Anyway..." A shrug. "We will be leaving tomorrow, so I need you to pack your bags. When you pack, think both warm and sexy. Can you do that?" He glanced at his watch. "I don't believe that even took a full minute." He turned on his heel and headed for the door.

"Stop."

He stopped. "You don't want me to leave. I get it." He looked back at her. "Because you feel that hard attraction between us, too. But, hey, if we're going to be working together, you need to—"

Dex broke off. Just stopped. Because he'd been talking out of his ass while he tried to figure out how to play the scene with her, but while he'd been rambling, Lacey's expression had just become ever-so-revealing. Wonderfully revealing. At least, for a fleeting moment, anyway.

"You're crazy." She leapt to her feet. Her face flushed. "There is no attraction between us."

Well, well, well. He was attracted to Lacey. He'd be insane not to be. The woman was sensuality personified. All of that tumbling, dark hair. Those deep, dark eyes. Her plump, red lips.

The curves of her body. The huskiness of her voice. The way she smelled so good and—

"And we are not working together!" She stormed toward him. "Eric would have called me if I had been assigned to work with you."

He exhaled. Turned to fully face her. "You're right. You haven't been assigned to work with me." That was the frustrating part. "Eric said the choice was yours."

Her gaze searched his.

He could feel her confusion, but he wasn't about to reveal too much. In his world, *need-to-know* was a true way of life. "I still have a few minutes, so how about I lay some things out for you?"

A grudging nod came from her.

"I need someone with your skills to help me on a case."

"There are plenty of skilled agents at the CIA," Lacey dismissed. She tucked a thick lock of hair behind her ear. "I don't buy that in all the massive ranks of folks at your agency, you can't find at least one person to do the job."

"I can't use one of my agents. I need someone unaffiliated." A pause. "I need you." Her in particular. As to *why* it had to be her, well...*need-to-know*. She didn't need to know that part, not yet. Maybe never. "The case starts tomorrow. It will continue for an indefinite amount of time. We'll be traveling to Colorado, so you'll need to pack clothes that you'd take on a ski trip. And...like I said..." He had to clear his throat because of the mental image that popped into his head as he added, "Something sexy."

Her hands went to her hips. "Why in the world would I pack something sexy? *If* I happened to be crazy enough to sign on for this case. And, by the way, I'm not."

The lock of hair had fallen forward again. He wanted to brush it back and let his hand linger against the smoothness of her cheek. *What in the hell?* His hand fisted. "You'd be going in undercover. So would I. The clothes are to help with the ruse. Make it more believable. If you come in a burlap sack, that *won't* be believable."

Her incredible eyes—deep chocolate with flecks of gold—narrowed. "Just what is this undercover mission, exactly?"

Well, it was now or never. Since a man only had one chance to get this deal right...Dex dropped to one knee in front of her.

"What are you doing?" Lacey's voice notched up.

He reached for her hand. Curled his fingers carefully around hers. "Lacey Amari, would you do me the honor of being my wife?"

Her lips were parted. Her eyes now huge. Shock covered her face.

He waited, knowing this was the big moment and—

"No, absolutely not. I would *never, ever* marry you."

CHAPTER TWO

Dex Ryan had just asked her to marry him. Impossible. Insane.

She shook her head and even gave her arm a little pinch on the down low, just to make sure she hadn't fallen asleep in her bedroom and that this whole scene wasn't some crazy nightmare.

Nope. She felt the pinch.

Still down on one knee, Dex exhaled slowly and stared mournfully up at her. "I was afraid you'd say no."

"Of course, I said no! I'm not marrying you! You don't love me. I don't love you and—"

"Relax. Love doesn't need to be involved. It would strictly be an undercover ruse. Not legally binding in any shape or form." He rose to his feet. Cocked his head. "Unless you need that. If it's easier for you to get into character by actually marrying me, I'd be game. I would be—"

"*No.*" She put her hands on his chest. *Very strong* chest, by the way. Ignoring that thought, she pushed him toward the door. "I'm not going to be your undercover fiancée. That's not happening."

"Pity." He backed up and went along with her push easily enough. "Would it help if I told you that lives were on the line? That this was a matter of national security?"

She stopped pushing. Her hands pressed to his chest. Once again, she couldn't help but notice he had a very muscled, powerful chest. Her fingers stretched a tiny bit and—

Lacey caught herself. Her hands yanked back. "I need to know more."

"I can't tell you more. Not until you're on the case."

She glared.

He stared. And she realized that his eyes were actually quite beautiful. Deep gray. Super intense. They seemed to see right through her. Or, *in* to her.

"I know why you're working at Wilde," he murmured.

Her spine straightened. "I know, too. Because I respect Eric as a boss and because I enjoy helping people."

Dex shook his head. "You're smart. Very smart. I bet you haven't even left a trail there, have you?"

OhmyGod. She could feel the color draining from her face.

"At first, you tried to use a regular PI to get the job done, but when he turned up jack, you knew you had to step up your game. If no one else was going to help you, you had to help yourself. You turned your whole life around. Changed all your plans as you devoted yourself to finding the truth."

"You should leave," she whispered.

"You got Eric to hire you—because, hey, on paper, you look great—but then, once you made it into his inner circle, you helped yourself to Wilde resources. You've been using his tech and his agents to help you with your own investigation ever since you walked through the door of that business. And Eric has no clue."

This was bad. Very, very bad. She'd intended to tell Eric everything—especially after all the recent developments at Wilde. When they'd found out that they had a traitor at Wilde, she'd known that she had to tell Eric the full truth about herself. But...

The situation at Wilde was strained enough. And maybe...maybe she'd been afraid that he'd kick her out.

Her lashes swept down as she considered the situation. Eric hadn't just hired her for her skills. He'd hired her because she was family. A connection most people didn't know about. She'd used that connection as her in at Wilde. She hadn't thought her secret investigation would be a big deal. She had just intended to use the firm's resources, then slip away. But...

Eric Wilde is a good person. Eric and his brother Ben—they had treated her with nothing but kindness and respect and if they found out the truth, if they found out that she'd been using the company's resources...

What if they turn on me? She would be alone again. No family.

"So, the way I figure it..." Dex drawled. "I could walk out of this door right now. The door that you were pushing me toward. And I could go to Eric. I could tell him what I learned. Could get him to search through his system and see what you've been doing." He nodded. "Or..."

She waited.

He didn't finish. Instead, Dex frowned at her. "Did I upset you?"

A stupid tear had leaked down her cheek. "No, you made me deliriously happy with joy." She swiped away the tear. "Yes," she snapped. "You've upset me. I had a killer day. A gun was shoved into my face—"

A muscle jerked along his jaw. "Tell me the fucker's name and he's dead."

What? "He's in custody, so you don't have to worry about him." Her chin jutted up. "On top of everything else that happened, now I'm having to deal with you. You're threatening me. No, check that, I think you're *blackmailing* me—"

"Blackmail." He winced. "That is an ugly word."

"Yes. It is. And you're the one *doing* it."

"I'm not blackmailing you." He shook his head. And he closed the distance between them. His hand lifted toward her face. "You have a little bit of the tear drop left here." His jaw was hard as his fingers lifted and carefully swept over her cheek. "Silk," he whispered.

"Excuse me?" When he'd touched her, Lacey's heart had thudded so hard and loud that she hadn't been able to hear that last part that he'd said.

His hand lingered on her cheek. His gaze seemed to burn into her own. Why was her chest tight? Why did it seem so hard to breathe?

The man was threatening her. Blackmailing her. Yes, it sure sounded like blackmail to Lacey, no matter what denial he might want to spit out.

And yet she was standing there, her whole body reacting to him like she was waiting for some kind of first kiss or something.

Ridiculous. Obviously, she was still reacting to the adrenaline. And not to him. Not to some kind of insane, primitive, super-hot attraction to Dex.

She caught his wrist, much like he'd caught hers before. She curled her fingers around his and—

Felt scars.

Her eyes widened as she flipped over his wrist.

"The cuffs left quite a mark. No worries, though. It was a long time ago."

She stared at the old, white lines that curled around his wrist. Lines that cut across his skin much like tight handcuffs might have done. But to scar him that way...

"Had to get out of them, so what was a little pain? The mission depended on my success. Just so you understand who I am, I didn't start at the top. I started in the field, where there is blood and betrayal and death all around you."

Her fingers were sliding over his scars, as if she could take away the pain. But the pain had ended long ago.

"We all carry scars, don't we, Lacey?"

Her head tilted as she looked at his face once more. Her fingers lingered around his wrist.

"Some are just hidden on the inside," he continued, "where it's ever so much harder to see them. But those scars are the ones that can hurt you the most."

He was right. She swallowed the lump in her throat and let go of his hand. "I think your five minutes are way up."

"True. They are. But you haven't heard my full offer yet."

She backed up a step. Lacey definitely wanted some space between the two of them. "There wasn't an offer." Her voice sounded all crisp and cool. She was rather proud of herself for that tone. "There was blackmail."

"There you go, talking dirty to me again."

One eyebrow rose. "When I talk dirty, you'll know."

His smile flashed. A shark's eager grin. "Is that a promise?"

Her lips clamped together.

"No?" A long exhale. "Guessing it's not a promise. Unfortunate. My hopes were up."

She did not understand him. "I'm going to bed. And, no, that is not some offer. It's me telling you that your time is up, and I'm exhausted." So exhausted that she'd actually let a tear slip out in front of him. She didn't cry in front of anyone. Her pain wasn't for the world to see. It was hers. Hers alone. "So I'd like to say this has been fun—"

"Hasn't it? I mean, we've had quite the first date."

First date? No.

"I got your other would-be suitor on the floor with barely any effort. Seriously, you must have been disappointed with how easily the man caved to me. Then, to make the evening even more unforgettable, I proposed. How many first dates have given you so much excitement? And, now, for the final reveal..."

She turned away. *Enough.*

"For the final reveal, I'll offer you what you want most."

Her steps faltered. "You have no idea what I want most."

"Are you kidding? Have you *met* me? I'm like the 'all knowing Oz' from—"

She spun toward him. "Maybe my memory is sketchy, but I thought that Oz guy was a fraud. Just pretending he knew everything and that he had all the power. When really, he was just a man hiding behind a curtain."

Dex's head inclined toward her. "I'm the real deal."

She snorted. "You're—"

"Your parents were murdered."

She sucked in a breath.

"You hired a PI to find the truth a while back, but he wasn't good enough to get the job done. You went to work at Wilde because you wanted to use their network to find out the truth. You wanted to catch the killer. To find out *why* they died."

Lacey didn't confirm or deny his charge.

His expression was inscrutable as Dex added, "Instead of thinking that I'm blackmailing you, how about you view it as me offering you a deal? You agree to be my partner on this one assignment—just one little case—and I can help you get what you want most."

"You're lying to me."

"I lie to many people." A nod. "I do it without barely thinking."

Tension knotted at the base of her skull.

"But I'm not lying to you. I have resources that Wilde can't tap. You want to find out what really happened to your parents? I can give you that answer. And you don't have to pay a dime for the truth. Eric Wilde can go on thinking that you came to join his team because you wanted to be part of the family."

She wondered if his use of the word *family* had been deliberate. Did he know—

"One assignment. You pretend to be my fiancée. You follow my orders unconditionally. We take down some very bad people. Then you get what you want most."

Her sweaty palms were pressing to her thighs. "I need to think about this."

A sigh slipped past him. "What's to think about?" And, once more, he eliminated the distance between the two of them. "I'm offering you what you want."

He was. And she *knew* he had resources she could use. If he kept his word and didn't tell Eric...

What do I have to lose?

"Tell you what," he offered with a roll of his broad shoulders. "To show you how cooperative I can be...How about you sleep on it? I'll give you until five a.m. to tell me your decision. That way, you can rest for a little while. You can clear your head. And you *won't* be able to later say I rushed you."

"You're giving me a few hours. That still falls into the rush category."

"Yes, well, time is of the essence. The plane leaves at seven so..."

The plane? "So you're pretty certain I'll agree."

His gaze swept slowly over her face. "I'm learning a great deal about you right now."

His words held an unsettling ring of truth.

Dex rattled off an address. "I'll be in the presidential suite there," he explained. "So when you decide, come to me. I'll be waiting." Then he turned and walked for her door. "Sleep well."

As if she'd be able to sleep *at all.* "Why me?"

"I already told you." He didn't look back. His hand reached for the door. "You're smart. Obviously capable. You know how to fight. And Eric doesn't just bring anyone on his staff. I will be able to count on you when things go dark." He hesitated. "Besides, I also need someone who would suit me as a believable fiancée."

Um, what did that mean?

"There are some things that can't be faked." His voice was little rougher. "I need the people watching us to believe that I want you so badly I would do anything to have you. That I can't keep my hands off you."

"I...I think a guy like you could fake most things."

Now he did look back. "Why bother faking when it's real? Makes everything so much easier."

Wait, wait, *wait.* Had he just said...was he telling her that he really wanted—

"Good night, Lacey. Sleep well." A quick wink. "Maybe you'll even dream of me."

"If I do, it will be a nightmare." She would not even think about the one time—*one time*—that maybe, kinda, sorta, she'd had a sex dream about him.

My dry spell must end soon.

He laughed. The sound was warm and rough and sexy. "Whatever you need to tell yourself." He slipped out of her home.

She hurried forward and shoved the door closed behind him. Flipped the lock. Squeezed her eyes closed. "Dammit."

Leave it to Dex to get her all tangled up like this. Arrogant, controlling, hot Dex.

Hot?

She stomped away from the door. She had until five a.m. She was going to shower. Going to crash in bed. And *not* going to dream about him. But first things first...Lacey grabbed her phone and called Eric Wilde. He answered on the third ring.

"Lace? What's happening?"

"Dex Ryan is happening."

"Oh." No surprise. Definite resignation.

"You *knew* he wanted me to work with him?" Just to be clear.

"Yes, he mentioned it. But I told him that there was no way you'd agree."

Her hold tightened on the phone. *No way, except Dex figured out what I want.*

"Lace? You there?"

"I'm here." She wet her lips.

"Look, I don't care what the man told you, you don't have to take the case."

"But you have a relationship with him." A frenemy kind of thing. "I know how things work. He's CIA. You do favors for him. He does favors for you." She peered toward her front door, almost expecting Dex to pop up again. "If I say no, what happens to Wilde?"

"Not a damn thing. I can handle Dex."

Can I? "He wants me to leave with him at 7 a.m. He wants me to pretend to be his fiancée."

Eric swore. "Tell me you're not going to do it! You know how that guy is!"

Arrogant.   Incredibly   manipulative. Dangerous. Diabolical. And...

He had scars on his wrist. Deep scars from where he'd fought to escape cuffs. He'd been so careful as he brushed away a tear from her cheek. He'd offered to give her what she'd desperately sought since her parents had died. The truth.

And, of course, he'd blackmailed her. Not like she could forget that part of the night.

"Uh, Lace, you didn't answer. You *aren't* going to take the case, are you?"

She didn't reply.

"Are you?"

***

Dex whistled as he lifted the cup of coffee toward his mouth. He'd ordered the early delivery from room service, and it had arrived right on time.

Ten minutes before five a.m.

Steam drifted off the black liquid, and he lightly blew over it. His gaze darted toward the fingers of his right hand as they cradled the mug. The knuckles were a bit bruised. He'd decided to make a little side trip before returning to the suite after his visit with Lacey.

Sometimes, there was just work that needed to be done. Work that required a personal touch.

He sipped the coffee and let the caffeine surge through him.

The clock on the table ticked closer to five a.m. Ever closer.

And his phone rang. The ring tone was set to some kind of SciFi TV show. *Antony.* Dex put down the mug and pushed the phone toward his ear. "Someone is up early."

"You know I didn't go to sleep." Antony's voice was disgruntled. "I kept searching for intel on your lady, and I just sent it all to your email. You are welcome."

"Someone is feisty in the morning."

"Do not start with me, Dex. I stayed up all night for you. I found out everything about her. Everything from the woman's bra size—34C, by the way—to the number of lovers she's had."

Dex's muscles tightened.

"I sent you their names and pics, in case you were curious—"

"Are you trying to make me angry, Antony?" he asked silkily. "Because that's my fiancée you're talking about."

Antony sucked in a breath. "What the—no, I didn't mean—" He broke off. "She...agreed then? Even without all this intel I gathered, you got her to agree?"

Three minutes until five. "The sun isn't up yet. You know I told you that I'd have her agreement by sunrise."

"But you can be wrong," Antony muttered. "Sometimes, like it *can* happen. Statistically speaking, it is more than a possible occurrence. She could tell you no. Tell you to go to hell, in fact." He seemed to warm to the topic. "She could tell you—"

A knock sounded at the suite's door.

Two minutes until five.

"Got to go, Antony. My soon-to-be fiancée just arrived." Dex kept the phone to his ear as he rose and stalked to the door. A quick glance through the peephole showed him that, yes, Lacey was there. A black, rolling piece of luggage was at her side. "Why don't you get some sleep? Oh, and Antony?"

"What now?" Definitely disgruntled.

"I get that we're friends. But friendship can only go so far. Don't ever fucking talk to me about her bra size or ex-lovers again. Where my fiancée is concerned, I'm very, very jealous and possessive."

"But—but—" Antony stammered. "Are you punking me? She's not even your real—"

Dex hung up on him. He tucked the phone into his back pocket and swung open the door.

CHAPTER THREE

"You are right on time." Dex gripped the door with one hand. "I've got to say, punctuality in a partner is a plus."

In response, she glowered. He doubted that Lacey would like to be told that glowers were cute on her. But they were. Come to think of it, though, she pretty much always looked good to him.

She'd pulled her hair back in a messy bun, and loose tendrils escaped to tease her cheekbones. She wore jeans, black boots that rose to her knees, and a long, flowing red sweater.

"You're dressed for the cold. Guess that means we're ready to roll." He nodded. "Excellent. We can head downstairs. I'll have my driver take us to the airport—"

"I have *not* said that I'm agreeing to this situation yet."

"Lacey..." He drew her name out. He liked her name. It was sexy. Just like she was. Fit her to a T. "You're here with a suitcase at your side. Of course, you're agreeing." Why waste time pretending otherwise?

She huffed out a breath. Her glower became more ferocious. Even cuter. And those deep, dark eyes of hers darted to—

"What happened?" She was peering at his bruised knuckles as he gripped the wood of the door. "Did you hit your hand on something?"

Something. Someone. "Yes. A few times. No worries. I'm good." He dropped said hand and backed up. "Come on in. You obviously want to talk before we hit the road, and I have hot chocolate waiting for you."

"Wait!"

He didn't wait. He went inside because he was utterly certain she'd follow him. Sure enough, she did. The door clicked closed a moment later. He sat on the sofa. Motioned to the waiting hot chocolate that sat on a nearby delivery cart.

Her luggage bumped into the edge of the sofa as she studied the whole scene with suspicion. "How do you know I like hot chocolate?"

Dex let out a long-suffering sigh. "Because I am the all-knowing—"

"Don't say that to me again." She plunked down next to him. Her thigh brushed his leg, and he tensed at the contact. "You had me investigated, didn't you?" Lacey reached for the mug of hot chocolate. Whipped cream covered the top of the liquid, and caramel and chocolate syrup had been skillfully layered in an artistic design on the fluffy cream. She took a sip and moaned.

His brows shot up. That was certainly a fun new sound from her.

"Heaven," she declared and sipped again. "Okay, I know what you did. You had one of your techie agents dig into my life. That's how you know I like hot chocolate." She angled toward him. "That's also how you knew about my parents.

I bet you dug into my financials, didn't you? Found a record of where I'd paid the PI? I think there are laws about that kind of intrusive search."

He leaned toward her. His eyes were on her mouth. His hand lifted, and his thumb slid slowly, sensually, over her lower lip.

He was close enough to see the widening of her pupils.

"Wh-what are you doing?" Her breath caught.

"You had a little whipped cream on your lower lip." A sight that had been tempting as all hell. He brought his thumb to his lip. Sucked away the whipped cream.

She watched him with her deep, dark eyes.

"You're right," he growled. "Heaven." But he was talking about how *she* tasted.

She looked back at the hot chocolate. Back at him. Then— "No."

"No, what? No, you don't like the hot chocolate? Because judging by your moan, you—"

"I meant...no. No, I am not sleeping with you."

"Okay."

"I'm not."

"Noted."

"I get that you want me to pretend to be your fiancée, but that's all this is, got it? Pretend. When we're alone, you're not crawling into my bed." Her cheeks had flushed. The flush made her even more beautiful.

"For the record," he murmured, "I feel compelled to point out that I don't generally *crawl* into a woman's bed. Not my style. First, I'm invited. Very eagerly invited."

She snorted.

His lips wanted to curl. Because even that snort of hers—

No. Stay focused. "I'm eagerly invited," he continued blandly, knowing the role he had to play. He was always playing a role. With everyone. Everyday. Sometimes, the deal got old, but it wasn't as if he had a choice. He'd given up the luxury of being his true self long ago. "And after I get my invitation, I don't *crawl.*" Hardly. "Sometimes, I pounce. Sometimes, I jump, and sometimes, well, I just wreck the bed because the lady I'm with...all we care about is pleasure."

Her breath was coming a little too quickly. She licked her lower lip. Then Lacey told him, "Don't pounce, jump, or wreck anything."

Now he *had* to smile. "Unless I get an invitation?"

"I wouldn't hold my breath on that one."

But he could hold his breath for an extremely long time. Fun fact, he'd been a SEAL before joining the CIA. Definitely top secret info. "You understand that since we're pretending to be engaged, it has to look real, right? That is one of the reasons I wanted you for this job. The attraction that we have for each other is obvious."

She glanced away. "I'm supposed to know what you're talking about?"

Now a faint trickle of anger slid through him. "This is a dangerous case. Lives will be on the line. While we are in the field, I expect you to tell me the truth. I'm telling you the truth right now. Do me the same courtesy. If you can't, forget the job. Walk away now."

"Someone is grumpy first thing in the morning."

He blinked. *Grumpy?*

Her gaze cut back to him. "Fine. If you must know, I do feel a vague, unreasonable attraction to you."

He waited.

"Maybe not vague," she allowed. "But it *is* unreasonable. You don't have a nice reputation. I've been warned you're exceedingly dangerous and manipulative. I've seen you in action that way, courtesy of the Wilde case that first brought us together, and I—"

"When I'm with you, I'm not the same man that I am when I'm around others." A very honest statement. He was never the same with different people. "The attraction I feel for you is not some vague, unreasonable thing. It's strong. Damn near consuming. Each time I see you, I think you're more beautiful than the time before. You're smart, capable, and you know how to stay cool under fire. Sexy as fuck." He drank some of his coffee. Then revealed, "Not having to fake an attraction will make this go much easier. We'll be in a romantic setting. We will be there with other couples."

"Is this like a couples' retreat deal?"

Not exactly. "Letting our natural attraction show will be beneficial. But don't worry. The show won't carry over when we're alone." He paused.

She nodded.

"Unless there's that invitation."

Her delicate jaw hardened. "It's not coming. You will not be getting an invitation from me."

How disappointing. He glanced at his watch. "The private jet is gassed up and ready to go. We should be on our way."

She sipped a little more of her hot chocolate. Then she quickly licked her lips to remove any lingering whipped cream.

Pity. He could have licked the cream away for her. Perhaps another time.

"I'm assuming that I'll get a fake name? You'll give me a persona and you'll have a cover, too."

He didn't have a suitcase. It would be packed and waiting for him on the plane. "You're going in just as you are. You *are* Lacey Amari. Everything you say will be one hundred percent true about yourself."

Surprise washed across her features. "Wait...what? Why?"

"As for me, I'm Dexter Ryan. That's how I'll be introduced. And if anyone wants to research me, they'll find a fun background waiting to be discovered." A background he'd carefully crafted. He always had plenty of false info darting around the world.

She reached for his arm. Her fingers curled around him. "Dexter Ryan isn't your real name."

"Is that a question?"

Her lips firmed. "*Is* Dexter Ryan your real name?"

"If you're asking if I was born with that name, no, I wasn't. But it is very real." He could feel the warmth of her touch sinking through his body. Why did he enjoy her touch so much? Something to consider later. "The name is real, just as I am very real. I will keep you safe on this mission. You can trust me on that. You'll come back safe and sound, and I'll hold up my end of the deal. We'll find out about your parents."

"Thank you." Soft. Grudging.

Delightful.

He laughed. "Was that so hard?" He leaned in close, mostly because he liked to pull in her delectable scent. "Better be careful, or you'll start to think I'm not the big, bad wolf of the story, after all."

"Are you?"

The question made his heart lurch. Dex kept the smile on his face as he caught her hand. Lifted it off him. And then brought it to his lips. His mouth feathered over her knuckles. "I'm the baddest wolf out there," he assured her roughly. "Never forget that."

***

The plane would be touching down in Colorado soon. She could see the white-capped mountains stretching around her. They were heading to a private strip, in a town called Fortune. She'd never heard of the place before, but it was fairly close to Aspen on the map.

She'd done an internet search on the hotel— or rather, the lodge they were visiting. Very, very expensive. Very private. An exclusive getaway for the rich. If you wanted to disappear and escape from tabloids or from corporate chaos, you headed to Fortune.

Her phone rang.

Dex was up in the front—freaking flying the plane. They had a pilot, but Dex had taken over shortly after takeoff. His control issues were showing. As if she hadn't already realized that Dex liked to be in command of everything and everyone around him.

Her phone rang again. She pulled it out. Saw Eric's face on the screen. She answered the call and put the phone to her ear. "You checking up on me already?"

"Are you safe?"

"Yes. I'm good." High in the air and far away from threats. For the moment. "But I do appreciate the call." Very...family-like.

Because he was family.

His sigh drifted to her. "I think this is a mistake."

She glanced toward the front of the plane. Dex had just left the cockpit. Interesting. She'd rather thought he'd land them. But he was approaching and frowning at her—no, at her phone.

He heard it ringing. He came to see who called me.

Control issues.

"There's something you should know," Eric continued grimly. "August Shay was attacked last night."

She shot upright in her seat. August Shay had been the man who put his gun in her face. The perp who'd been stalking her recent client. The guy who—

Should have been in a maximum lockdown. "Was it other prisoners? Did they jump him?"

"No. The guards swear August was in a separate cell. And, no, the guards didn't do it, either. But then, I can't be sure who hit him because the security feed mysteriously cut right before the time of the incident."

Dex strode toward her. "Who's on the phone?"

She waved him away as Eric told her, "When Layla headed into see the prisoner this morning..."

Layla. She knew he meant Detective Layla Lopez. Lacey had become fast friends with the other woman since beginning her job at Wilde.

"When she went in, hell, he confessed to the murders of two women."

"*What?*"

"August had stalked and killed them. Women who all looked just like Jessica Harper."

The Broadway star he'd been after. "OhmyGod."

"He even told the cops exactly where to find the bodies. Someone got to him last night, Lace. Someone scared the hell out of him. Scared him so much that August confessed everything. He's going to be locked up for a very, very long time. I'd be surprised if he ever gets out again."

Her throat had gone dry.

Dex slid into the seat across from her. "We'll be descending soon. You should buckle up." His hands went to his own seatbelt.

Her gaze lingered on his bruised knuckles. She swallowed. Twice. "Thank you for letting me know about August. I appreciate it, Eric."

"Are you sure you feel good doing this mission with Dex?"

Good wasn't the right word. And Dex was staring straight at her. "I'll talk to you soon," she promised Eric. Then she hung up.

Dex shook his head. "Afraid that's going to be a no-go. When we leave the plane, that phone will stay here. I'll give you a new one, don't worry, but it will have some security upgrades, courtesy of the agency."

The agency. He meant the CIA.

"Please don't call Eric or anyone else at Wilde." His tone dropped. "This is a very delicate situation, and I don't need to be worrying about outsiders."

She fumbled and managed to secure her seatbelt. "You didn't tell me how you got those bruises." She couldn't take her gaze off them.

"Sure, I did. You asked if I'd hit something, and I said yes."

Another swallow. "Did you hit something..." She dragged her eyes up to his face. "Or someone?"

He stared back at her. The pilot made an announcement that she only vaguely heard.

Then Dex said, "If you have a specific question for me, why won't you ask it?"

Fine. But she'd start with a statement, not a question. "August Shay just confessed to killing two women."

"Um. Yes. I know that already. Hate to spoil the reveal, but I tend to get intel very fast."

Her breath hitched.

"Did *you* know..." He leaned forward. "That those two women were also petite brunettes? That he shot them in the head?"

"I—" *No.* She hadn't known that. Eric hadn't exactly had time to describe the victims to her.

"You didn't tell me that you were pretending to *be* Jessica Harper during your recent investigation and that the reason August put a gun in your face was because he thought you were her. You are his type, after all. And I bet you blended perfectly when you took her place and used yourself as a victim."

Had that been anger humming in his voice? Why would he be mad? "I wasn't a victim. I was acting to draw him in. I was—"

"I don't want you to be a victim. I want you to be a kickass agent who doesn't let anyone get close to hurting her. Do you understand me? Every moment that we are in Fortune, you stay on your guard. You do not let anyone catch you unaware."

"I can do the job." Was he doubting her? "In case *you* didn't know, I disarmed August easily when he pulled the gun. Just as I'd planned. I took him down, and I saved the client. Now August is in jail, and, apparently, that is where he will stay for a very long time."

The plane was descending. She felt the shift in angle, and her hands clamped around the edges of the arm rests on either side of her body.

"You still haven't asked me what you truly want to know..." He didn't move at all. Just kept leaning casually toward her.

"Did you go to see August Shay last night?"

"Yes."

Just...yes? "And you hit him?"

His expression didn't alter. "Still not getting to the real point." A slow exhale. "Don't you really want to know if I beat the guy until he confessed?"

Yes, she did want to know that. Because she'd seen some damning evidence. "Your knuckles..."

"I went in for a chat. I didn't like hearing about the gun in your face. August didn't like being locked up. So I guess we were both feeling stressed. He came at me, swinging, so I swung back." A shrug. "Here's the thing, I swing pretty hard."

She thought of the tall, muscled August. His bright blond hair. His soulless blue eyes. The way he'd smiled when he'd pulled the gun on her. "Eric said someone scared him into confessing everything."

A faint, almost mocking laugh. "And do you think I'm a scary man?"

He didn't look scary as he sat across from her. He appeared confident. Casual. Relaxed.

But she could feel the danger swirling beneath his surface. "Yes." A firm nod. "I think you can be a very scary man. I think you're probably the worst enemy that anyone would ever want to have."

"Good thing I'm not your enemy."

Goose bumps rose on her body.

His head cocked to the right. "August put a gun to your head. He killed two women who looked exactly like you. *You* were the one who took him down. Don't you think—with a man like that—he might have now become fixated on you? That if he got out, he'd turn his obsessive compulsion on you?"

Well, now that she was learning all the details about August and his crimes, she was thinking—

"Couldn't very well let that happen to my new partner. So I went to have a talk with him." His bruised knuckles flexed. "During the course of our talk, he realized the error of his ways. He confessed to his crimes. You know what? I think he even started to like the idea of prison."

That made zero sense. "Why would he do that? Why would he *like* prison?"

His gaze was lethal. Chilling. "Because he liked the idea of having bars between him...and me."

She couldn't look away from him. "You *are* a scary man."

"I protect what's important to me. If I have to be scary to get the job done, so be it." His stare swept carefully over her. "You don't ever have to be afraid of me. You understand that, don't you?"

She wasn't so sure what she understood.

"We've landed."

They had?

"I'll go change." He unhooked his seatbelt. "Got to make the right entrance."

Yes, yes, the job. *Focus on that.* "Should I change, too?"

He'd already risen to his feet. "You don't need to change a fucking thing. You're perfect as you are. Remember that."

He stalked away from her.

And her breath expelled in a long rush.

***

She was terrified of him. Not exactly a surprise. Maybe he should have put off that little chat with August until after the mission.

But he put a gun in her face.

Nah, no point in putting off that particular come-to-Jesus meeting. Besides, now two other families had closure regarding the murders of their loved ones. And August Shay would rot in a jail cell. Win, win.

Dex glanced into the small mirror. Rolled back his shoulders. He was wearing crisp black dress pants that had been tailored to fit him, a white dress shirt with the top three buttons undone, and a blazer. For a moment, he shifted through a few different facial expressions as he tried to get just the right look that he needed—

Do you even know who the fuck you are any longer?

The question slipped through his mind. Slowly, very slowly, his expression hardened. His eyes went cold even as his jaw became rock hard. A killer stared back at him.

Yes, he knew exactly who he was.

A light knock rapped against the door. "Dex? I'm thinking maybe I should change. I mean, I just glanced out the window and you have a limo waiting for us. The outfit I'm wearing doesn't—"

He opened the door, and he made sure that when he saw Lacey, he had a warm grin on his face. "How many times do I have to tell you...you're perfect as you are?"

Her head tilted. Her gaze slid over his face. Lingered on his mouth. "I have to tell you, I think that grin is the scariest one you have."

His smile slipped a little.

"Because you somehow do this thing where the grin goes up to your eyes, so it looks real, and maybe that's the scary part. Even *I* want to believe it, but..."

"You don't," he concluded softly.

"I've caught a few of your real smiles. They were fleeting and brief, but they stuck out in my mind. Now that I know what those look like, it's hard to be fooled again."

Well, well. He leaned toward her. "And that's why you're perfect," he told her. "Absolutely perfect."

She swallowed.

He wanted to kiss her. Actually, he was pretty desperate to do just that. "You be exactly who you are on this mission. I'll be the one who pretends."

"Why do I feel like that's the story of your life?"

Because it is. "The show starts the minute we step off this plane."

"Okay."

"Be prepared for what's to come."

"I am." She sounded utterly confident.

"Let's see, shall we? Better run a quick test first." Then he closed the last bit of distance between them and put his mouth on hers.

Her lips were parted and open, and when his mouth touched hers, heat pulsed through Dex's body. Heat. Lust. Need. His tongue dipped into her mouth, and fuck, she tasted sweet. As sweet as he'd dreamed. Because, sure, he'd had his share of fantasies about Lacey Amari. The woman was the sexiest thing he'd ever seen.

She didn't back away from his kiss. Instead, her fingers curled around his shoulders and she pressed closer to him. Pressed that hot, tight body of hers flush against him, and she opened her mouth even wider.

Yes.

His cock surged toward her. Long, hard, fully erect. Her tongue met his. She kissed him with a light delicacy, a careful hunger, and he wanted to wreck that care. He wanted to make Lacey light on fire with lust. He wanted her nails clawing at him. He wanted her mouth frantic. He wanted her as hungry as he felt.

"How's that?" Lacey whispered against his mouth.

"I think you can do better."

"What?" Her eyes blazed at him. "You did not just say—"

He had. Mostly just to stir her up. "You're holding back. I can feel it."

Her lashes flickered. "It was a first kiss. I'm supposed to jump your bones with a first kiss?"

"Jump my bones anytime," he invited.

Her cheeks flushed.

Did she have any idea how gorgeous she was? "You're my fiancée. You're mad about me."

"Mad is the right word, but you're using it the wrong way in this instance."

He grinned.

Her breath caught. "There it is."

Then, before he could say anything else, she used her hold on his shoulders to pull him forward once more. This time, when she kissed him, the fire nearly ignited his whole body. He could feel her hunger. Her need. Her desire. She kissed him as if she'd never wanted anyone more, and he responded the exact same way. His hands dropped to her hips. He wanted to pick her up, pin her against the nearest wall, and plunge deep into—

"Better?" Lacey panted as she pulled her mouth away from his.

Better didn't even come close. "You know you're fucking fantastic." An automatic reply.

Her lashes fluttered. "What?"

"What changed? Because I need you to be this same way always." Wait. Shit. He'd meant, um... "Always, you know, when we're performing for the others here."

She licked her lips.

He would have happily done that for her. Licked. Sucked. Maybe even given a faint bite on her plump lower lip.

"You changed," she answered. Her voice was husky. Way too sensual for him.

And he didn't know what she meant.

She backed away a step. Straightened her shoulders. "You stopped pretending, I saw your real smile again, and I—"

"You what?" he asked when she stopped.

"I liked your real smile." She spun on her high heel. "The limo is waiting. Let's go."

He didn't move. If she would kiss him like that again, he'd give her his real smile any damn time. Over and over again.

***

"The target has landed."

His fingers tapped on the computer screen as he watched the security feed. "Yes," he snapped. "Obviously, I can see that for myself."

"They're walking to the limo."

Was this shit for real? "Again, I can see that for myself. That's the whole point in you sending me a *video* feed." He didn't need a friggin' play-by-play of things he could figure out for himself.

As he watched the feed, he saw Dex's hand linger on the woman's lower back. A possessive touch. Interesting.

She slipped into the limo first.

Dex quickly followed her.

"I want to know who she is." Dex Ryan had been a thorn in his side for too long. "Obviously, he's working some angle, and I want to know exactly what's happening—"

"Um, this is like a lover's retreat place, so I mean, I think I can basically guess what is going to happen if you want me to—"

"Get her name. Get her background info. I want to know everything about her."

Why did he have to deal with such an idiot? "You know what? Fuck it. I'll deal with this myself."

The limo drove away. Dex and his lady were off to their final destination.

Time for the games to begin.

CHAPTER FOUR

"Do you kiss all of your fake fiancés that way?" Dex asked as he lounged against the leather seat in the back of the limo.

"Yes." An absolute, honest answer.

It was too dark for her to clearly see his expression, but she felt the sudden stiffness of his body. Someone obviously hadn't liked her answer. She faked alarm. "Oh, I'm sorry? Did you think you were special? Hate to break it to you, but I do kiss all of my fake fiancés that exact same way."

His fingers drummed on his knee. "Because I'm the only fake fiancé you've ever had."

Bingo. "Not like I go around town and pretend to marry men every day."

"That's good to know." His voice was a growl.

A nervous laugh escaped her as the car slowed. "You sound jealous."

"I am." He turned fully toward her. "When it comes to you, I am very, very jealous." His hand rose and cupped her chin.

"I don't even have a ring yet," she mumbled because Lacey suddenly was feeling way out of her element. *It was the second kiss. I knew I should have held on to my control. But he gave me that warm smile, and I just...*

It had felt like seeing behind the mask, and she'd reacted. She'd let her walls fall down in return, and she'd kissed him as if nothing else mattered.

"Don't worry, I'll take care of that problem right away." His mouth swept toward hers.

And she might have leaned toward him. *Eager much?*

The limo's rear door opened. "Sir, we are here."

Dex's lips brushed over hers.

Part of her was all...*He knew the driver was coming. The kiss is deliberate. Just for show, tricky bastard.*

But another part of her was like...*I'll take more, please.*

She had to yank up her walls again, ASAP.

"Time for us to go, darling," he rumbled against her mouth. "I hope you're ready for a week you will never forget."

"Promises, promises," she responded. Then, because one good show deserved another, she caught his hand in hers. She brought his palm to her lips. Pressed a tender kiss to the center of his hand.

Dex hissed in a breath.

Then she sensually nipped the pad of flesh under his thumb. "I hope you're ready for what's coming," she added, voice husky.

For a moment, he didn't move at all. His gaze just locked on her. Even though the back door was open and cold air swept inside, she could have sworn that in the space between her and Dex, the temperature notched up several degrees.

"Uh, sir?" The driver cleared his throat. "The bellman already took your bags, and I think someone from concierge is waiting for you."

She let go of Dex's hand. But he immediately grabbed her hand back and twined his fingers with hers. Dex climbed from the car and tugged her with him.

Outside, yes, it was definitely colder. She shivered and knew that her outfit was not warm enough. One sweater wasn't going to do it up here. Winter temps in Georgia were a million miles removed from icy temperatures in the mountains of Colorado.

When she shivered, Dex immediately wrapped his arm around her and pulled her against his body. "Don't worry, I'll warm you up."

Oh, yes, she just bet he would. The doorman held open the door as they hurried inside, and, sure enough, there was a man in a dapper concierge uniform waiting for them. He had a clipboard in his hand and his shoulders were squared. His ID tag indicated his name was Charles Hatch, and as they closed in on him, Charles quickly said, "Mr. and Mrs. Ryan, welcome to—"

"We're not married," Lacey corrected as she kept her tone all smooth and steady. "I'm Lacey Amari."

Someone brushed by her and headed for the elevator. The stranger was bundled in a thick coat, and she had a quick impression of blond hair and a square jaw.

"But I thought—" Charles glanced down at the clipboard. Then he looked at Dex, and the poor fellow's expression could only be termed horrified. "I am so sorry." His voice was hollow. Whispery.

But Dex laughed. His warm, rich laughter seemed to echo around them, and Lacey could feel the gazes turning in their direction. There weren't very many people in the spacious lobby. Merely a few couples. And after a quick glance, they went back to their business.

She had to admit, the lodge was impressive. She'd been told by Dex that this was an old structure, on the historic registry. Marble floor beneath their feet. A massive, crackling fireplace in the middle of the main entrance room. Huge, elaborate arches up on the second floor above them. The arches were carefully carved, and her gaze lingered on the deep, sweeping designs that had been cut into them.

Because she was staring so hard at the arches, it took her a moment to realize...

Dex had bent on one knee near her.

Her head slowly turned to him. "Dex?" Her voice sounded breathless. A nice touch, she thought.

He smiled at her. The smile seemed to warm his eyes.

Don't believe that warmth. It's not real.

He reached into his pocket and pulled out a blue box. Very distinct, turquoise blue. He opened the box, and the ring glinted at her as the light hit the facets in the diamond ring. He took the diamond from the box and held it up to her. The round, heavy diamond looked like pure perfection.

It also looked as if it probably cost more than her apartment.

"I've never met anyone like you," Dex told her quietly. "From the moment you walked into my life, I knew I wanted you to stay. There is nothing I would not do in order to keep you by my side. Despite the hell that I see too often in this world, there is good out there. I know it when I look into your eyes."

Um...okay. His proposal wasn't the whole...*I'll love you forever and ever* kind of thing, but it actually fit him. It *sounded* genuine.

"Will you marry me?" Dex asked as he waited on his bent knee.

Will you pretend marry me? "Absolutely." A wide smile curved her lips. "I was starting to think you'd never ask." Like, seriously, why hadn't he proposed in the limo? Knowing him, probably because he wanted to make a big production of the event. *Create a show. Attract attention.*

She reached for the ring, and she let her fingers tremble a bit as she slid it onto her ring finger. "Oh, Dexy..."

He blinked. His brow furrowed.

Wait, had that been too much? *Dexy?* Probably. Yes. Too much.

He bit his lower lip. Was he trying not to laugh at her?

"It fits perfectly," she continued quickly. No big surprise that the ring fit. He'd done so much research on her that the man probably knew her bra size. And wasn't that a whole lot of info for him to know?

He rose and pressed a tender kiss to her lips. "You've made me the happiest man in the world."

Doubtful. Highly, highly doubtful, but he was putting on a good act, so... "I love you," she said as she pulled back and gazed into his eyes.

Only...

Something happened.

There was a crack in his expression. She saw it. For one faint moment, she could have sworn there was...*Yearning?* "Dex?" Her heart ached. "What is it?"

He swallowed, and just like that, the super spy was back. "I want to be alone with you."

Now her heart wasn't aching. It was racing.

He turned to the concierge guy and rattled off the name of some stupid expensive champagne—one that happened to be her secret favorite in the whole world because she'd had it at one of the Wilde company parties and she'd *loved* it—and she knew the choice of champagne could not be coincidence. He'd done that deliberately. Another way of showing how much he knew about her.

So she just had to sigh and say, "Oh, Dex, you remembered." She could put on a good show, too.

He gave a quick nod. "Every single thing about you."

Okay, she didn't think he was lying with that particular statement.

"Sir...I-I am so sorry. There was a notation in your file. I thought it said you were married, but now I guess it meant..." Miserably, Charles trailed off.

A warm laugh slipped from Dex. "It meant I was going to propose and that I'd reserved the

Whisper Floor for the special event." Dex looked upward.

She followed his gaze and once again found herself studying all of the elaborate arches. Wait, Whisper Floor? Was that what he'd called it?

"I'm so sorry," Charles apologized again.

Lacey focused on him and saw the poor man's face was mottled red and sweat beaded his brow. "Please don't be sorry," she told him sincerely. Why on earth should he feel miserable when everything was a hoax? "This moment was perfect. I would not want it any other way."

Charles's head bobbed as he shot her a grateful smile.

"But we'll still take that reserved time on the Whisper Floor," Dex noted. "I think my fiancée will quite enjoy it."

"Promises, promises," she told him with a coy look. She had no idea what was up on the Whisper Floor but the man was acting like it was a big deal, so she'd play along.

She *had* to play along, didn't she?

"The key to your suite." Charles offered it with a flourish. "You'll go straight down the hallway, beyond the main lobby. The private elevator is to your left, and if you should need anything during your stay, please know that I am at your service."

"Thanks, Charles." Dex took the key and traded off a tip all with one casual wave of his hand. "I will remember that."

Charles took a sly glance at the tip. And immediately perked up. "Yes, sir. I am here for *you*."

All right, then. So...were they done with the proposal? Ready to actually get to work? Because, so far, there had been no action. She was itching for some action.

Dex curled his arm around her hips, and they began to walk away from Charles. Then he paused. "Oh, one thing you can do for me. We want to hit the slopes first thing in the morning."

Lacey controlled a flinch. Dear God, they did?

"I will make arrangements," Charles promised. She almost expected him to salute.

"Great. Double Black Diamond, that's always how I roll."

Sweet mother of...

She didn't say another word, not until they were inside the private elevator. When the doors closed, Lacey immediately blurted, "I can't ski."

Dex crossed his arms over his chest and leaned back against the glass wall of the elevator as they began to ascend. "Great performance out there. When you looked into my eyes and said you loved me, I could almost believe you."

"I don't love you. And I *can't* ski."

"Really?"

"You know this," she accused as she closed in on him. "You know everything about me."

He inclined his head. "I try."

"Then *why* would you attempt to kill me on a Double Black Diamond course?"

"Relax, love. You won't be skiing. I'll keep you safe."

She wanted to scream at him. The last thing she felt was *relaxed*.

"Do you like the ring?"

"It's beautiful." She didn't even glance at it. "What is my job here, exactly? Other than to fawn over you? Because I have talents. Lots of them that are being wasted, and I don't exactly enjoy playing arm candy—"

"You've already completed the first phase of your assignment. You helped me to attract the attention I wanted."

The proposal. "I knew you deliberately waited before giving me the ring."

"I do like to make a good entrance."

The elevator dinged, and the doors opened.

She started to head out, but Dex put a hand on her shoulder. "Let me check things first, would you?"

Lacey tried to ignore the pulse of heat that his touch had created. "I can handle myself." Did he expect an attack already?

When he moved forward and pushed back the edge of his blazer, she saw his holster. *Oh, yes. He does expect an attack already.* "You had that on in the limo?"

"Sweetheart, I had that on in the plane." He slipped out first and glanced to the left and then to the right. "Okay. Clear."

"I want one. I don't understand why you get a weapon and I don't. That's hardly fair."

"You like knives, not guns."

Yes, she did. The very first time they'd met, she'd pulled a knife on him. Ah, memories.

"There's going to be a lovely present waiting for you in the suite. Don't worry. I have you covered."

Then he opened the suite's door and took her into a lover's paradise.

A fireplace—nearly as big as the one downstairs—dominated the middle of the main room. The flames flickered. A big, floor to ceiling window showed the soft snowfall and the killer view of the mountains in the distance. Beyond the main sitting area, she saw an open door that led to the bedroom. Inside that bedroom, Lacey glimpsed a massive, four-poster bed. Such a big, big bed. The covers were turned down—black, silk sheets. Faint, romantic music played from somewhere, and she could swear that she even caught the faint scent of vanilla in the air.

She tiptoed her way in the bedroom. Noticed that there was yet another fireplace in that room, one near a very heavy, elaborate bookshelf. And across from that bookshelf, a floor to ceiling window provided another killer view of the mountains.

A wrapped package waited on the bedside table. The present he'd promised? She glanced at it. Then at him. Of course, Dex had followed her into the bedroom.

Dex waved toward the box. "Go ahead. It's for you, after all."

She hurried across the floor, and the lush carpeting swallowed the sounds of her steps. She opened the package—far too quickly because she was feeling like a kid at Christmas—and when she pulled the beautiful blade from its sheath... "It is perfect." She smiled and lifted the knife toward the light.

"I think you like that more than the diamond."

Her gaze jerked to him. "I—"

Dex's phone rang. He glanced at the screen. "Sorry, it's the office," he said without looking up at her. "Have to take this. I'll be in the hallway and when the luggage arrives—and the champagne I ordered—I'll make certain everything is sent into the suite."

"Thank you, Dex," she blurted. "I really like the present."

His gaze lifted. Held hers. "Keep it close. When you value something, keep it very, very close."

A few moments later, the suite's door closed behind him.

Her hand curled around the handle of the knife. "Don't worry. I will."

***

"You made a serious mistake, Dex." The voice was low. Taunting.

"Sorry, I think you have the wrong number," he responded cheerfully. "But go fuck yourself and have a good—"

"Don't play your games with me. I know where you are."

"Is that supposed to scare me?" Now genuine curiosity filled his voice. "I never know with you. You do keep me guessing." *Almost* a compliment.

"You think you can play your games and never get hurt. You think there isn't blood on your hands—"

"I never said there was no blood on me. There's always blood. It covers you, too, and if you try to pretend it doesn't, you're just lying to yourself." *Truth hurts, doesn't it?*

"You're going to be sorry. You think you're the smartest guy in the whole freaking world, but all you are is a fake. There is no real Dexter Ryan. You have no soul. You have no conscience. You have—"

"I have her," he inserted flatly. He could see that the elevator was rising. He needed to wrap this shit up. Their luggage was about to be delivered. Hopefully, the champagne, too. Thanks to Antony, he knew Lacey loved that particular champagne.

Rough laughter grated in his ear. "Like I'm supposed to care that some dumb bitch agreed to marry you?"

Dex tensed. "Don't talk that way about my fiancée."

"You don't care about her. You're just jerking that woman around. Trying to look normal when we both know that you don't have a normal emotion in—"

"Talk about her again, and you'll regret it."

Again, laughter burst from him. "The mighty Dex is revealing a weakness? A chink in his armor? I don't buy it."

"I don't care what you buy. Here's what I know. *I. Have. Her.*"

Silence. As if the words had finally registered.

"Did you truly think you'd find her first?" Dex continued and it was his turn to laugh. "I've always been better than you. More motivated.

More driven. Always been willing to do whatever it takes."

"Don't lie to me."

"I have her, and if you want to deal, you will stop this bullshit stuff where you're calling and you're hiding in shadows and you're playing *your* games. I'm not in the mood to play any longer."

"It's not her."

"I'm sure you heard her name when you brushed by us in the lobby." *Yeah, I spotted you. Like that required even half an effort.* "Check her out. See what you discover. When you're done, you come to me and we'll deal. Turns out I'll be on the slopes tomorrow with my *fiancée*. Maybe we'll both see you there."

"Dex—"

The elevator dinged. "My luggage is about to arrive." The doors opened. *Sweet. The champagne is there, too.* "And my champagne is ready. I'm off to celebrate with Lacey. Chat later." He hung up the phone.

Within moments, the luggage had been delivered, the champagne was chilling by the bed, and Dex was alone with Lacey. She stared out at the view, and a soft smile curved her full lips. "This is beautiful."

He didn't look at the mountains. "Stunning."

Her head turned toward him. The faint smile was still on her face.

I love you. For a moment, he could hear her giving him that declaration again. She hadn't meant those words. She'd been acting, just as he had been. But he'd almost wanted to believe her.

He'd wondered...what it would be like to be loved by Lacey Amari?

But that wasn't going to happen. Not today. Not ever. He was using her. And when she found out the truth...

Shit. Lacey would try to kick his ass.

"How about we open that champagne?" Dex asked. "I could sure as hell use a drink."

"Was everything okay at the office?" She took a quick step toward him.

Okay? Not by a long shot. In his world, though, things were rarely okay. Most of the time, the world was on fire. He'd learned to deal with the heat. "All going to plan," he assured her cheerfully. That *was* the truth. Nothing was okay, but everything was happening exactly as he'd intended.

He just...

He hadn't realized that he'd started to feel this weird ache when he looked at her. Was it longing? Need? Yes, he desired her. He'd known that from the beginning. But he could separate his emotions. His lust. There was the job. Then there was her. Not like he'd get this setup confused in his head and think that they were *actually* a couple. Not like he'd fall for her.

He popped the cork on the champagne. Poured some into a long flute and the bubbles spilled over the side.

"Wow, I think that's enough." She laughed and reached for the glass. Her fingers slid over his.

He usually could do a smooth-move champagne pour in his sleep. It wasn't like him to make a mess. "I spilled it. I gave you too much."

"Yes, well, it's okay." She took the glass from him. "What's a little spilled champagne between friends?"

But they weren't friends.

A smile played along her lips. "You have to put some in your glass or we can't have a toast."

Of course. So why was he just staring at her? He poured champagne into his flute and *didn't* make it overflow this time.

Lacey lifted her glass. "What shall we toast to?"

"How about...To all the things we wish we could have...but are out of our reach."

Her nose scrunched. *Cute.* "All right," she agreed slowly. "But that is a shitty toast."

He blinked. The words had just come out of his mouth. Mostly because he was staring at her and wanting her far too much. "Shitty?"

"Toasts are supposed to be good. They are supposed to be celebrating something. If you're longing for something out of your reach," she stepped even closer, "then you need to do something about that. Maybe reach out and take it."

Oh, he wanted to do something. But...

The job. Do the job. Not her.

"Know what? I'll give the toast." She raised her glass a little higher. "To the best fake engagement in the world and to the man who will finally give me what I've always wanted."

For one crazy moment he thought...

But no.

She didn't mean hot, screaming sex. His bad.

She meant the truth about her family. That was what she wanted. Unfortunately, it was what she would get, too. His glass tapped against hers. "Here's to making dreams come true."

Dreams. Nightmares. Sometimes, they were the same thing.

But I won't let you be hurt, Lacey. I will protect you. No matter what. He wasn't the total bastard that most people assumed. He was just a partial bastard. And when it came to Lacey, he was finding that he didn't want to be a bastard at all.

She took a sip of the champagne. A low, sexy moan pulled from her.

Of course, his eager cock twitched.

Then she lowered the flute and licked her lower lip. "My favorite."

I know.

"But you knew that," she continued carefully as her long lashes swept down to conceal her gaze from him. "You must think that gives you an advantage over me. The fact that you know so much about me. That you believe you know all my secrets."

His gut clenched. There were some secrets he knew, that he was using, that she had no clue about. "Lacey..."

"Except here's the thing. One of the things you *should* have learned is that I'm really good at reading people. And I can read you." Her lashes lifted. "For some reason, you are almost exceptionally easy for me to read."

No way. "That's something no one else has ever said before." *No one* had been able to see past—

"You lied to me."

His hold tightened on the fragile stem of the champagne flute. "Excuse me?"

"Things are not okay at the office for you. In fact, I suspect things are very, very bad right now. I want the truth. I want to know exactly what's happening. Exactly how I'm involved and exactly how we are going to end this case and catch whatever bad guys are waiting for us."

Uh...

She brought the champagne glass to her lips and downed the rest of the contents in a fast gulp. "Absolutely fantastic. I will be wanting more."

She...

She put down the glass. "Start talking."

CHAPTER FIVE

He'd told her jackshit and working blind really wasn't her forte. If Dex intended for her to be his partner, then he had to stop leaving her in the dark.

Immediately.

She stared into the mirror, pulled her hair over her shoulders, straightened her spine, then nodded. Okay. She was good to go. Lacey turned and headed out of the spacious bathroom and when she stepped into the suite's main area, Dex was waiting on her.

He wore a black suit, an expensive, white shirt under the jacket providing a flash of contrast. He was adjusting the sleeve of his jacket when he looked at her, and for a moment, she felt almost frozen.

Dex cleaned up very, very well.

She'd known that, of course, but...

He is hot. The kind of hot that could make a woman forget almost everything else and just go with the urge to walk across the room. Wrap her arms around him. And kiss him like her very life depended on it.

Not that she was going to do that. But she could see where some other woman might feel so inclined.

Sex and danger oozed from his pores and that powerful combination filled the air like an aphrodisiac. Why, oh, why, had she always had a thing for dangerous men?

Weakness.

His gaze slowly swept over her. "You look stunning."

She hadn't brought the dress. Because when he'd told her to pack, he'd left out the part about having some sort of fancy, gala-type dress at the ready. She distinctly remembered him telling her to dress for the cold...and to bring something sexy. A Cinderella ball gown had not been on her list.

But he'd waved his magic wand and gotten one to appear.

Sleeveless, the A-line, black dress fit as if it had been made for her body. It was a sweetheart, floor-length dress designed with cascading ruffles that appeared right after her waist. The material cinched around her waist before swirling loosely around her hips and legs. And that loose material was absolutely perfect...for hiding her knife.

She'd strapped her new knife and sheath to her right thigh. A lady had to be prepared when she went to the big ball.

And, whoops, she'd been staring at him too long. Lacey cleared her throat. "You look very handsome. All suave and sophisticated."

"I do try." He let go of his sleeve and offered his arm to her. "Shall we?"

Why the hell not? She took his arm, and they strolled from the suite. The high heels she wore gave her a little added height boost, but he still swamped her in size and as soon as they stepped into the elevator, the space sure did feel extra small.

"It's a tradition to have this winter ball at the lodge. After the ball, you and I are scheduled to have our time on the Whisper Floor. Don't worry. We'll only stay at the ball for about thirty minutes. The point is for us to be seen. For us to talk to the others."

She nodded. "Because one of them is the target."

He'd admitted that much to her when she'd demanded that he tell her the truth earlier, so perhaps she hadn't quite gotten total jackshit from him. What he'd told her was... *The target is at the lodge. My intel told me he'd be here. Your job is to help lure him out.*

Her mission, not that she had any choice but to accept it.

"I'll be called away after our first dance," he added. "Or, at least it will look that way. When I leave, you circulate. You're so fucking sexy, you won't have trouble attracting attention."

Her eyebrows shot up. "But I thought this place was primarily for couples. If people are involved, I doubt the guys will be lining up—"

"Oh, did I say it was only for couples?"

Actually, no, now that she thought about it, he hadn't. She'd asked if it was a couple's retreat and he'd—

"That's my mistake. Sorry." Dex shrugged.

Her eyes narrowed. "It's hard to work with you."

He seemed to consider those words. "It may surprise you to learn that I have been told that before."

It did not surprise her even a little bit. "It's hard when you keep omitting important points, twisting the truth, and *lying*."

"I want to kiss you."

She blinked. "What?"

The elevator dinged. The doors were about to open.

He brought his face close to her left ear. "I want to kiss you. I thought you might appreciate a moment when I wasn't lying."

Her breath caught.

The doors had opened. Once more, he offered his arm, and soon they were in the ballroom, and, yes, it was as fancy as she expected. Glittering chandeliers. Elaborate arrangements of flowers everywhere. A live band played on a raised stage while white-coated waiters offered hors d'oeuvres. The smell of money seemed to hang in the air.

She'd done plenty of undercover assignments with the rich and famous, so she knew how to blend in at these scenes. But being able to blend in didn't mean that she *liked* these events. They always made her feel uncomfortable. Like someone would realize she was a fraud and didn't belong.

"You are the most beautiful woman in the room."

Surprise rushed through her. He sounded as if he meant those words. But this *was* Dex—

"And, in case you were wondering, that was another true statement." He inclined his head toward the dance floor. "Let's dance and that will allow me the chance to whisper all sorts of secrets in your ear."

Well, that certainly sounded interesting.

She let him lead her onto the dance floor, and when his hands curled around her hips and he pulled her close, a spark of electricity fired her blood. They swayed easily together. It was almost as if they'd danced dozens of times just this way.

"See?" Dex murmured. His head had lowered. His lips feathered over her ear. "Bet you're regretting not agreeing to dance with me at the club when I made the offer. Now that you can see my fancy footwork in action, the regret must be weighing heavily on your soul."

A surprised laugh sputtered out of her. She was looking to the side and, at her laugh, she saw a blond man's head turn toward her. He glanced at her quickly, then away.

"You're staring at the blond," Dex continued as he kept his mouth near her ear. "He's one of my targets."

How had Dex realized she was—

"Name's Roman Valentino. Money to burn, powerful connections to far too many countries, and certainly a person of interest for us."

She noticed Roman was dancing with a pretty brunette. The woman's dark hair was pulled back into an elegant twist. She wore a white gown that curled over one shoulder and hugged the curves of her body.

"And who is the woman?" Lacey asked.

"His bodyguard. Heather Madding. They pretend to be involved, but they're not." Dex's mouth moved down until it hovered over the curve of Lacey's shoulder. "You smell delicious." He pressed a soft kiss to her shoulder.

"I-I thought this place was for lovers. A retreat—"

"Not exactly. Oh, sure, plenty of lovers come here. It's the perfect place to sneak away. But others visit, too. For a variety of reasons. In order to get in, you just have to be willing to pay the price."

She was betting the price was very, very high.

"The lodge promises complete privacy, and sometimes, people in my line of work need a location like this one."

Now her gaze swept the ballroom. "So...are there other spies here? Is that what you're telling me?"

"Sure, there are...others...in my line of work here."

That certainly seemed like an extremely careful answer.

"There are also celebrities. A fashion CEO. A famous chef. And, if you take a look to my left, you'll even see a familiar face."

She darted a quick glance to the left. "That's Jonathan Radcliff."

"You mean Duke Radcliff, don't you?"

She didn't really bother with titles much. "I worked his protection detail about two months ago." She'd kept him—and his new wife, Elizabeth—safe. The new wife was currently in

Jonathan's arms and staring up at her husband with an expression of utter bliss on her face.

He looked back at her the same way. As if the whole universe revolved around her.

Must be nice. The thought slipped through Lacey's mind before she could stop it.

Just then, Jonathan glanced over and spotted her. A broad smile swept across his face. "Lacey!"

Heads turned at his call. More attention that went to him, then immediately to her.

And Lacey got the uncomfortable feeling that this entire scene was a set-up.

Wait, had Dex arranged for Jonathan and Elizabeth to be there?

Jonathan and Elizabeth were approaching, both with friendly smiles on their faces.

Dex pressed another kiss to her shoulder. "Delicious." Then his head turned toward the approaching couple.

Jonathan beamed while Elizabeth pretty much glowed. Lacey liked the couple. They were both kind and *real*, and the idea that Dex might be using them in some way...no. *I won't let him hurt these two.*

Jonathan stood at about six-foot-one, with firm shoulders and dark hair that had begun to thin just a little. His features were warm and even, and he had faint laugh lines around his mouth from frequent smiles. Elizabeth's dark hair skimmed her cheeks and stopped just at her chin level in a stylish bob that accentuated her sharp cheekbones. Her eyes were warm and wide, and her lips were painted a sleek red.

"Lacey, it is so wonderful to see you!" Elizabeth pulled her in for a warm hug. "When Jonathan sprang this surprise trip on me, I had no idea what to expect. But this place is like a dream and seeing you here—it's just even better!" Elizabeth was American, a teacher who'd been hired to work with Jonathan's nephew. But once Jonathan had met the teacher his nephew raved about so much, he'd been hooked.

Elizabeth let her go and looked expectantly toward Dex.

Lacey knew she should probably make introductions.

"Are you working on a case, Lacey?" Jonathan asked as he leaned in close. "I must say, I find your work fascinating!" Then he gave a hard nod. "She saved my life, you see. Twice, in fact. I owe this woman a debt I will never repay."

For a moment, Elizabeth's lower lip trembled. "Me, too," she whispered.

Lacey felt her cheeks burn. "I was just doing my job. You don't owe me anything." Her left hand lifted and pressed to Dex's chest. "But I'm not here on a case, Jon. I'm here..."

"Because I can't spend another moment of my life without her," Dex inserted smoothly. "And I asked Lacey to be my wife."

Elizabeth's eyes widened. She even gave an excited little bounce. That was Elizabeth—always moving. Always happy.

Dex offered his hand to Jonathan. "Dex Ryan."

Jonathan shook his offered hand. A faint furrow appeared between his eyebrows. "I've heard that name...haven't I?"

"I'm pretty infamous in certain circles." A waiter passed by with a tray of champagne. They all took glasses and Jonathan laughed, as if Dex had made a great joke.

He hadn't. The man *was* infamous.

Lacey put the glass to her lips, and her gaze darted around the ballroom. She could *feel* eyes on her. And...

The blond. He stood against a tall, white column. There was no sign of the woman who'd been with him earlier. The man's gaze was locked straight on her. She could have sworn she saw...

Fury.

Yes. He was staring at her with absolute rage in his eyes. *No, not me.* Dex. He was focused on Dex. Her breath caught because she knew that couldn't be good.

The blond's hand began to slide toward the inside of his tux—"Dex?"

The lights went out. The ballroom was plunged into complete darkness, and, somewhere, a woman screamed. That one scream was followed by another and another.

Great. Hello, panic. Here we go.

"Everyone, calm down." Dex's commanding voice rang out. "I'm sure there is no cause for alarm. Just a temporary outage so..."

Every instinct she possessed screamed at her, and she kept seeing that blond's hand slide toward the inside of his tux. So maybe...screw calm. *"Everyone, get down!"* Lacey shouted.

"What?" Dex asked. "What are you—"

She threw her body into his just as a gunshot rang out.

More screams. Footsteps rushed by as people frantically moved for the exits, and a spiky heel slammed into the back of her hand.

"Dammit!" Lacey swore. "*That hurt.*"

Beneath her, she felt Dex's entire body harden. "You're hit?" He rolled her, moving quickly so that he was on top and his hands flew over her. "Where, baby? Tell me where, and I'll make sure that you're—"

The lights flashed back on. The brightness was disorienting. She had to blink a few times and Lacey found herself staring straight into Dex's wild gaze. A gaze that was frantic and worried and—

"I'm not hit," she said as her hands pushed against him. "Are you?" She knew the sound of a gunshot, and one had fired.

He released a breath, as if he'd been holding it, and Dex grimly shook his head. "No, I'm good."

Good didn't seem to be the right word.

He rose, slowly, and his gaze surveyed the room. Half of the ball attendees had already fled. As for the others, they were crouched in corners. She did her own visual scan of the area. No one appeared to be armed. There didn't seem to be any casualties.

The blond guy is gone. Because she was specifically looking for him, Lacey noticed his absence. Roman Valentino wasn't crouched in any corner.

"I say...I think that's a bullet hole." Jonathan's voice wobbled as he pointed toward the wall that was less than two feet away from Dex.

And, yes, he was correct. From what she could tell, there was a bullet embedded in the wall.

Security personnel raced into the room. And right behind them, she saw Charles—their concierge guy—enter the ballroom with fluttering hands and a look of panic on his face.

"It's a good thing you grabbed Lacey and ducked," Jonathan continued as he clapped a hand around Dex's shoulder. "I do believe one of you might have been shot, if you hadn't, ah, what's the phrase? Hit the deck?"

Lacey smoothed back her hair. There was no reason the shot would have been aimed at her. Obviously, Dex had been the target.

And she'd saved his ass. *Boom*. She'd be sure to tell him exactly how much he owed her as soon as they were alone and—

"We're getting out of here." Dex locked his fingers around her wrist. "*Now*."

But they needed to investigate. They had to take stock of the scene. See if the shooter was still there. Go find Roman Valentino. They—

"And I didn't grab Lacey," Dex snapped over his shoulder to Jonathan. "She grabbed me." He was hauling ass to get them out of there. In her heels, she had to race to keep up with him. As they blew by Charles, Dex glanced down at her. "I didn't anticipate the shot. That shit should never have happened." His eyes burned with fury. "Believe me, there will be hell to pay."

CHAPTER SIX

"I don't understand what's happening." Lacey wrapped her arms around her stomach and peered at Dex as they stood on the second floor of the lodge—the so-called Whisper Floor. "You brought me here to help with a case. How can you be surprised when gunfire erupts if we are working a mission?"

He clenched his hands into fists because his fingers were shaking. What in the hell was that shit about? His fingers never shook. He was always freaking rock steady. But this...

Right after the shot, he'd wanted to flee the ballroom with her, but the pricks from hotel security had stopped to interview him and everyone else. Well, those still present, anyway. A shooting at this place was a nightmare for management. By dawn, half of the guests— probably far more—would be gone. The lodge was known as a beacon of safety and secrecy, and for this to happen...

Unacceptable.

She stopped hugging herself and her hands fell to her sides. "You should at least thank me for saving your ass."

And you should scream at me for risking yours. "How did you know a shot was going to be fired?"

"Because I saw the blond guy—Roman— staring at you as if he hated you with every fiber of his being. Just as I was realizing he was hate-glaring at you, I saw his hand reaching for the inside of his tux. That was right before the lights went off. My instincts screamed, and I reacted."

Dex sucked in a deep breath. "Good reaction." But Roman as the shooter made no sense to him. The shot was far too risky to make in the dark, especially with Lacey *right there.* "You didn't mention this to the lodge's security team."

Her delicate eyebrows arched. "Was I supposed to do that? Do you want them knowing this intel or do you have other plans in place?"

He already had other plans in motion, and she obviously knew it.

"You didn't want another agent for the role I'm playing," she noted. "That was why you brought me, an outsider, into whatever web this is, but I'm guessing that doesn't mean other CIA operatives aren't here."

Again, she was right. He did have other operatives in position, and they were currently scrambling. They'd be in charge of the investigation, not any locals.

A lock of hair slid over her cheek. He reached out—just as she moved her hand to slide the lock back—and their fingers tangled.

Lacey went still as her gaze held his.

"Thank you for risking yourself to protect me." Dex had to force the words out. The very fact that she *had* been in jeopardy...*unacceptable.* Someone would pay.

"It's part of the job description," she told him breezily. "Protect and defend, and it's why you brought me out here so—"

"No," he growled when his control snapped. He could actually hear the snap. "Not the job description." He locked his hands around her and hauled her against him. His mouth crashed into hers as need and fear and lust surged through him.

The need and lust were easy to understand. He wanted Lacey. He thought she was the sexiest woman he'd ever seen. The longer he was with her, the more he wanted her.

The fear—that was different. He wasn't usually afraid of anything or anyone, but the idea of something happening to her, of her being hurt when she stood right beside him...

Can't happen. Won't happen.

Her lips were parted beneath his, and Lacey kissed him back with the same raw need that he felt. The kind of need that made him want to rip away her clothes, forget everything else, and just get lost in her.

The kind of need he didn't usually feel because he controlled his emotions, not the other way around. But with Lacey, everything was different. She was different.

And he was becoming different the longer he spent with her.

Her hands curled around his shoulders. Her body pressed to his. A soft moan built in her throat and he absolutely wanted—

"Ahem."

Dex wanted to be alone with her, not dealing with bureaucratic bullshit.

"Mr. Ryan, I must insist on speaking with you again. Multiple witnesses believe that you were the intended target, they put *you* nearest the location of where the bullet hit, so I just need to go over some safety protocols with you."

Dex slowly lifted his head and gazed down at Lacey. Her lips were red from his mouth. Her gaze—languid, sensual—held his.

"Charles is waiting for you," she said softly. Her voice was the best, huskiest temptation ever.

"Charles can fuck off," he replied. He'd been in the middle of other things.

"Ahem." That ahem sounded offended. "Sir, it is of the utmost importance that we speak—"

"He's one of your agents," Lacey continued without even missing a beat. "So go and give the man his instructions then come back to me."

She'd tagged Charles? Since when?

Lacey eased away from Dex and glanced over at Charles. "Am I to assume that this area is secure? No one else is lurking in any corridors up here?"

Dex turned his head toward Charles.

"The floor is secure," Charles agreed. His back was ramrod straight, and the man's expression was carved into tense lines. Dread practically poured from the fellow.

It should. Charles *was* on Dex's payroll, so to speak, and the man should have made sure that no freaking shooters were in that ballroom.

"Let's have that chat, Charles," Dex said silkily.

Charles flinched. He turned away.

Instead of immediately following, Dex caught Lacey's hand in his. "Stay here. I'll be back as soon as I can."

"Shouldn't I go investigate? Talk to the other guests? Find out who the hell is trying to shoot you?"

Not me, love. I'm not sure the bullet was for me. "This is a safe spot." The safest one at the moment. "I'll be right back." Then, before he gave in to the urge to pull her into his arms and maybe never, ever let go, Dex released her hand. He left her and strode after Charles.

***

Being on the second floor—the Whisper Floor, as Dex had called it before—gave Lacey a killer view of the scene below. Women in gorgeous gowns and men in expensive suits were rushing about in a frenzy. Some of the lodge staff members stood to the side, and she noticed the way they carefully eyed certain guests. *Ah, so you're an agent. And you're an agent...*

From a distance, it was easy to see what might get lost in a crowd. She could even see Dex as he and Charles huddled together.

Then Dex looked up. His intense, gray stare landed on her. She remembered the kiss. The passion that had nearly knocked her off her feet.

Lacey found herself backing away from the balcony. From him. She edged back toward the arches—

"Don't trust him."

Lacey stiffened when she heard the low warning. The whisper had just seemed to sound right in her ear. She whirled even as her heart raced but...

No one was there.

No one stood near her. No one stood anywhere close by at all. The arches stretched around her as her head turned to the left and the right. Odd. She had been so sure that she'd just heard a voice.

Absolutely certain...

She moved away from the arches and looked over the balcony once more. On the floor below, Dex was leaning in close for what appeared to be a very heated conversation with Charles. Poor Charles. The man looked like he was facing the devil himself.

Maybe he was.

But...

Her lips pressed together. *Dex kissed me like he'd go crazy without me.* And for just a moment, she'd felt the same way. Like she couldn't get close enough to him.

Adrenaline.

And...more.

Her hand curled around the wooden top of the balcony. Then her head lifted, and her gaze darted over the second floor. *That whisper had seemed so real.* Yet no one else appeared to be there.

Whisper Floor.

Body stiff, she headed back toward the arches. Then she turned, surveying the—

"He's lying to you."

Again, a whisper, just teasing her left ear.
And, again, *no one was there.*

***

"I want to know what the fuck happened, and I want to know now. If there was a man or a woman in the ballroom with a gun, I should have known the minute I stepped inside." Pissed didn't even begin to describe the way Dex felt.

"Yes, sir." Charles nodded.

"This isn't some amateur-level operation. I told you how important it was. I was counting on you, and you're screwing this to hell." He stepped closer. "Lacey could have been shot. If she'd been shot, everything would have been lost. *Everything.*"

Me. I would have been lost.

He stiffened. Glanced up. For just a moment, he caught sight of Lacey as she leaned over the balcony. Her expression was pensive. Then she looked away, and her gaze seemed to sweep toward the arches...right before she stepped back.

Oh, shit. The arches.

He bounded away from Charles and rushed for the stairs.

***

"He's using you. Don't believe a word he says."

No one was beside her, but the words were spoken as if another person was less than a breath away. Lacey bent and smoothed her hands over the cascading fall of her dress. Then she frowned at the fabric. Held it in a loose grip before straightening. Slowly, she circled around the edges of the Whisper Floor. With every step, she kept that loose grip on her dress, as if she was keeping it raised so she wouldn't trip on the long fabric, and when she got to the far right...

She saw the shadow from the corner of her eye.

Lacey yanked the knife from the sheath on her thigh, and she attacked. She lunged forward and shoved the knife against the throat of the man who'd stood under the arches in *that* section of the second floor.

The blond. Roman.

He blinked at her.

She pushed her knife harder against him. "You've got something to stay to me?" Lacey snarled at him. "Say it to my face. I'm not a big fan of people who lurk in corners and whisper ominous shit to me."

His lips parted, but he didn't speak.

"Whisper Floor," she snapped at him. "Took me a minute to remember why that seemed so familiar to me." She didn't take her gaze off her prey. "Read about another hotel with arches like this place once. Down in Mobile, Alabama. Article said you could speak into one end of an arch, and someone all the way on the other end could hear you."

"Move...the knife."

"I don't think so. That knife stays exactly where it is and you tell me why you are up here trying to warn me away from my fiancé."

"Because he's using you."

Tell me something I don't know. "He loves me," she threw right back, not missing a beat. "All of me. He knows exactly who I am."

"Yes...fuckin' bet he does."

What? Her lips parted.

"Lacey!" Dex roared her name as he bounded up the stairs. "Lacey! Baby, where—"

"I'm here, and I have a new friend," she called to him.

Dex ran to her side. Stopped. Whistled. Then, voice amused, Dex said, "Oh, darling, you're already using your engagement present. So very happy that you're enjoying it."

Sweat trickled down Roman's left temple.

"This jerk was hiding in the corner, whispering into the arch about how I couldn't trust you."

"Was he now." Only Dex's words weren't a question.

"When a man hides in a corner near a woman, it makes you think he might be planning to attack. So I attacked first." She rolled one shoulder in a shrug. Her grip on the knife never wavered. "That's who I am. A fight-first-and-question-later kind of woman."

Roman's gaze jumped to Dex. "Call...her off."

Lacey's stare hardened on him.

"Are you implying that my fiancée is some sort of attack dog? Someone—something—to be *called off*?" Dex's voice wasn't amused any longer. It was furious. Rumbling with dark intent and power. "Because I will kick the living hell out of you if you disrespect her by word or deed, so watch your damn self."

"She's not your fiancée. Obviously...bodyguard."

Now Lacey laughed. "What is it about Dex that makes you think he would need a bodyguard? Obviously," she used the word deliberately, "he can take care of himself."

Roman's eyes widened. "You're...actually...marrying him?"

"I'm wearing the ring. Did you miss it? It's pretty big, so I'm surprised you didn't notice it." As she stared into his eyes, there was something about him that nagged at her. She didn't think they'd ever met before, but there *was* a familiarity there. Something she couldn't quite place. "How do I know you?"

His expression shut down.

Dex's fingers slid to cup her shoulder. "He's not going to fight. He's going to walk away. Aren't you, Roman?"

Roman gave a jerky nod. The blade nicked him.

"I hope you've satisfied your curiosity with this little meet-and-greet," Dex continued, still using his I-will-destroy-you voice of fury. "Because it's time for your ass to go, Roman."

"Consider it satisfied."

Lacey slowly lowered her blade. "My curiosity isn't satisfied." In fact, it was working toward a fever pitch.

Roman swiped away the trickle of blood on his neck.

"Why were you warning me about Dex?" Lacey wanted to know.

"Because he's an asshole," Roman replied flatly. "You can't trust him."

Interesting. His tone had just told her..."You hate him."

Roman's stare flickered toward Dex. "You can say that. And to think, we were once best buds."

"Friends make for the worst enemies," Dex tossed out.

Okay, there was apparently lots at play between them. Time to cut to the chase. "Did you shoot at Dex in the ballroom?" she asked Roman.

"No." An immediate reply.

And one she didn't buy. "You were reaching inside your jacket before the lights went out—"

"Because I had a telephone call to make. I was reaching for my phone. I didn't shoot at Dex." He swiped at his neck again and left a faint smear of red near his Adam's apple. "Now, we're done. I've been assaulted and treated like a criminal, so I think my night is complete." With that, he stalked toward the stairs—

"Did you shoot at Lacey?" Dex's question rang out, hard and stark.

Roman stilled. Then whirled to face him. "What?"

"You said you didn't shoot at me. Fine. I buy that, especially since I'm not so sure I was the target."

Whoa, whoa, whoa. Lacey shook her head. Why would anyone in the ballroom be shooting at her? She'd done nothing wrong! She hadn't even known most of the people in there!

Roman's gaze lingered on her. "I did not shoot at Lacey."

"Did *anyone* on your team fire the shot?" Dex gritted out.

"I will fucking find out," Roman vowed.

Then he was leaving. Rushing away in a storm of fury. She didn't move, not until she was absolutely sure he was out of sight and then— *"What in the hell, Dex? Why would someone want to kill me?"*

His lips thinned.

"This is insane. You have me operating in the dark. You're making me work blind even when I am saving your ass." He was also dead wrong. Because no, surely nobody had wanted to kill her. This scene must be about him. Huffing out a breath, she hitched up the cascading bottom of her dress to reveal the sheath strapped to her thigh. "I swear," Lacey fumed as she shoved the knife into the sheath, "you are driving me to—"

He caught her chin. Tipped her head up. Kissed her.

Not some hard, heavy, desperate kiss.

But...

Softer. Careful. Like she was something very, very precious and he was afraid she'd break on him.

She wasn't the type of woman to break. He should know that. He seemed to know everything else about her.

But as the kiss lingered, she realized there was more at play. He was kissing her with such tender care. Maybe it wasn't as if he thought she'd break...

More like...

I'm something he can't lose?

And how in the hell was she even getting that from a kiss? What was the man doing to her head? Was he making her as crazy as he was? She let go of the gown and pushed against his chest. "Stop."

Immediately, he tensed.

"Not here," she added. "Let's get back to our suite. We need to talk, now, and I want to be sure someone isn't lurking around a corner and trying to whisper in my ear."

"Is that what the bastard was doing?" His eyes glittered. "Whispering about me?"

"Not here," she repeated. She moved away from him and her dress fluttered around her. She was far, far too conscious of the weight of her weapon against her leg. "Come on."

"Where you go, I follow."

Lacey slanted a glance over her shoulder at him. "Do I look like I'm in the mood to be mocked?"

His expression was unguarded. Intense. Focused solely on her. "And does it look like I'm mocking?" he asked quietly. "Where you go, I will follow. I'm starting to wonder if that is going to be the story of my fucking life."

***

Someone had been shooting at Lacey Amari? That was truly what Dex believed?

Roman marched back into his suite—he and Heather had taken the honeymoon suite because it worked as a great cover. He'd heard the blast of the shot in the ballroom, but knowing how Dex attracted enemies in swarms, he'd just figured someone had targeted the SOB.

But if the shot had been intended for Lacey...

Everything changes.

"Heather!" Roman called for his bodyguard and the woman he'd trusted implicitly with the secrets of his life. "Heather, we have a situation we have to handle!"

The door to the bedroom was slightly ajar. He'd given her the bedroom, and he'd planned to crash on the couch. At his call, she didn't reply.

After the mess in the ballroom, he knew she'd gone to canvas the area, but they intended to meet up in the suite.

He headed for the bedroom door. Rapped lightly with his knuckles. "Heather? Listen, there is something I have to tell you about—"

The door inched open beneath his knuckles.

The room was empty. No Heather.

Roman heard a rustle of sound behind him. He turned—

Too late.

Something hit him in the side of the head. A blow hard enough to send him stumbling into the door. Then another blow followed. A third.

If any hits came after that, he didn't know. Roman was out cold.

CHAPTER SEVEN

His plan was shit. He'd made a major tactical error, and Dex didn't like to make errors. He followed Lacey into their suite and shut the door. He took a moment to flip the locks into place, and then he pressed his back to the wood of the door as he studied her.

"You have way too many secrets, Dexter Ryan." She lifted the heavy fall of hair off her neck, revealing the delicate column of her throat. He wanted to cross the room and put his mouth to her throat. To kiss her. To drink in her scent.

He wanted to fuck her.

Because he wanted her so very badly, he locked down the muscles in his body and didn't move at all.

She stared at him and seemed to wait for a reply. When none came, a soft sigh escaped her. Lacey dropped her hair. "I'm guessing you're not about to share your secrets."

"Don't remember that being part of our deal." He hated the wooden tone of his voice. He didn't want to be wooden with her. He wanted to be real. But he couldn't be real with anyone. *And you don't get to start now, jackass. So suck it up.*

"Our deal. How could I forget?" She nodded. "The deal where you blackmailed me into taking this job."

Dex winced. "Blackmail is such a dirty word," he muttered.

Her head cocked. Her hand trailed down the side of her neck, as if she'd realized how absolutely obsessed he was with that portion of her body and wanted to torment him even more for fun. It was strange because he'd never gotten stuck before thinking that a woman's neck was particularly sexy. He was more of a breast guy. And legs. He loved legs. Or hips and—

Screw it. I love everything about Lacey.

"Dirty words." Her voice was husky. She kicked off her high heels and stalked toward him. Her dress rustled. "Do you like dirty words, Dex?"

Oh, the dirty words he could imagine coming out of her mouth...

She stopped right in front of him. "Because if you don't *like* dirty words, then you shouldn't threaten dirty things."

"I haven't threatened—"

"You said that you'd tell Eric that I was using the resources at Wilde."

Guilty. He had done that.

"Look me in the eyes right now. If I were to walk away tonight, would you still tell him? If I got fed up with your secrets and your games, would you go to Eric and tell him that I'd held back on him? That I used Wilde?"

Fucking *fuck*. She was pushing him into a corner.

"Answer me honestly. We both know I can tell when you lie."

Only sometimes. But she was still far more accurate than others. "No."

Her eyes widened. If you stared into eyes like hers too long, a man could lose all control. Lose everything. *For her.*

Lacey leaned even closer. "Did you ever intend to tell Eric the truth?"

"No." It had been an empty threat. Why would he want to do anything to hurt her? Not then. Not now. *Not ever.*

Her sensual lips parted.

"But I *did* intend to keep up my part of the deal. I am going to find out who killed your parents."

Her gaze searched his. "Roman told me not to trust you."

"Roman...isn't he a stranger to you?" Dex asked carefully. "A man who whispers in shadows. Why believe him over me?"

"Because you just admitted to lying to me." A pause. "You know about my relationship with Eric, don't you?"

"Relationship?" He blinked innocently.

"Stop it." Her hand flattened on his chest. Her touch burned him to the core. "Don't play games."

But I don't know how to stop. It's as basic as breathing as this point.

"You had some tech guy dig up everything possible on me, didn't you?"

"Antony is very good at his job," Dex allowed. "But he is way more than just a tech guy. He'd be insulted to hear you thought his skills were limited. Very fragile ego on that one."

"Antony?" Her brows shot up. She kept right on touching him. Without the heels, she seemed even more delicate. Fragile. But she wasn't.

She had her knife strapped to her thigh.

Sexy.

Her scent was driving him mad. He inhaled a big, delicious whiff and admitted, "I didn't need Antony to find out the truth about you and Eric. I knew that before I ever approached you with my offer."

"You mean with your blackmail."

Unable to help himself, Dex leaned a little closer to her. "You're the one using the dirty words, sweetheart."

Her tongue swiped across her lower lip. "I can get dirtier," she promised.

Please, yes, do it.

"What do you know about me and Eric?"

Maybe if he shared with her, she'd trust him more. Her trust was going to be absolutely necessary in the coming days. "I know he's family. Part of the only family you think you have left." Holy shit, he'd just fucked up. He needed to watch his wording better. "Eric...and his brother, Ben. They're related to you."

She gave a slow nod. "Yes. My mother was their father's sister. He didn't even know about her. Turned out that Grandpa Wilde—who is long gone now—had an affair back in the day. My mom was given up for adoption, and I never knew about them."

"How did you find out?"

"Don't you already know?"

He did, but... "Sometimes, I like for you to tell me things. When you *trust* me enough to tell me things..." And, yes, he'd emphasized trust right there deliberately. "It means more."

A startled blink. "Why should the things in my life mean anything to you?"

"Because you mean something to me." His hand lifted. His fingers smoothed down her cheek. Ever so carefully. Lacey's skin was like silk. "I like for you to tell me your secrets. I like for you to trust me."

"Can I trust you?" She leaned into his touch.

Instead of answering her, he bent and brushed his lips over hers. A soft, gentle caress. "With your life," Dex swore against her mouth. He meant it. He would do anything to keep her safe. He wasn't going to let anyone hurt Lacey. Hurting her was not part of any plan that he had.

He forced his hand to fall away from her. Forced his head to lift when all he wanted was to lock his mouth tightly to hers and take and take and take. Dex cleared his throat and walked around Lacey. Ditching his suit jacket, he headed for the chair in the corner of the room. Dex threw himself into it and grabbed the arms of the chair. He held on a little too tightly. "Why don't you go get some sleep?" His voice was gruff. Hard.

Yeah, like my voice is the only thing hard. His dick was shoving out at full attention. His fingers dug into the chair arms. *Do not move from this spot.*

Lacey turned toward him. One hand went to her hip. "You like kissing me, don't you, Dex?"

Pretty much more than he liked breathing. Instead of confessing that rather unsettling truth, he gave her a cocky smile. And a wink. "You like kissing me, too, sweetheart."

"Absolutely." She stepped toward him. The bottom of her dress trailed over the floor. "I'm very picky about my lovers. I don't trust easily."

Don't want to think about her and other men. Don't want to have to go out, hunt them down, and kick all their asses.

He didn't speak.

Lacey kept advancing on him. When she was about a foot away from his chair, she bent and lifted the cascading falls of her dress.

Oh, sweet hell...

Her legs were freaking perfect. And she had that knife strapped to the top of her thigh and it looked so hot. Every bit of moisture dried from his mouth, and Dex found himself angling forward far too eagerly. "Wh-what are you doing?" Damn. Had he just stuttered? He never stuttered.

Lacey released a soft, sensual laugh. Her left hand casually removed the knife and the strap. "Can't very well to go bed with a knife strapped to my thigh." She put the weapon on the nearby table. Slowly let the dress fall back to the floor.

Dex looked up at her face. The drumming of his own heartbeat was far too loud in his ears. He got caught by her gaze and couldn't look away. Curious, intrigued, he asked, "Are you playing a game with me?"

"I don't play games. I think that's more your thing."

Okay. Fine. *Guilty.* "Then what are you doing?" Dex's voice came out more growl than anything else.

She inched closer. So close that if he reached out, he could curl his hand around her waist. He could pull her down on top of him. The chair was one of those over-stuffed creations, easily big enough for two. Dex could imagine pulling her down onto him. Those perfect legs of hers would straddle him as she scooped up the dress again, and then she'd be pressed hard right to—

"I'm trying to come to a decision."

He swallowed. "Want to clue me in as to what that decision is about?"

"I think you know." Soft. Sensual. Then she advanced.

He sucked in a breath but—

She moved to the side of the chair. *Not on my lap. Not in the chair with me. At the side.* Still very, very close.

Her index finger extended and slowly stroked down the column of his neck. And if he'd thought that his pulse was racing before, he'd been wrong. At her touch, his heart pounded so fast that his chest shook.

She leaned over beside him. Since the top few buttons of his shirt were undone, it was easy for her to trail her fingers down his chest. Easy for her to reach out and caress him—

He caught her hand. Trapped it there. "Don't play." His head turned toward her.

"I'm not."

"You should go to bed." A hard warning.

"But if I do, I'm afraid I'll just be in the dark, still trying to make this decision."

Cards on the damn table. "You trying to decide if you want to fuck me?" He made the words deliberately rough. Maybe part of him wanted to scare her away. To warn her...*you're not getting some gentleman with me. People are right when they call me a bastard. An asshole. Don't offer me what I want so badly. Because I'll take it.*

If he took her, he might not be able to let go.

The last thought caught Dex off guard. He'd always been able to let go. To everyone and everything. Nothing mattered long enough to keep.

He was still staring into her eyes. *She might matter.*

"Don't be an ass, Dex," Lacey chided.

"I can't help it." The words just spilled out. "Second nature."

She shook her head. "I don't think so."

He was caressing her inner wrist. Moving his fingers slowly. Tenderly. "Your last lover was named Tim Wraith. He was the drummer in that rock band that's everywhere these days." Picturing the jerk with his tats and million-dollar smile...*I can make a rock star vanish.* He could. Wouldn't even be that hard. "You met Tim when Wilde was hired to upgrade security for the band's tour. After the security contract ended, you became involved with Tim."

"I don't like that you know everything about me."

"I don't know everything." It was the things he didn't know that were driving him crazy. "I don't know why you broke up with him. Word on the street was that he wanted to marry you."

She looked away. No, she looked down. At her hand. The hand *he* held. And at the ring on her finger.

Not Tim's ring. *Mine.* The thought was savage. And wrong. This wasn't for real. The engagement wasn't real. Nothing that was happening between them was real. So why did everything feel so fucking real?

"Word on the street was wrong." She spoke with little emotion. "Tim didn't want to marry me. He wanted to own me. There's a difference. He wanted me to leave Wilde. He wanted me to give up my life. He wanted me to follow his band and support him. Guy was nice at first, but the longer I was around him, the more demanding and moodier he became. He was good on paper, not so good in reality." She bit her lower lip. Seemed to debate something in her mind, then told him, "Tim knew about my parents. He knew I wanted to find out the truth about them, but he kept telling me to let the past go. Kept telling me I had to focus on the future. On what we had. But it turned out that what we had wasn't strong enough to last." A faint shrug. As if she'd let go of some weight. "Tim wanted the spotlight all the time. The last thing I wanted was to be in the light."

There was no longing in her voice when she spoke of Tim. Good. She wasn't hung up on the guy. Even though he'd written a damn song about her for his band. Some "Come Back to Me" bullshit of a song.

But Lacey wasn't going back to him.

She was standing right by Dex.

Lacey's gaze held his. "Your turn."

He wanted her mouth. "My turn for what?"

"Who was your last lover? When were you together? Why did it end?" Her smile held an icy edge. "Because it's only fair that if you know my secrets, I know yours."

Fine. "Nicole Martin. Nine months, no, maybe ten months ago. It ended because I was lying to her every single minute we were together. She thought I was an insurance salesman who traveled a lot."

Lacey snorted. "Insurance, seriously?"

Why did he find that little snort she'd occasionally give so cute? "I got tired of lying. That's why most of my relationships end. Though, I don't think they really are relationships. Things don't typically get that far." Why was he telling her all of this? But he kept going, almost as if he was warning her... "I don't let people close. No one can know the real me. I'm a dangerous man, and I do very bad things. It's better to keep involvements brief. If you don't have ties, then you don't have weaknesses."

"But you're not lying to me. I know who you are. I know what you do."

"You know who I am." He inclined his head. "But, sweetheart, if you had any idea about all of the things I want to do to you right now, you'd back away. You'd get your sexy body and scent away from me. You'd walk into that bedroom. Shut the door. Maybe even lock it."

She didn't back away.

"I want you." This was the truth. "More than I can remember wanting anyone. As you just found out, it's been a long fucking time since I've been with a lover, and having you right here...let's just say you're a big temptation and I am trying helluva hard to keep my hands off you."

"Yes, your dry spell is longer than mine. Guess it's hard to find lovers when you're out playing puppet master. If you're not careful, you'll let some sort of secret spy into your bed and then all kinds of drama will ensue."

Was she mocking him? When he was about to go insane for her? "Lacey..."

She tugged on her hand. He let her go. What else could he do?

"It's been a long night." Her words sighed out.

Getting longer by the moment. Wait. Was that the night or his dick?

Voice low, she continued, "We did the ex talk. We survived a shooting. Got the adrenaline all pumping."

Was she about to push off their attraction as being due to the adrenaline? If so, *I'll call bullshit.*

"I've wanted you from the beginning. I haven't always liked that attraction," Lacey confessed carefully. "It wasn't...convenient."

Her word choice drew a startled laugh from him. "I am not a convenient man."

Her gaze lingered on his smile. "No, you're not." She released a quick breath. "I realized something tonight. You know, when the lights went out, the gun fired, and I found myself straddling you in the middle of that ballroom."

His chest tightened. "What big revelation did you have?"

"I realized that I don't want you hurt."

Surprise rushed through him. "You don't have to worry about me, I'm—"

"I find I am worrying. I find I'm...caring. I didn't expect that."

He couldn't breathe because the tightness in his chest had expanded so much.

"So, having said all that...let's skip the dirty talk about blackmail. This isn't about blackmail any longer. I'm here with you because someone has to watch your ass, and I'm the best one for the job."

"Lacey—"

She bent toward him. Put her lips close to his ear. "But I have other dirty talk. Like this...I want you."

Fuck, yes.

"I want you right now. I want to see if things between us will be as good as I can imagine, and I can imagine a whole lot." Her fingers trailed over his chest, and she undid a few more buttons on his shirt. "I want you naked. I want to be naked with you. And for tonight, I just want us. No holding back. No lying. No scheming. Just two lovers coming together in the dark."

Her scent was all around him.

"Think you can handle that?" The tip of her tongue slipped over the shell of his ear.

He broke. There was only so much a man could handle, and when he'd been fantasizing about a woman for this long...

He grabbed her by the waist and hauled her into the chair with him. The fabric of her dressed bunched up as she straddled him. She stared into his eyes, her breath panting, her lips parted, and her hand was still on his chest. Right over his racing heart.

"I can handle that," he rasped.

Her head lowered toward his.

His mouth jerked up to meet hers. This kiss wasn't slow or careful. It was as if a wall had been shattered between them—no, a dam, and the need was rushing free. Thundering between them like a river out of control. He thrust his tongue past her lips and tasted. He was a fucking starving man, and all he wanted to do was feast on her. She gave a little moan that he greedily drank up even as his right hand slid down her waist, down to her legs, and he yanked up the soft fabric of her dress even higher.

Then he was touching her thigh. So smooth and soft. His fingers trailed up more, moving slowly toward the one spot he wanted to touch the absolute most and—

He tore his mouth from hers. Stared into her eyes. Felt everything in his world center only on her. "You're not wearing panties."

A smile curved her lips. "Good of you to notice. I—"

She didn't get to finish. He took her mouth again. Harder, rougher. His control was gone. She'd been in the ballroom, dancing in his arms, her body so tight to his, and she hadn't been wearing underwear. If he'd known that, they never would have gotten out of the suite.

His fingers slid over her bare flesh. *Bare.* She was hot and wet already, and he eased a finger into her and nearly lost his mind because she was so wonderfully tight.

Lacey arched toward him.

He thrust a second finger into her even as his thumb worked over her clit. His touch was demanding and worshipping at the same time. He could touch her for hours. Days. He wanted to learn every single detail about her body. What she liked. What made her moan—

She moaned.

That. She likes that. So he did it again. Stroked the way she wanted. Had her riding his hand in a fast rhythm as he rubbed her clit again and again with his thumb and drove his fingers into her.

This time, she tore her mouth from his. "*Dex!*" Need throbbed in her voice. She was on the cusp of pleasure. He could feel it in the tightening of her delicate inner muscles around him. He'd never seen a more beautiful woman.

His mouth pressed to her throat. He licked. Sucked. Kissed his way down to the bodice of her gown even as he kept working her with his fingers. As if he'd stop touching her. Hell, no. He wanted to feel her come against his fingers. Then against his mouth. Then around his dick.

Oh, the plans he had for her.

The bodice was in the way. He wanted it gone so he could see her breasts. Lick them. Touch them.

"*Dex!*" She jerked against him as the pleasure hit her. A hard, hot climax that was sexy as hell. Her hips bucked and her head tipped back, sending her hair tumbling over her shoulders.

His cock was long and thick. So eager to dive into her silken heat.

But I get to taste first.

His fingers kept stroking her as she rode out her climax. Until she was giving soft moans and the eyes she'd squeezed closed slowly opened.

He couldn't speak. He was far, far past the point of speaking.

"Dex?"

He stood and held her easily in his arms. He carried her straight to the bedroom. Lowered her onto the bed. The dress's fabric pooled around her waist. The lights were on and for a moment, he just stared at her sex.

He'd touched her. Made her come around his fingers.

Her thighs were spread, but as he stared at her, she began to slowly pull them together.

"No." Dex shook his head. That one word had been savage. He didn't look away from her sex. He couldn't. He caught one of her legs. Then the other. He pulled Lacey toward the edge of the bed. Bent between her spread thighs.

And tasted her.

CHAPTER EIGHT

Dexter Ryan was going down on her.

And it felt...*amazing.*

Lacey's nails scored over Dex's broad shoulders as his tongue slid over her clit. She bit her lower lip to hold back the frantic cry that wanted to erupt. She was so sensitive from her orgasm, and every lick of his tongue was making her hips surge toward him.

In part of her mind, she was thinking...*This can't be happening. I know how bad he is. This can't...*

But a much, much louder part of her mind was screaming...*This is finally happening. He's so good. Better than good. OhmyGod, I'm about to come again!*

He drove his tongue into her. The orgasm hit, and pleasure swept her away. A surging blast that blew through every single cell of her body. No way should sex be this good. Sex this good was addictive. Insane.

Once-in-a-lifetime.

She shoved the thought away as quickly as she could. Aftershocks were still riding through her body. Aftershocks from her second orgasm, and he hadn't even taken off his pants yet. What was he waiting for?

Her eyes opened. She hadn't realized that she'd closed them again. But when her lashes lifted, she saw him slowly raise his head.

Never in her whole life had a man looked at her that way. His gaze glittered with desire. With a need that wouldn't be denied. He licked his lips as if he had to taste her one more time. His jaw was clenched. His expression fierce.

For a moment, her heart seemed to skip a beat. Then she heard herself say, in a husky, sensual voice she barely recognized, "If we're going to the next step, those pants have to go." *Bam. Bam. Bam.* Her heart pounded.

His eyes narrowed. Without looking away from her, he stripped.

Wow. Dex had been hot with clothes on. His shoulders had been broad. His muscled build apparent. Without clothes...

Sex god. The man could have made one hell of a living as a stripper. He had abs for days. Strength that made her stomach quiver. Power was evident in every long, muscled line of his body. And when it came to another *long* part of his body...

Big deal. Very, very big deal. "Uh, Dex..."

He reached for the nightstand drawer. Yanked a condom from a box there. The suite came equipped with condoms? That was awfully convenient.

He rolled the condom on and reached for her.

Having sex with the ball gown on. No way was she slowing down to take the thing off. She wanted him right then. And he wanted her that way, too. Her hips were at the edge of the bed, her legs dangling over the side. He lifted her hips up now, as he stood beside the bed, and he put his cock at the entrance to her body. The thick head stretched her as he pushed in...

She shoved up with her hips.

And took in every long, wonderful inch of him.

He sank fully into her, and her sex clamped greedily around him. Thick, hard, full. *Perfect.* The pleasure bordered on pain because she was so sensitive from her releases and because he was so big, but there was no way that she'd stop. She wanted more, so much more and—

He was stroking her clit again. Making her body open up and yearn and soon she wasn't bordering on pain. There was only pleasure. He thrust in and out. Her body met him in perfect rhythm. Their breaths panted. Their hearts raced. They drove toward release with feverish intensity. Her hands clamped around his shoulders. Her nails raked down his arms.

"Harder...faster...Dex, *yes!*"

He yanked her off the bed. Pulled her all the way up into his arms and she gave a cry of surprise. He was so strong. She hadn't realized just how powerful he was.

He spun around. Put her back against the wall. Upright this way, she was fully open to him. Her legs locked around his hips as he pounded into her, and she loved every single thrust. Loved it so much that she bent forward and pressed a kiss to his neck. Then a bite.

"*Lacey!*" Dex roared her name.

But she was coming again, and everything but pleasure seemed distant. The release was so powerful that her vision dimmed. She clung to him and rode it out. An endless wave. Not a pop of pleasure. Bliss that stole her breath and swept her into some kind of mindless, pleasure-soaked oblivion. She shuddered and trembled and held on tight, and when the aftershocks rippled through her, she enjoyed the hell out of those, too.

Then he held her even tighter. Thrust deeper. Harder. Came with another rough cry of her name. She looked up, blinking to clear her vision, and saw the pleasure wash across Dex's face. The primitive satisfaction made him savagely beautiful, and she couldn't look away.

His breath shuddered out.

Reality crept back to her. One slow moment at a time. She became aware of the feel of her dress as it bunched at her waist, trapped between their bodies. She felt the hard wall behind her. The aches in her muscles. The dryness in her throat that told her she'd been moaning—and maybe even screaming a whole lot. And she saw his eyes—the expression in them changed. Warmed.

Pleasure. Possession.

She couldn't help but wonder....was she looking at him the same way?

And, oh, dear God, had Dex just made her come three times?

***

You weren't supposed to fall asleep in the arms of your enemy. But she had.

Lacey's eyes flew open with a start, and she realized that, nope, she hadn't dreamed the sensual activities from the night before. The whole amazing-sex-with-Dex scene hadn't been some feverish fantasy that slipped into her head while she slept. Obviously not, because a warm, strong arm was wrapped around her, and when she turned her head a little bit, she found herself staring right at Dex's face.

His very handsome face. A face that looked a little softer in sleep.

Three times. I came three times with him last night. Then he'd stripped off her dress. Taken her to the shower and...

Okay, fine. Four times. I came four times with him. By the time they'd made it back to the bed, they'd both collapsed from exhaustion.

She'd slept with the man she considered to be her enemy. And her fiancé.

And she had no idea what the heck she was doing.

But he looked really peaceful when he slept. Without the blinding power of his gaze, he was softer. Easier and—

From the nightstand, she heard the vibration and quick peal of sound that told her a text had just come through on Dex's phone. Instantly, his thick lashes shot up. His gaze settled straight on her. And, of course, he didn't slowly wake up. No gradual return of awareness in his gaze, no sir. Just a fully aware, fully focused stare. Right on her.

"Were you watching me sleep?" Dex asked, voice rumbly and quiet.

"I...what?" Her voice rose on the *what* question. "I just woke up," she mumbled.

The phone vibrated again.

Without breaking eye contact with her, he stretched out one hand and grabbed his phone. He didn't look down at the phone as he asked her again, "Were you watching me sleep?"

She could feel herself blushing. How embarrassing. "Look, it's not my fault you look so freaking cute when you sleep."

His brow scrunched. "Say that again."

She would not. "You're the one who slept in *my* bed."

"Our bed. Our suite, remember?"

She prayed for patience and an easy way out of the haze of embarrassment that surrounded her. "I woke up, opened my eyes, and found your face about two inches from my own. I mean, where else was I supposed to look?"

A slow smile teased his lips.

"Why don't you check your text?" She rolled away from him and yanked the sheet with her. Lacey wrapped that sheet around her body, toga-style, so that she didn't flash him.

Seemingly unconcerned with the fact that he had on zero clothes, Dex sat up. He frowned at her. "Why are you covering up? I love your body. Didn't you get that clue last night when I kissed every single inch of you in the shower?"

Her cheeks burned even hotter. She had gotten that clue, yes.

His expression tensed. "Are you having regrets? Is that what this is about? You woke up, saw who you were in bed with, and had a change of heart?"

Now her own eyes turned to slits. "Are you crazy?"

He rose from the bed. One hand gripped his phone, and he still acted as if he wasn't naked. He *was* naked, though. Naked and turned on and her gaze kept dip-dip-dipping down to peek at him.

"Not crazy at all," he rasped. "Just trying to figure out what you're thinking."

"I'm thinking..." *Eyes up. Eyes up.* She pulled her eyes up. "I don't regret four orgasms." Oh, shit.

He quirked an eyebrow. Started to smile once more.

"What I meant was..." *Who the hell would regret four orgasms?* "I think we need to take a step back and focus on the case. It's not the middle of the night any longer. We have a job to do." The weight of the ring felt heavy on her finger. "You just got a text that you haven't even looked at yet. Surely having this conversation with me can't be more important than the mission you're supposed to be running."

His smile froze. Then..."What if it was?"

He was losing her. "Dex?"

Swallowing, he glanced down at the phone. His shoulders straightened as he read the text. And... "Fuck me."

"I did. Last night." In the interest of total honesty... "I'll probably do it again, but this isn't the time."

His head whipped up.

The look in his eyes was making her all hot. "What's in the text?"

"A morning meeting." His voice had gone guttural. Dex cleared his throat. "Roman is asking for a chat."

"Is that good news? Or bad?"

"Could be either. Or both." He hadn't replied to the text. "He knows about my skiing plans today."

"You mean the fake skiing plans." Better be fake. "Remember, I told you that I can't actually ski."

"There's a cabin not too far from the ski lift. He wants me to meet him there."

Her toes curled against the carpeting. "This whole scene reeks of being some kind of setup. When someone asks you to meet in a remote cabin, typically, the best response is to immediately say—"

"Yes." He fired out a quick text.

"Uh, no." She hurried around the bed and moved toward him. She paused long enough to pick up his pants and toss them at him.

He caught the pants with his left hand.

"When someone invites you into a trap, you don't reply yes. You reply no. They should have taught you this in spy school." She huffed out a breath. "Did you forget that he may have tried to kill you last night?"

"Roman said he didn't, and like I told you, I think the shot was aimed at you."

Which made zero sense. "Me and my long list of enemies."

His eyelids flickered. "You'll go with me. I'll enter the cabin. You'll stay outside to make sure we don't have any unwelcome guests."

She wanted to grab the man and shake sense into him. So she did. Her hands curled around his muscled arms. "That's not smart! You could walk in there and get blown to hell! This screams trap. Trap, trap—" The sheet fell.

Of course, the sheet fell. Just slithered right on down to the floor.

Dex could have been a gentleman and kept his gaze up. Sure, she'd ogled him moments before, but it would not have killed the man to maintain eye contact with her and...

Nope.

He was looking down. And whistling.

She let go of him, bent, and yanked her sheet back up. "You don't care that you're walking into a trap."

He shrugged. "I picked the location. I know what I'm doing."

"What?" Her voice had gone way too high-pitched. She was surprised the nearby window hadn't cracked. "How could you have picked the location? You just told me that *he* said—"

"When I let it be known that I was going skiing on the Double Black Diamond trail, *I* picked the location. The only place to meet up there is this cabin. My men will have been watching it since dawn. Those were their orders, and they'll keep eyes on the place the whole time we approach. If there's trouble, they will be there to back you up."

"*Us* up. They will be there to back *us* up." Her hold tightened on her sheet as she held it in place. "You like to think you are two steps ahead of everyone else, don't you?"

His head inclined toward her. "I try to be three steps ahead."

Sure he did. "Does that always work out for you?"

She didn't think he would answer. Then, softly, "No. Not always."

"What happens when you aren't ahead?"

He glanced away. "People die."

Not the answer I wanted. But it had been the one she feared. "Okay." She released her breath. "Let's get dressed and get to that cabin. And you'd better be three steps ahead of whatever plan Roman has." She spun away, intent on getting a quick shower before she—

He curled his arm around her and hauled her back against him. She looked up in surprise right before his mouth took hers. The kiss was long, hot, and thorough.

Dex's tongue was wickedly talented. As she'd learned last night.

His head slowly lifted. "To circle back to your earlier comment, I'm glad that you want to fuck me again. But how about we change that from a probably to a definitely?"

Easy enough. "I definitely want to fuck you again." She caught his jaw and pulled him back down toward her. This time, she was the one who pressed her mouth to his. She liked to think her tongue was pretty dang skilled, too. She took her time kissing him, then nipped his lower lip when she was done. "So let's wrap up this case."

His hold tightened on her. "I want you."

She wanted him, too. But she forced herself to step back. To break contact with him. And to keep walking away until she could shut the bathroom door.

***

"Is the team in place?" Dex glanced at the closed bathroom door. As soon as Lacey had turned on the shower, he'd made the call to the team leader.

"Yep. Been here since dawn. No one has entered the cabin yet."

"We're coming. He'll either arrive before us or right after. Keep the agents hidden." Three agents. All trained snipers.

"So...I hear congratulations are in order, boss."

Dex expelled a hard breath. "I will kick your ass, Larry."

"Dammit, you know I hate it when you call me that."

"Take it up with your mama. She's the one who gave you the name."

"Yeah, but plenty of people call me Lawrence. You're the dick who insists on calling me Larry. And when you say it, you know other people do, too."

"I call you Larry because I'm the dick who knows every secret you possess." True story. He knew all the guy's secrets, so he knew that he could trust Larry one hundred percent on this case. "The goal is to protect Lacey Amari. You get that? I want her under surveillance at all times. When I'm in the cabin, she goes nowhere without me."

"What are you expecting? That someone is going to rush out of the snow and grab your fiancée? Whisk her away and you'll never see her again?"

The bathroom door opened. Damn. That had been fast. Lacey's hair was wrapped in a towel, and a white, fluffy robe covered her body. The warm water and steam had made her cheeks pinken and as she stood there, all freshly scrubbed and absolutely beautiful, he had the quick thought of...

No one can take her away. I need her. "You heard the order," he said flatly. "Screw it up and it will be the last mistake you ever make, Larry." He hung up.

She frowned. "Are you making friends again?"

"Excuse me?"

Her hands went to her hips. "I've noticed you don't seem to exercise a lot of tact when you talk with folks."

"I can be extremely tactful." When the situation called for it.

"You're still naked, you know."

"I'm glad you noticed." He waved a hand in front of his body. "Look your fill. I'm not shy."

Her lips curved the faintest bit. "I noticed."

His eager dick noticed her noticing. *What I wouldn't give to take her again...No, dammit.*

The case. Do the job. Dex tossed his phone onto the bed. "I have to get dressed, we have to go for a big showdown, and you know...get shit done." He headed for the bathroom. "But you can admire my ass as I walk away. I won't hide behind a sheet like you did. So very rude."

"Dex!"

He looked back at her.

"You *do* have a great ass."

"Thanks for noticing."

"Be serious with me. Everything is going to be all right this morning, isn't it? You talked to your agent—though without any charm—and all is good to go? Because I'm still operating in the dark for the most part. I'm trusting you."

He rubbed the center of his chest. It had started to ache. "You can absolutely trust me to keep you safe."

She nodded.

He closed the bathroom door. Didn't bother glancing toward the mirror. There was no damn way he could look at himself right then.

You are such a fucking bastard.

When she found out the truth, just how much would Lacey hate him?

CHAPTER NINE

Her teeth were chattering. The higher up the mountain they'd gone, the colder it had become. Lacey was bundled in a thick, puffy black coat, with a ski cap on her head and a dark scarf wrapped around her neck, but she was still freezing her ass off.

When you lived in the South, you considered a cold day to be fifty degrees. She was not made for these Colorado temps.

The snow crunched beneath their boots as she and Dex made their way to the small cabin. They'd ridden up the ski lift in silence, and the view had been incredible. If it weren't for the fact that her cheeks had turned numb and they were heading out on a dangerous mission, she might have even enjoyed the ride. Thought it was romantic.

But...

Yeah. It was a mission.

"There aren't any tracks here," Lacey said as she surveyed the white ground leading toward the old cabin. "I don't think Roman has arrived yet." She knew that fresh snow had fallen in the hours before dawn.

Dex paused and stared at the ground, then he studied the cabin.

He'd insisted that she bring a gun with her, not just her knife. The gun was holstered beneath her jacket. He was packing, too, and his expression had become increasingly hard as they neared their destination.

"I'll be waiting inside for him," Dex said. "You find a spot out of sight so you can watch the scene. Don't talk to him when he arrives. Don't have any contact with him at all, understand?"

"Not like we're best friends," she muttered. "And I don't think there is any place out here where he can whisper some dark warning to me."

Dex's head turned toward her. "Take no risks. If anything happens, if you feel threatened, shoot."

"I can take care of myself." She pulled her gaze off him and eyed the cabin. "Just why are the two of you having this big, important meeting?"

"Because I have something that is valuable to him," Dex replied slowly. "He wants it back, but I've decided not to give it to him."

Her attention shot to Dex. "Does he *think* you're going to give this item to him today?"

"He thinks we'll make a deal. That in exchange for intel I need, I'll turn what I have over to him." His jaw hardened. "That's not going to happen. I'm keeping what I have."

"Because it's valuable." She nodded. "And you think you can use it against him in the future?"

"No, that's not—" Dex began, voice almost angry. Then he caught himself. "What I have—it turned out to be more than I expected. The value can't be equaled."

Okay. "Sometimes, Dex, you have got to just learn to say what you mean." She huffed out a breath and a little cloud appeared before her mouth. "You'd better get inside, and I need to get hidden."

"My men are out here. They're watching our backs right now."

She hadn't spotted them—and she'd been looking—so his team had to be very, very good.

He motioned toward his ear. "I'll turn my comm link off when I go inside. What I need to talk about with Roman is classified."

Of course, it was. This was Dex, after all.

"But if there is trouble, I'll turn it back on, and I'll call you and the rest of the team through the link." He stepped toward her. Her head tipped back. His gaze had dropped to her mouth, and she could have sworn that he was about to kiss her.

While they were *on* the mission, about to meet up with the bad guy? Someone was being a rule breaker. She swayed toward him and—

"Get your gun out, Lacey. If someone attacks you, shoot the bastard in the heart."

Well, all right then. Not a kiss. Just a fierce warning.

Dex turned on his heel. His boots crunched over the snow as he marched for the cabin.

She blew out another breath, ignored the chatter of her teeth, and prepared to get down to business. She would protect Dex's back. They'd end this mission.

Then she'd finally discover the truth about her family.

***

"I see you," the shooter whispered. Staring through the scope, there was no way to miss the target. It would be such an easy shot. Like so many others had been over the years.

The wind was just right. The direction perfect. The bullet would fly through the air without so much as a whistle of sound, and in the next breath, the target would be down.

It was supposed to be a heart shot. Head shots were preferred, but this time, the client had been very, very specific.

Heart. To send a message.

When the bullet hit, it would tear through skin, muscle. Bone. It would sink into the heart and blood would explode. The victim would fall back, and the white snow would turn red.

It would be a beautiful sight.

Just wait...

It was almost time.

Another glance through the scope. This time, a slow sweep around the full area.

Ah...Dex was entering the cabin.

Wait...Just wait.

He'd be coming out again soon enough.

***

When he opened the cabin's door, Dex already had his gun in his hand. He had a key to the cabin—one he'd taken from the lodge—and the door creaked as it slid open.

Darkness waited inside. Gaping and cold.

Lacey had been right when she'd noted that there had been no signs of footprints outside. And

Larry had assured him that no one had gotten into the cabin since dawn.

That left before dawn.

In order for Roman to have been there that long, sitting in the cold...well, that was unlikely, given what he knew about the fellow. Roman was dangerous, deadly, but he didn't exactly rough it on any cases. The arrogant asshole tended to think he was too good for shit like that.

Still...

"I'm here," Dex called out. "So if you're hiding in the dark, come out now before I get all jumpy and shoot your ass."

Nothing.

He hit the light switch. The place was supposed to be supplied with power via a generator but—

The lights didn't come on.

Bad sign number one.

Dex's shoulders tensed a bit more. The windows were covered with heavy drapes, so no light slipped inside. He used his left hand to lift up his phone. He tapped the screen to access the flashlight option, then swept it carefully over the floor.

Was that a drop of blood? Over near the closed door—the door that led to an old storage room. Because, yes, he'd gotten schematics of the cabin. He'd wanted to know what waited for him.

Always three steps ahead.

He advanced toward the door. That wasn't just one drop of blood. It looked like two. Maybe three.

Bad sign number two.

There wasn't a good reason for blood to be on the floor. And it was fresh. Not faded by time. Someone had been bleeding fairly recently in that cabin. Could have been an employee who'd gotten cut while doing maintenance but...

He didn't think so.

His heart wasn't racing. His hands weren't shaking. As per usual on a mission, he was stone cold. Dex's mind and emotions became detached as he focused on the goal. He'd learned long ago that there was no room for error on a case like this. Emotions led to mistakes.

He stared at the closed door. Made sure his body wasn't in front of it. The last thing he wanted was for bullets to fly through the wood and sink into him. Even though he was wearing a bulletproof vest beneath his coat, there was no sense in taking any chances.

Always three steps ahead.

"Roman, if you're in there, you need to say something right now. Or else I might just start shooting. A stray bullet could hit you in the head, then we'd never get to have our little talk."

There was...a mumble.

Dex frowned.

Another sound...a groan? Something that sounded like growling.

Shit. He grabbed for the doorknob and shoved the door open.

Even as the door flew open, Roman lurched forward in his chair. His arms were secured behind him, and his legs were taped to the legs of the chair. Gray tape covered his mouth, and blood poured from his hair line. His eyes were wide and frantic as he tried to talk from behind the tape.

"What the hell?" Dex demanded.

Roman heaved toward him. The chair toppled and sent him slamming sideways into the floor. Pain flashed on Roman's face even as he kept trying to talk behind his mask.

Dex didn't step toward him. He activated the comm link in his ear. "Larry, something is wrong." *Understatement.*

Roman growled behind the tape.

"You got eyes on the area?" Dex pressed his team leader.

But Larry didn't respond.

For just a moment, fear trickled through Dex, but he shut it down. He shut everything down. Emotion led to mistakes.

"Dex?" The soft voice on the comm link belonged to Lacey. "You need me? You want me in there?"

His gaze darted to a frantic Roman. Dex leaned down and ripped the tape off Roman's mouth.

"It's a fucking trap!" Roman snarled as his breath heaved. "Someone knows! Someone is going after—"

A gunshot blasted from outside.

Lacey.

Dex whirled and ran for the door.

"Don't leave me like this! Cut me free!" Roman roared.

Dex didn't stop. "Lacey, talk to me," he snapped.

Only she didn't respond via their comm link. Fuck. Fuck. *"Lacey!"* This couldn't be happening. He'd planned. Three steps ahead. He...

He saw her boots. Lacey was on the ground. Sprawled as if she'd been heading toward the cabin but had been stopped. Stopped because...

She'd been shot?

He rushed to her. Her dark hair spilled over the white snow. Her skin was too pale. She looked fragile and broken, and if some sonofabitch had taken his Lacey from him, Dex would absolutely lose his freaking mind because she mattered to him more than anything else. He crouched over her. Reached out to touch her.

Lacey's eyes flew open. "Dex?" There was confusion in her gaze. A flash of fear. Then... "What in the hell are you doing?" She grabbed him and jerked him toward her, rolling him so that she was now on top of his body.

So that she was protecting him?

Fuck, no. "Not happening." He twisted his body. Rolled them again.

"Bullet...missed me," she panted out. "Mostly because...shit, I slipped on the damn snow."

She'd slipped on the damn snow? That was why she hadn't been shot? *Fucking miracle.*

But he couldn't count on another miracle occurring. They were in the middle of a white field of snow. Perfect targets. His team—the snipers who should have been covering their asses—were radio silent. He and Lacey had to get to cover, and they had to get to cover right the hell then.

He grabbed Lacey and leapt to his feet. He kept her curled in front him, his left arm a vise around her as he rushed forward. His right hand gripped his gun, and he swept it around the area as he looked for a target. For some bastard to take out because he was not about to lose this fight.

"Two men down," Larry's rough voice broke in Dex's ear just as he reached the cabin. "Shooter is retreating. So...freaking sorry. Going after him now, but...bastard tagged me in the leg..."

Dex stood inside the safety of the cabin. Lacey was in his arms, yanking and kicking back at him because he knew she wanted to be free so she could protect *him*. If he'd been an average opponent, she would have knocked him on his ass. He wasn't average.

Roman staggered out of the storage room. Torn bits of tape clung to his ankles and wrists. "She's okay." A wide smile split his face. "She's safe!"

Safe...

Dex looked around the cabin. A shooter had been outside. The only safe place for cover had been the cabin. The only place that he could take Lacey had been...the cabin.

He shook his head.

Fucking hell. He was there. Lacey was there. Roman was there. *All in the cabin.*

Before Dex had arrived, Larry had assured him that the cabin was secure. That no one had been inside since dawn. *That's because the SOB got in during the dark hours before dawn. He left Roman out of commission. Let the falling snow cover the tracks. And I'm betting he left us a surprise behind.*

Holding Lacey, Dex raced for the back of the cabin. He knew there was another door back there. Another way out.

"Dex, talk to me!" Lacey raged. "Tell me what's—"

The door wouldn't open. Someone had nailed the fucker shut. *He wants us forced out the front.* Because their enemy had another plan of attack waiting near the front of the cabin? Because he'd left a deadly surprise there?

Not happening.

Dex kicked at the door. Once. Twice. He had to let Lacey go so that he could use all of his strength on that door. On the next kick, the door flew outward. He caught Lacey's wrist. "Stay low and stay with me!"

"Why are you running out there?" Roman had surged toward them. "The shooter is waiting! We need to stay in here until your team arrives! I know you have a damn team out—"

"Get your ass out, too," Dex thundered at him. "Because if we stay here, we're dead."

Roman shook his head.

Your choice. Dex focused beyond the back door. There was a line of trees about thirty yards from the rear of the cabin.

"Run like hell," Dex ordered Lacey. "Don't stop. Don't look back." He would draw the shooter's fire. He would make himself the target so she could get clear.

"We're safe here." Roman lumbered closer. "Don't you get that?"

"Not if there is a bomb here, jackass!" *Not if the bastard left one here because he knew he could force us all into this cabin. Herding us. Like sheep.* There was no time to waste. Dex ran out with Lacey. He wanted to hold her tight and never let go, but he needed to protect her. He needed to draw the fire if the shooter was still close.

Be gone. Larry said you were retreating. Fucking be gone.

Dex made sure that when Lacey left the cabin, he was beside her. He shielded her body as best he could.

"This doesn't make sense! Why are you protecting *me?*" Her question huffed back at him.

He looked toward the tree line and saw the glint of light. A gun. Pointed at them.

***

The shooter's breath slid out on a soft sigh. A change of position had been necessary when those prick agents of Dex's had managed to return fire.

But this was better. This was perfect. Odds had been high that once he'd sought shelter in the cabin, Dex wouldn't then immediately run back out the front door. No, a rear exit had been expected. The nails had even been put in the door so that Dex would think the intent *was* to force him out the front. Or to keep him in the cabin.

Wrong.

Dexter Ryan had been studied carefully. This plan was perfect.

Lacey was in the scope. So close.

Right to the heart.

The shooter squeezed the trigger.

***

Lacey didn't have a chance to cry out. One moment, she caught the glint of light in the woods. And in the next—a fist punched her in the chest.

Her breath caught in her throat and the impact sent her staggering back. Her boots slipped over the snow, and she stumbled. She hit the ground and that fist kept burning against her. Her hands flew toward her chest.

"Lacey!" Dex was over her. Staring at her with wild eyes. "Oh, God, baby, you're hit."

CHAPTER TEN

Why was Dex looking so crazed? His eyes were wild and his face had contorted into lines of fury.

"Bullet...proof vest," she gasped. He knew she was wearing one beneath the puffy coat. He'd insisted she wear the thing. *Extremely grateful for that insistence right about now.*

But he covered her chest with his fingers. "No! Don't do this to me!" he roared.

Um, what?

His gaze cut to her face. "Play dead," he whispered.

Again, *what?*

Footsteps scrambled near them. Her eyes drifted closed.

"She's hit?" Roman's voice, and he sounded gutted. Why would he be so upset by her wound? The man didn't even know her.

"Stay the hell away from her or I will shoot you where you stand!"

She didn't move.

"*I didn't do this! I wasn't involved!*" Roman's voice was still all gutted and desperate. "*I swear it!*"

"I want a chopper here now," Dex blasted. She knew he was talking in his comm link, and since she had her earpiece in place, too, she heard the reply.

"*They're en route now. I'm in the woods about twenty yards from you. Shooter is moving. Fuck. I'm so sorry, boss. Me and Taylor lost him for a second. We've got him now. Taking aim—*"

A gunshot blasted.

Lacey didn't move. Didn't flinch.

"Stay the fuck back, Roman," Dex warned. "You take one more step this way, and it will be your last. That gunshot was my team taking out the shooter."

And, on cue, Lacey heard in her ear, "*Shooter is down, but alive. Shit, Dex, you won't believe this...it's that sexy bodyguard of Roman's.*"

"Keep her alive," Dex ordered. "Because I'm talking to her." His hand was still on Lacey's chest. His voice rose as he seemingly turned his attention back to Roman. "You didn't have anything to do with Lacey getting shot, huh? Then why the hell is *your* bodyguard the one my men just caught in the woods? Why the hell is she the one who shot Lacey in the heart?"

"The heart? No, my God, *no!*"

His voice was broken. That made no sense. Roman sounded like he was shattering over her would-be death. And he'd just met her yesterday.

"Finally...found her..." Roman mumbled. Snow crunched beneath his feet.

"I told you to stay the hell back!" Dex snapped. "And *I* found her!"

"Finally found...my sister...and someone is taking her—"

Her eyes flew open. Her head whipped toward Roman. "What did you just call me?"

Roman gaped at her. "You're...not shot?"

"Bulletproof vest." Were there tears on his cheeks?

She felt callused fingertips slide over her jaw. Her head turned back toward Dex as he leaned over her.

"Lacey..." He breathed her name like a caress. "You can't play dead very well, can you?"

"Why did he call me his sister?"

Dex's expression hardened just as she heard the whir of approaching helicopter blades.

"Dex." She said his name again, harder, rougher. "Why did he call me his sister?"

He swallowed. "Because that's what you are, sweetheart. You're Roman's sister."

***

She stared out of the suite's window at the white snow, and Lacey rubbed her chest with slow, circular motions of her hand. Dex watched her in silence. She wasn't yet aware that he'd entered the room, and he enjoyed drinking in the sight of her.

She'd been shot today. Even knowing that he'd insisted she wear the bulletproof vest, he'd nearly lost his mind when she fell. So much for locking down his emotions. When Lacey was around, his control was shit.

"Are you just going to stand there," Lacey asked as she kept gazing out of the window, "or are you going to explain what the hell is going on?"

So she had known he was there. Her posture and her expression hadn't changed at all when he'd slipped into their suite. It had been four hours since the hell scene at the cabin. Two of his team members were in the hospital. Luckily, the man and woman were both going to survive. Larry had managed to only get a deep graze on his leg before he'd taken out the shooter, so he was already back at the lodge.

As was their perp. Heather Madding was secured in the basement of the lodge. Except it wasn't exactly a basement because this whole facility? It held plenty of secrets. And one of those secrets was that the basement floor could only be accessed with special clearance. If you had that clearance, then you'd discover a holding room, a cell, security equipment...basically, a CIA field office.

While Heather was in custody, he had eyes on her. Soon enough, she'd be transported. But that transport wouldn't happen until Dex had his chance to question her again. During his first round of questioning, she'd refused to say a word to him.

But that would change. Especially when he let Roman have a run at his ex-bodyguard.

"Dex?" Lacey prompted.

Where to begin? "There's a lot at play right now."

Her shoulders squared.

"More than you can imagine," he added carefully.

"I've got a pretty phenomenal imagination, thanks." Her voice had gone arctic. Her head angled toward him and, yep, as he'd feared, her gaze was ice cold.

He felt the chill sweep over him even as he heard himself say, "I have orders, too, you know. You might think I'm the big boss at the CIA, but even I have to answer to someone."

She laughed. The sound lacked the normal musical quality of her voice. "I don't know that I believe that."

His lips thinned. "Then do you believe that some things are class—"

Lacey held up one hand. "Don't." The word bit off. But not with anger. Anger he could handle. The word poured from her with pain wrapped tightly around it. "Don't you dare stand there and tell me that you can't tell me about *my life* because things are classified."

"Baby..."

Wrong thing. *Wrong* thing to say.

Her eyes turned to slits as she stalked toward him. She wore jeans, black boots, and a long, white sweater. She looked like the most beautiful woman in the world to him but she *looked* at Dex...

As if he were a stranger.

She stopped right in front of him. "I am not your baby."

But I want you to be. I want you to be so much, but I don't get to say it. I don't get to tell you how I really feel. I don't get to tell you that I almost lost my mind when that bullet fired, and I saw you fall. I have to keep this stupid fucking mask in place and play the asshole when all I want to do is grab you, pull you close, and never, ever let go. "You're my fiancée. Terms of endearment are expected between us."

She yanked off the ring. Before she could throw it at him—and Dex knew that was exactly what she intended—his hand caught hers. His fingers wrapped around her hand as he forced her to keep the diamond ring cradled in her palm.

"It's not over," he told her softly. *We're not over.* "You can't give it back yet." The fantasy had to last a little longer. Especially because he'd miscalculated.

"It's over unless you tell me everything, and you tell me now."

Would she walk away from him? *Walk into danger?* He couldn't let that happen. "Fine. I think I know who killed your parents."

Her eyes widened. "Then tell me. Don't just—
"

"Roman's father." Couldn't she ever consider that maybe he didn't want to tell her everything because the news would hurt her? *Dammit, I hate her pain.* Yet here he was, bringing that pain to her over and over again. "I believe that Roman's father was responsible for their car crash."

"What? Why? How—"

"His father and your mother had an affair. A very long affair."

She shook her head. The denial was clear to see on her face. "No. My mom loved my father. He was a good man."

"Yes, yes, he was a good man, and Roman's father..." *Your father, baby, your real father.* "He wasn't so good. He was a dangerous man who took what he wanted. He met your mother when she was a young dancer doing a tour in Europe. They...connected. And over the years, she kept coming back into his life."

Once more, Lacey shook her head. "She wouldn't do that." Her voice had gone ragged.

"Maybe he kept pulling her back. He had a lot of power and influence." People hadn't exactly been known to say no to him. Until her mother. "But from what I can gather, shortly before the accident, she finally broke it off with him. Said she never wanted him in her life again."

"From what you can gather." She swallowed. "You mean with your network of spies and intel. You used them to find all of this information, and you kept it from me."

Yes. He had. He was still keeping secrets from her. *I don't like hurting her.* But she deserved as many truths as he could give her. "When he couldn't convince your mother to leave her husband and come back for good, he was enraged."

"So enraged he killed her?"

Tread carefully. "When your parents died, they were driving in your father's car, weren't they?"

"Y-yes."

"Your mother wasn't supposed to be there. She should have been out of town that day. Only your father should have been in the vehicle, but your mom returned home early to surprise him."

Lacey's lips parted, but she didn't speak.

"Roman's father paid someone to cut the brake lines in the car."

"He wanted to kill my dad," she whispered. Tears gleamed in her eyes.

"Kill him or hurt him. Instead, he wound up with a crash that killed them both."

"You knew this from the beginning." A tear rolled down her cheek. "You are a bastard, you know that?"

"I know." He couldn't look away from her tear-filled eyes. *"Please, don't cry."* The words tore from him. Gruff. Rough. "Please." When had he ever used the word please with anyone but her? But Jesus, Lacey was crying, and he couldn't handle it.

"You made me cry, you jerk!" She swiped her hand over her cheek. "You just stood there and told me that my mother had a lover who killed her and—"

"You wanted the truth. I'm trying to give it to you." *Because I want to give you everything.* "I didn't want to tell you right now. I wanted to wait, try to find a better time—a better way...You're the one who insisted."

"Don't piss me off even more." She sniffed. Another tear leaked from the corner of her eye.

Her tears were breaking him. She could have just taken her knife and plunged the blade into him, then twisted. He was pretty sure it would have felt the same. *I hurt her.* "I want to hold you."

Her lips trembled. "Don't say stuff you don't mean to me."

He wasn't lying. "I thought you could tell when I was telling the truth."

She wasn't looking at him. Her gaze had turned away. Hell. As if she couldn't stand the sight of him. Not like she'd be the first person to hate him. He tended to leave a path of hate in his wake. Kind of his thing.

But she mattered.

"I guess I didn't know you as well as I thought," Lacey mumbled. "And don't I feel stupid? Here I was, thinking I could see the real you, but that was just another lie."

You can see me.

She walked away from him. Raked a hand through her hair. "Why the hell does Roman think I'm his sister? That just makes—"

She stopped. Didn't say the rest even though he knew she'd intended to say...

That just makes no sense.

Because she knew—deep down—that it did make sense. Dex had told Lacey that her mother had been involved with Roman's father. That the affair had continued for years.

She turned back toward him. Slowly. "No?" A question. Almost a plea. "He's wrong?" She was asking him to tell her it wasn't true. He could see that. In response, he wanted to lie. He wanted to say anything necessary to take the pain from her eyes. He would do *anything*—

A knock sounded at the door. Not just a knock. Pounding. A fist slamming into the frame over and over again.

Lacey flinched.

"Dex!" Roman roared. "Open the door before I break it down!"

Dex didn't move.

Lacey's eyes darted to the door, then away. Her shoulders hunched. Lacey had seemed so strong to him. Her body was delicate, yes, but a strength had always burned from within her. In this moment, though, she appeared far too vulnerable. Almost breakable.

"I want to see her!" Roman snarled. His fist thudded into the door again.

Lacey shook her head no.

That was all Dex needed. "You can go into the bedroom, and I'll talk to him."

"I just—I can't talk to him." Another tear slipped down her cheek. "I'm not..." She bit her lower lip. Seemed to struggle for words. Then... "Dex, help me."

He surged toward her.

A bitter laugh tore from her lips. "I can't believe I said that! You aren't helping me. You've been manipulating me from the beginning. You don't care about me. You've screwed me over in more ways than—"

"I care about you more than I care about anything else in this world." Absolute truth.

She was finally—finally—staring into his eyes. And he hoped that she could see the truth of his words. A truth that he was fully realizing.

The missions, the work, the agency—screw it all. When it came down to the job or to Lacey, he was picking Lacey. "I will never hurt you again."

"I don't believe you," she whispered back.

He nodded. Her response hurt, but... "I'll prove it." His hands lifted. Hovered over her shoulders. "May I...touch you?"

"Open the fucking door!" It sounded like the wood was about to break.

There were agents outside of the door. Unfortunately, Dex needed Roman's cooperation. So the agents were supposed to watch him, supposed to make sure he didn't leave the premises, but there had been no rules about him not pounding the shit out of Dex's door.

He'd have to go change that rule.

Once more, Lacey's gaze flew to the door. "I'm afraid."

His hands fisted. She hadn't answered his question, and he damn well wouldn't push her. "I'm not going to let him in. I'll take care of him. You don't have to see him until you're ready."

"He's...my half-brother? You're...you said my mom and his father had an affair for a long time so...my father is..." She didn't finish.

He wouldn't lie to her. "He's not your half-brother."

Her shoulders sagged. Relief flashed on her face. "I knew my dad was—"

"Baby, I am so sorry." He was. He hated causing her pain. "Roman isn't your half-brother. Not half anything. He is *your* brother. You share the same biological mother and father."

"Dex!" Roman's fist hit again. The wood cracked.

"That's not possible." Lacey shook her head. "My mom was given up for adoption. She told me how much she wished that she could have met her biological parents. No. *No.* She wouldn't have lived a life with me and not—"

Voice gentle, he said, "Sometimes people have to make very hard choices in this world. Choices that tear them apart. There is more at play here than you realize. There is more to—"

"Open the door!" Roman shouted.

Her gaze held his. "Dex..."

"You don't have to talk to him right now." He whirled for the door and the pounding prick. The pain in her stare was making him crazed. He frowned at the spider-web-like cracks in the wood of the door. He flipped the locks and yanked the door open—

Then had to shove his hand against Roman's chest when the other man barreled forward. "I want Lacey!"

Dex's jaw locked. "You're not getting her."

Roman tried to shove past him. Dex shoved back. Harder. He pushed the other man into the hallway.

"Let me see her!" Roman bellowed.

"You're scaring the hell out of her right now." Dex's voice was low. Hard. "Is that what you want?"

Roman glanced toward the suite, then back at Dex. "I...want my family. It's what I've always wanted."

Dex knew that. He'd originally intended to use that longing against Roman. *But that was before—before, hell...Lacey.* "She just found out that her father killed her mom *and* the only dad she's ever known. I had to deliver that news to her—"

"You should have told her from the beginning!" Fury darkened Roman's face. "You're an asshole and you had no right to—"

Dex surged toward him. "She's hurting. She is not ready for you right now. I told you not fifteen minutes ago to give her a little time. Your bodyguard shot her in the chest this morning! *In the chest!* Now she got this news from hell thrown at her. It's too much. Lacey wants time, and I'm giving it to her." *I'm giving her whatever she wants.*

"I didn't know about Heather! She knocked me out in my room last night, and then I woke up tied to that chair."

Yes, and that was another problem they had to face. No way did Dex buy that Heather had been able to transport Roman all the way from the lodge to the remote cabin by herself. Had to be at least a two-person job. *Which means there are more players involved.*

"I am not leaving until I talk to her." Spittle flew from Roman's mouth.

"How do you even know she's the right woman?" Maybe he could throw some doubt at Roman. "Have you run some DNA test that I don't know about? Hmm? Have you considered I was lying to you when I said I found her? Come to think of it, you assumed Lacey was your sister. I said that I'd found 'her' but I never specified who—"

"Dex." Lacey's voice. Soft but firm and coming from behind him.

"It's okay," he reassured her without glancing back. "Roman is going to calm down and take a walk."

Roman tried to rush past him. Dex grabbed him, shoved his arm under the guy's chin and pinned him against the nearby wall even as the two agents who'd been ordered to guard the suite just stood there and gaped from a few feet away—

Way to be helpers, fellows.

"*Don't.*" Lacey's fingers slid over Dex's shoulder. "I shouldn't have told you to send him away. Let's go inside. We all need to talk."

Roman glared at him. Dex glared back, but when he turned his head toward Lacey, he made sure his expression showed no rage. "Are you certain?"

She nodded and said, "Absolutely not."

Aw, Lacey, baby, you make me feel—

"But I think we have to do it anyway," she finished quietly. Her fingers pressed into him. "Let's go inside."

If that was what she wanted, then okay. Dex let go of Roman. Stepped back. At first, Roman didn't move. He just stared at Lacey. There were so many emotions swirling in his eyes. It was hard to read them all but...

Longing.

Fear.

Fury.

Dex moved subtly closer to Lacey. That fury of Roman's wasn't a good sign, and it was something Dex had worried about. He'd feared that Roman might not truly be the loving brother who'd finally found the sister he'd sought for so long.

After all, Roman had been raised by a sadistic bastard for most of his life. He'd only gotten to see his mother on rare occasions. He'd been told that she chose her daughter over him. That she'd wanted the daughter to stay with her.

He'd been told that his mother had thrown him to the wolf.

Now Roman *was* the big, bad wolf.

"You look like her," Roman accused, and there was no missing the anger that seethed in his words.

Once more, Dex moved his body. A careful, deliberate movement that put him between Roman and Lacey. He held the other man's gaze and wanted to make certain that his message was absolutely, one hundred percent clear.

If you want to hurt her, you'll have to go the hell through me.

CHAPTER ELEVEN

She wasn't a coward. All right, fine. She wasn't normally a coward. But when she'd told Dex that she hadn't wanted to see Roman, she'd been afraid. *Her brother? Roman was the son of the man who'd killed her mom?*

Only there was more to figure out because...her dad wasn't her real dad? God, everything was so confusing. Her chest ached— both from the impact of the bullet hitting the vest earlier and from the pain that grew straight out of her heart—and she just wanted to shut out the world for a little while. Jump under the covers of a bed and pretend that her world hadn't been wrecked.

But running and hiding had never been her style. And she could not, would not, start now.

She led the way back into the suite. Dex followed at her heels, with Roman crowding behind him, and when they were inside, no one sat down. There was way too much tension for that. Roman stared at her with eyes that swirled with emotion, while Dex stood at her side. Dex was expressionless. Nothing showed in his eyes or on his face, but she could feel tension pouring from his body.

"I haven't done a DNA test. Didn't need to," Roman announced grimly. "I still have a pic of my mother. Once you started throwing the shit in my face that you'd found *her* first..." He pointed at Lacey. "I acquired some info, dug enough to figure out that, yes, it all fit." His lips twisted into a grim smile. "Though I'm sure you have done a DNA test, haven't you, Dex?"

*Throwing the shit in my face that you'd found her first...*The pounding of her heartbeat was so incredibly loud even as the pain of betrayal cut like a knife.

She'd known that Dex was using her. Obviously. He'd been so adamant that she had to help him on this case. Saying he needed her special skills. *Bullshit*. She wanted to scream at him and rage and rage and *rage*.

But she didn't make a sound of fury. Her control was too thin. She would not lose it. She needed answers. By God, she was going to get them. "Have you done a DNA test?" she asked Dex in a slow, stilted voice.

"No, baby, but...it fits. You fit."

She wasn't even sure how to interpret his words.

"I can do the test, if you want it," Dex offered, "and I can have the results for you immediately. Say the word."

A DNA test. When she'd first started investigating the death of her parents, she'd had no idea it would lead to this. "The results will tell me who my father is."

Roman lunged toward her. "I know who your father is. I know who your mother is." He jerked his hand toward his chest. "And I know who your brother is." Bruises darkened the skin around his hairline, and a white bandage covered a section of his forehead. "I've always known you were out there. I didn't have a name for our mother. She was a ghost in my life. A ragged picture I kept while I lived a world away. I didn't even know about you until the old bastard died. You were the last thing he talked about. The daughter *she'd* chosen."

Her temples pounded in tune with her heartbeat. She stared hard at Roman, trying to see a similarity, but there was none. His hair was blond. His eyes blue. She didn't look like him. She looked like her mother. Her dad. Her mom had even told her—so many times—that she had her dad's laugh and...

"Dex is using you. You can't trust him," Roman said quietly. He offered his hand to her. "Come with me. We should talk without him around us. Then you need to get the hell away from him, as fast as you can."

She stared at his hand. Then looked into his eyes. The rage in his gaze made her uneasy. So much about this mess made her uneasy. "You told me I couldn't trust Dex last night. Right after someone tried to shoot at him...or at me."

Now she got why Dex thought she'd been the target. *Maybe share important details sooner, Dex!*

Lacey hissed out a breath. She couldn't think straight. She'd been hit with so much, and she just kept circling back to Roman. Her brother. The man who stared at her with a mix of longing and rage in his eyes.

"You can't trust him," Roman seethed. "No one can trust him. He turns on his own agents and leaves them in the wind."

Dex took a hard step toward him. "The hell I do."

Roman's laugh held a bitter edge. "We both know I'm speaking from personal experience. You left me. You should have just put a bullet in my brain yourself."

What? Her gaze flew between the two men.

And Dex...smiled.

Goose bumps rose onto her arms. That smile of his was icy cold. Lethal. As she stared at Dex's smile, she felt as if she was staring straight at a stranger. This wasn't the Dex she knew. This wasn't the Dex who'd brought her to orgasm again and again. Not the Dex who'd looked at her only moments before and told her to please, please not cry.

"If I'd wanted a bullet in your brain," Dex said easily, "then one would be there right now. I've had plenty of opportunities over the years. You know that. Have you ever considered trying to be grateful to me instead of pissy? I got you out of the mess you were in, and I let you keep living. Instead of telling me thanks, you've been nothing but a pain in my ass."

It looked as if the two men were about to come to blows. Right there in front of her. "Stop it."

Both of their heads whipped toward her.

"I'm not looking for backstory shit between the two of you right now, though it's pretty obvious there's a whole lot going on there. Bromance gone bad, that it?"

The chill in Dex's eyes thawed a little as he looked at her.

Roman kept frowning.

"Why did your bodyguard try to kill me?" Lacey demanded. "Why did she drag you to that cabin?"

"I...don't know."

"That's not a good enough answer for me." She focused on Dex. Since he seemed to hold all the answers..."Why?"

"She hasn't told me...yet. I thought you might want to join me for the next round of interrogation."

Her face must have reflected her surprise.

Dex eased closer to her. "I don't like keeping things from you. You may not believe that, but it's the truth." His voice was low, but Roman was so close he had to be able to hear the words. "Whenever I can, I want to be one hundred percent honest with you." He reached for her hand, the hand that carried his engagement ring. She'd slipped it back on when he'd gone to confront Roman. "You matter, and I need you to get that."

Once more, Roman's bitter laughter rang out. "If Dex is talking, he's lying. That should be the first lesson you learn. I don't know what kind of promises he made to you, but he won't keep them."

Except he actually had. He'd promised to help her discover who had killed her parents, and he *had* told her. Or...maybe he hadn't. She lifted her chin and asked Roman, "Did your father kill my mother?"

"Kill *our* mother, you mean? Yes, I think he did." He shrugged.

"Why?" Ice covered her heart.

Another shrug. "An accident." Said casually. As if her mother had tripped and skinned her knee. *An accident.* "She shouldn't have been in the car with that guy."

That guy. *My dad. The man who taught me how to ride a bike. Who held my hand when I went trick-or-treating and stayed up late on Christmas Eve with me so that we could watch for Santa Claus.* That guy.

"He was my dad. Not just some random guy." The ice around her heart shattered. A wild yell broke from her lips as she lunged at Roman. Her hands were fisted, and she wanted to attack.

Before her fists could land, Dex's arms curled around her stomach. "Baby, baby, just breathe." He pulled her back against him.

She was seeing red. Pain and blood and—

Roman smirked at her. "You've been living a lie. Time to take the blinders off. Your father was Gideon Valentino. Fucking monster. All-around sadistic bastard. Welcome to the family, sis."

"Get the hell out," Dex snapped. "Now."

She heaved in his hold. This was too much. Everything was crazy. Her head was spinning and—

"Is that why you nearly broke the door down?" Dex's hold on her was gentle, but unbreakable as he snarled at Roman, "You wanted to get in her face and hurt her?"

"She needs the truth! She needs—"

Dex looked down at Lacey. "I pulled you back because you might feel guilty later for beating the hell out of him. But don't worry, I won't."

She frowned. What was he saying?

"Step back would you, baby? Got to make sure you don't accidentally come between us."

His arms had fallen away from her. She stepped back.

"Thanks so much." Dex flew forward and plowed his fist into Roman's jaw. "I just fucking told her I wouldn't let her be hurt!"

Roman tried to punch back.

Dex dodged the blow. Swung again. *Hit.* "I made her a promise, then you dragged your ass in here and you told her news in the worst possible way. Like you're trying to piss me off. Stop hurting her! She loved Jason Amari. He was her dad, her father in every way that counted, and when you talk about him, you damn well talk about him with respect, you understand me? He's not some guy. He's her dad. That's what he'll always be."

It was like—like Dex had just read her mind. Everything he was saying was playing through her head over and over again.

Dex's breath heaved out. He backed away from Roman.

Roman's lower lip was bleeding. He brushed away the blood. "Why in the hell are you acting like it matters to you, Dex? This is all just a ruse for you. Another game." His gaze found Lacey. "You think he cares about you? At all? Bullshit. He doesn't care about anyone. The engagement is fake."

Well, sure, it was, but—

"If he's fucked you, it's because it was part of his plan."

Lacey could feel blood rushing to her cheeks.

"He has." Roman's hands fisted. Released. Fisted. "You fucked—"

"You know, there are many reasons why I don't like you. So many, many reasons." Dex rocked forward onto the balls of his feet. "The fact that you are standing in front of me, disrespecting my fiancée? That's currently at the top of my list. Stop it. Or you will regret it."

Roman's eyes blazed as he rushed for Lacey. His hands curled around her arms. "He's using you." His hold tightened. "Don't you see that? You're a pawn, nothing more. He pulled you in because he wanted to use you in order to get to me. But he miscalculated. My enemies are coming after you. They want you dead. Or hell, maybe it's his enemies that want you to die. Either way, by bringing you in, he's put a giant target on your chest."

His fingers were digging into her arms. "Get your hands off me."

He looked down at her arms. "I..."

"Now!" Dex shouted. He locked a hand around Roman's shoulder and hauled him back. Then Dex leveled his stare on Lacey. "You okay?"

Absolutely, a million times *not*. She was most certainly not okay.

He must have read her expression clearly because he locked his fingers around the back of Roman's neck and shoved him toward the door. "Excuse us for just a moment, Lacey."

He forced Roman out of the suite. The door slammed shut behind them.

Lacey stood there with her knees shaking. Before, she'd gone out of the suite because she wanted to see Roman. She wanted to hear the truth.

The truth was ugly and twisted. Learning about who had killed her parents hadn't given her closure. It had broken her heart. Ripped away the memories of a family that she'd treasured.

Her arms wrapped around her stomach. She had to get the hell out of there. Lacey strode to the bedroom and started packing.

Maybe I am running and hiding...because it hurts too much to do anything else.

***

"I always knew you were a soulless bastard, Dex, but to use her like this—to make her think you wanted to marry her, that you cared even as you screwed her over—that's a new low, even for you."

Dex kept a very cold smile on his face as he glanced at the two, wide-eyed agents. "Give us five minutes, would you?" He motioned for them to walk away.

They immediately rushed for the elevator.

When the area was clear... "I've been civil with you so far—"

"Civil? You nearly broke my jaw!" Roman rubbed a hand over his jaw.

"I've been *mostly* civil because you are her brother. I happen to know that Lacey values family, so I was trying to exercise care with you."

"Care, my ass, you punched—"

Dex stood toe-to-toe with him. "Drop the bullshit." His voice was flat. No emotion. "I don't have time for it. If I wanted, I could make you vanish from this lodge right now—vanish from the face of the freaking planet—and we both know it. Your bodyguard just tried to kill the fiancée of a high-ranking CIA official. I can have you shoved into a hole so dark and deep that no one will find you."

Roman licked a drop of blood from his lower lip. "So why haven't you?"

"Did you order Heather to attack Lacey?"

"No! Of course, not! I didn't tell her to do a damn thing!"

He already knew that. Back at the cabin, when Roman had thought that Lacey might be dying, the man's mask had ripped away. He'd broken in front of Dex.

"I didn't exactly order Heather to knock me out and drag my ass up the mountain, either!" Roman raged. "She's obviously working for someone else."

"Exactly. You're going to help me find that someone else. That's why you're not in that deep, dark hole...yet."

Roman swallowed. "You're going to send me in interrogation with Heather?"

"We'll go in together. I want to know who is targeting my fiancée."

"It's not real. Stop calling her—"

"I should be clear. I have every intention of marrying Lacey Amari. I don't know why you think it's not real, but I assure you, she is mine." He needed this message to be heard, understood, and taken to the grave. "I protect what's mine. I guard it closely. And when someone tries to take what I value, I destroy the fool who made that mistake."

A furrow appeared between Roman's eyebrows. "You expect me to believe you care about Lacey? You've never cared about anyone in your life."

"What I expect you to do is believe what I tell you. Someone hurts Lacey, I destroy that person. Simple enough." A pause. "You hurt her in that suite. I let you speak to her because Lacey wanted the truth."

"Truth freaking hurts, man."

Dex lifted his hand and pushed the knife he carried—a weapon he'd had hidden until this moment—against the front of Roman's shirt. Right over his heart.

Roman went absolutely still.

"Oh, do I have your attention now?" Dex asked silkily. "How wonderful."

Roman didn't even seem to be breathing.

"You wanted your sister. After your father died, you came to me. You begged for my help because her trail was ice cold. All you had was an old photograph. A twenty-year-old plus photograph. You didn't even have a name. I told you I'd find your sister. I kept my word." He pressed the tip of the blade into Roman's shirt. Let it nick the skin. "Now you get to keep your word. Do you remember the offer you made to me?"

The flicker of his lashes said that Roman did.

"Good," Dex praised. "So start keeping up your end of the deal. First thing you can do is go downstairs and stay with Larry until I join you. Remember Larry? I'm sure you do. When I come meet you, we'll head in for a not-so-fun little chat with your bodyguard." He slowly released the other man. Then Dex turned his back on him. A deliberate move.

"She didn't know about me?" A rough, angry question. "Lacey had no idea that her brother was out there?"

His hand had already extended toward the suite's door. Those cracks in the wood were a problem. He'd need to get a new door installed ASAP. "None."

"You believe her? Or is Lacey lying?" Pain creaked in the words.

Dex couldn't imagine what it had been like for Roman, growing up as he had. And he knew that Roman blamed his mother for leaving him to that hell. Part of Roman also blamed... "Don't do it," Dex warned him quietly as he looked back.

"Do what?" Roman's chin jutted up.

"I see it in your eyes. The longing for a family. For someone to love you. To accept you, scars and all."

"Screw you. I don't need anyone to love—"

"You want her love, but you hate her at the same time, and that's going to be a major problem. Because I can't have your hate around her. Lacey is not to blame for anything that happened. She never had a choice. No, I don't think she knew about you. Lacey values family. She values it one hell of a lot." So much that he'd been able to use that against her. *Fuck me.* "If she'd known, Lacey would have been the one hunting you."

Hope flared in Roman's eyes, only to be quickly smothered away. "Always manipulating, aren't you?"

"Not this time. Take my advice. Don't mess this up. Don't let that hate in you win. Do us both a favor, would you?"

Roman waited, as if he was actually curious to see what Dex would ask for in a favor.

Dex held his stare then said, "Don't be your father's son." Without another word, he left Roman. He shut the door quietly behind him.

***

Roman didn't move. His hands clenched and released, over and over again. His knuckles burned—mostly because he'd bruised and bloodied them when he'd tried so hard to get into the suite earlier.

He stared at the door. His sister was behind that door. A sister with his mother's eyes. His mother's cheeks. Her hair.

The mother who hadn't wanted him.

The sister who...hadn't known he ever existed?

When he'd thought that Lacey was dead on that mountain, that she was slipping away before he ever got to know her, he'd been terrified.

"Ahem." A throat cleared behind him. He'd known the agents had returned.

He sucked in a breath, then turned and stormed by them. He *had* once made a deal with Dex, and, dammit, he'd keep that deal.

Or he'd die trying.

Knowing Dex as he did, death was a definite possibility.

Roman stomped into the elevator.

"Perfect timing," Larry said with a grin.

Fuck. Of course, *he* was there. Tall, built like a friggin' tank, with a gleaming, bald head.

"Dex wanted me to keep an eye on you. Said I should plan to be in this elevator because you'd be coming to me."

Dex. Always playing ahead of everyone else. He'd known that Roman would demand to see Lacey. He'd had his guard dog Larry waiting in the wings. "Screw off, Larry."

"You know, I still carry the scar from that knife wound you gave me."

The elevator was descending.

Larry's fist slammed toward his face.

Because...why the hell not?

"Payback," Larry piped up happily. "Now, be good and don't call me a guard dog again. Hurts my feelings."

"Where the hell are you taking me?" Now his lip was bleeding even worse.

"Your girlfriend is waiting downstairs."

"She's not my girlfriend," he muttered. "She attacked me last night."

Larry merely lifted a brow. "Do you ever think you might bring out the worst in people?"

All the damn time. "Screw off, Larry."

CHAPTER TWELVE

She had her bag packed. Her fingers curled around the handle of her rolling luggage, and Lacey stared straight ahead with determination clear to see on her face.

Uh, oh. Dex approached her slowly. "Are we going somewhere?"

"No."

"Good." He exhaled in relief. "Because, you know, when I saw the luggage, I immediately thought we were—"

"There is no we. I'm leaving. Me. Just me."

Hard no, baby. Hard no.

"I'm getting out of this nightmare. I'm getting on a plane. I'm going home." She pulled her luggage forward. The wheels rolled across the floor. Her chin stayed up, her spine remained perfectly straight, and the tension poured off her in waves.

Dex stepped to the side so that he didn't block her path. With one hand, he motioned toward the door. "You are free to leave. You are certainly not my prisoner."

A snort.

His eyes narrowed. Normally, he loved that cute sound. This time...*okay, fine, I still think it's oddly sexy but...she doesn't believe me.* He'd never intended for Lacey to be his prisoner. "You are absolutely free to get on a plane and head back to your old life. But, if you leave, then you won't find out why Heather Madding tried to kill you."

He saw her hesitate.

"I'll find out, though," he rushed to reassure her. "Don't you worry about that. I am on the case. I'll find out, and I'll be sure to call you up and tell you what happened. So just go and wait for that call. Probably a good idea." He nodded for emphasis.

"You're playing me."

"What?" Dex put his hand to his chest. "I would never."

Her head cocked to the side. "My morning has sucked."

"Yes." He cleared his throat. "I can see how it hasn't been stellar."

"You think?"

Dex exhaled and dropped his act. "What can I do?"

Her hair slid over her shoulder. "Why did you want me to play dead?"

He blinked. "Excuse me?"

"After I was shot on the mountain, you wanted me to keep my eyes closed. You didn't want me to move. You wanted me to act as if I'd been shot in the chest. Why?"

"Because if you were dead, then no one else would try to hurt you. Or, rather, if whoever the hell hired Heather believed you were dead, then that would buy me time to hunt down the bastard."

"You don't think she was acting on her own."

He laughed. Turned away and headed for the window. He stared out at the mountains and wondered just who waited beyond his sight. "Heather is more of a for-hire kind of person. I warned Roman about her once. Told him that I thought her loyalties would always be for sale, but he didn't believe me. He should have listened."

"You...hold on, were you and Roman friends?" Her voice was closer because she'd crept up behind him.

She'd come to him. Not gone for the door.

"I don't have many people who truly fit the definition of friend." An honest statement, for her. "But once upon a time, yes, I trusted him. He trusted me. That's why when he learned he had a sister, Roman came to me for help in finding you."

Silence. Then, voice halting, Lacey told him, "You know I'm furious with you for hiding my past from me. I want to scream at you and call you every single name I can think of—and I can think of lots of names. Like, a whole lot."

Squaring his shoulders, he faced her. "Do it."

She didn't.

"Yell at me," Dex urged. "Tell me what a bastard I am. Get it out."

She'd let go of her luggage. With her eyes on him, she closed the last bit of distance between them. Her eyes were wide and deep. Her scent wrapped around him, and Dex wanted so badly to reach out and curl his hands around her shoulders. To pull her close and never, ever let go.

"Am I just some pawn to you?" Her question was husky. "That's what Roman said I was. Am I only a pawn to be moved around while you play your chess game with some enemy in the dark?"

"A pawn?" He had to laugh at the ridiculous idea. "No. Baby, you're the fucking queen."

Her eyebrows lifted.

"The most important piece. The most powerful one. The one I would protect at all costs."

"And here I thought the queen protected the king," she murmured back. "Actually, I thought she covered the asses of every other piece on the board."

"She does. That's why she's the most powerful. Everyone wants the queen." *I will always want you.* "I didn't tell you the full truth for a lot of reasons. The main reason? I knew it would hurt."

"How would you be hurt by—"

"*You* would be hurt. Not me. *You.*" But he'd discovered that her pain hurt him. Interesting. After years of being invulnerable, he'd found that his Achilles' heel was a sexy brunette. "When I learned how much you loved your dad, Jason...when I learned how much you wanted to find the person responsible for your parents' deaths, I knew the truth would hurt you. The more I got to know you, the more I hated to bring you pain. I always intended to tell you what happened to them. That wasn't a lie. I was going to keep up my end of the deal. But I wanted to tell you in a way that would cause the least amount of pain."

"You kinda failed there." She looked away.

He didn't. He kept staring at her because there was nothing else he wanted to see. *Just her.*

"The second reason I didn't tell you is because I don't trust Roman."

Her attention seemed to be on the mountains. "He obviously doesn't trust you, either."

"And the third reason is because I am working a classified case, and I know that's not what you want to hear—"

Her gaze jerked angrily back to his.

"But it's true. The case isn't over. There are people I must bring down. Dangerous people. I need Roman's cooperation in order to get that done. You're the key to his cooperation, Lacey. If you stay with me, we can end this. Just a few more days, that's all I'm asking."

Her mouth opened.

Fearing an angry refusal, he rushed to add, "I know it's asking a lot."

"Yes, it is."

"I need your help. But I will not make you stay. I'd never do that. Your choice. Walk out the door if you want and don't look back." *But I'll send a security detail to make sure you're safe until I'm satisfied this mess is over.* "Or stay with me and let's take down the bastard who ordered the hit on you."

She studied him in silence. He couldn't see past the veil of her dark eyes. What was she thinking?

Just how much does she hate me?

And why did it matter so much that she did?

Because I liked it when Lacey smiled at me. Because the world felt less dark when we worked together, and I was finally starting to feel like someone understood me.

"I want a new deal."

He blinked. Well, her response hadn't been a straight up no so... "Name your terms. You want money? I can pay." A lot. He had plenty of personal resources that he could put into play in order to—

"You'll pay me with intel. With that limitless supply of knowledge you seem to access." A brisk nod. "You'll help me figure out why my mother—*if* Roman is my brother, if she was his mother—you'll help me figure out why my mother left him and never told me about him. You'll help me figure out how she could have lived a lie for so long with me and my dad, but still been going back to visit that—that other man. Gideon Valentino."

"Done." An immediate answer.

"I'm not finished with my demands."

Didn't she get it? He would agree to anything for her.

It took a moment for the full ramifications of that thought to sink in. *Holy shit. I would do anything she wanted.*

"Why are you looking at me like that?" She squinted at him.

"Like what?"

"Like you've never seen me before."

"I always see you." *I just didn't always realize how important you would be to me. I will never make that mistake again.* "Continue with the blackmail."

"I—" She stopped. "I am not blackmailing you."

"I don't mind the dirty words. Keep going."

"I am *not* blackmailing you."

"You're saying you'll only help me if I agree to your terms. That's fair. Turnabout and all that. I got you. No worries."

"Dex..."

"You're not crying any longer."

She retreated a step.

"There were tears still gleaming in your eyes a few moments ago. Even one that trickled down right...here." His fingers slid ever so gently over the curve of her cheek. Then lingered. "But the tears are gone now. I think fighting with me—blackmailing me—is good for you."

Understanding flashed across her face. "A few moments ago, you wanted me to call you names."

A shrug of one shoulder. "I deserve them."

"Even now, you're trying to distract me from feeling so hurt."

"Is it working?" He loved touching her skin. His fingers slid down a little more.

Her hand flew up and curved around his wrist. "Yes. It is working. I don't feel like my heart has been cut out any longer. I feel like I want to get out there and find out what the hell is going on."

Because she was back in fighting form. His Lacey *was* a fighter. That was one of the things he loved most about her.

Loved? Wow. Hold the freaking phone...had he—

"Demand number two...you don't try seducing me."

He felt real alarm pulse through his body. "You don't want to be with me anymore?" Hell, sure she didn't. She was furious. Might even hate him. Not normally a problem because there were a whole line of folks who felt that way about him but—

"I don't want to be manipulated, Dex. If having sex with me last night was just some way of—of getting back at Roman, then I—"

He locked his hands around her waist, lifted her up, pinned her to the nearby wall, and kissed her. His tongue thrust past her lips, tasted the sweetness that he absolutely craved with every fiber of his being, and for a time, he just took.

She kissed him right back. With an angry passion at first. As if she were mad about the fact that she wanted him. But then the kiss changed.

Her fingers sank into his hair. Her body pressed closer to his. A sweet and sexy moan slipped from her as her legs rose and curled around his hips. She tasted so good. His best dream. He thrust his tongue into her mouth. Licked. Savored.

Lust surged through his body. He wanted to take her. Right then. Right there. He—

His mouth pulled away from hers. It took all of his strength, but he made his head lift. "Be clear about this. When I have sex with you, Roman is the last thing on my mind." Hell, no, he hadn't been trying to get back at Roman.

"Dex—"

"I want you. Have since the first moment we met. You want the truth?" He kissed her again. A deep, drugging kiss. "I've never wanted anyone as much as I want you. Sex with you isn't about manipulation. It's kind of about survival."

Another kiss. "Last night, I needed to fuck you as much as I needed to breathe." His hands were tight around her waist. "If you want to talk about seduction, all you have to do is crook that finger of yours at me, and you can consider me seduced."

Her eyes stared into his. Her cheeks had flushed, and her lips were red and plump from his mouth.

"You can forget demand number two," he rasped. He wanted her mouth again. Always. "Whenever you want me, say the word, and I'm yours." *I want you to be mine, Lacey.* He bit that part back, barely. Because when he thought about Lacey being his, he wasn't just talking about a hot time in bed.

He was talking about forever.

Now how do I make that happen?

Her breath came in soft pants. She still had her fingers in his hair. Still had their mouths so close together...

Let her go. Move back. If you keep holding her like this...

Slowly, he lowered her legs. Let go of her hips. She lowered her arms.

They stared at each other.

He should speak. "Any other demands?" Dex's words were guttural.

"We don't use sex against each other. That's...not involved in the case. That's separate." She licked her lips. "And I am *not* saying I'm having sex with you again. I'm saying that when we touch, we go supernova."

Yes, they did.

"And neither one of us should use that against the other."

No, they should just enjoy the hell out of the situation.

"Final demand and it's a big one."

He waited.

"I want the highest-level clearance it is possible for me to get. You've already been researching my background. Do whatever else is necessary so you can't stonewall me again by saying that things are classified."

Now this part was gonna be tricky. "You have to work for the agency..."

"I thought I already was. You are the agency, right?"

That's classified. Exactly what he did at the CIA and how much power he wielded—classified. "I can look into getting that clearance for you." He wasn't going to make her any promises, though. Because with Lacey, he wanted to try and not make promises that he couldn't keep.

He didn't want to let her down again.

"In return..." Dex reached for her hand. Lifted it up. The diamond engagement ring sparkled. "You'll continue with our ruse? You'll keep saying you're my fiancée, even to Roman?"

"Keep promising that I love you?"

"Yes." Gruff. "Keep promising that." He moved his fingers so that he was holding her hand—as if for a handshake. "Deal?"

"Deal."

Some of the heavy weight lifted from his shoulders. *She's not leaving me. I have time.*

"Then let's get busy, partner. We have a suspect that we need to interrogate."

CHAPTER THIRTEEN

"I want a lawyer." Heather Madding was adamant. "I'm not saying a single word without an attorney present."

"Oh, good news." Dex pulled out a chair and sidled closer to her. "I am an attorney, so consider your needs met."

He was? Lacey shot him a frown. They were in the basement of the lodge, but you'd never know it. The place looked like some sort of interrogation room at a police station—complete with one-way glass along the left wall.

When she'd entered with Dex a few moments before, she'd found Heather seated at a small table. Heather's hands were cuffed, and an agent—a guy with brown hair and assessing eyes and a posture that said he was always at attention—had stood behind her. Dex had dismissed the guard, and now it appeared that it was chat time.

"You're not my attorney." Heather sniffed. "I know my rights. I know exactly what I can and can't—"

Dex's laughter cut through her words. "That is adorable." He looked over at Lacey. "She thinks we're the police. Maybe Fortune PD?"

"I *know* who you are, Dex," Heather fired back.

"Good." Just like that, his laughter faded. "Then you know I don't take shit from anyone. You also know there aren't any rules that I have to follow when I'm questioning suspects, especially a suspect who tried to kill my fiancée."

Heather's gaze darted to Lacey. "I didn't miss." A pause. "Bulletproof vest?"

"You left me with a bruise," Lacey told her as she took a seat in the chair across from Heather. "Consider me not amused."

Heather seemed to weigh her. "You're not seriously marrying him."

"I've got the ring to prove it." She lifted her hand. Wiggled her fingers.

"He's a fucking psycho," Heather snarled.

Dex sighed. "Words hurt. They hurt." He leaned closer to Heather. "But you know what hurts more?" His voice had turned dangerously soft. "Being thrown in one of the government's off-the-books prisons. Being held there for years and years while you're forgotten by everyone you ever knew. That shit really, really hurts."

Because she was watching the other woman so closely, Lacey saw the faint tremble in Heather's lower lip. It was a tremble that was quickly controlled. Heather's lashes swept down over her cheeks while she apparently mulled things over, and then she tilted her head back as she lifted her lashes and asked Lacey, "When did you meet Roman?"

Unexpected question. "Yesterday," she responded honestly.

Heather appeared taken back. "But...you...you weren't with him before?"

With him?

She wasn't going to touch that question just yet. Instead, Lacey told her, "We have you dead to rights. You shot the agents in the woods. You were apprehended right after you took your shot at me. With or without a confession, you're going to the prison Dex promised."

Heather tapped the edge of her cuffs against the top of the table. "It wasn't anything personal. Just a job."

I take a bullet to the chest very personally. "Who were you working for?" Lacey asked.

"Nope." Heather exhaled. "Not going to be sharing that information. I am not going to tell you—"

The door opened behind Lacey. She looked back. Saw Roman. His furious stare was on Heather.

The man seemed to have so much rage bottled inside. She couldn't help but wonder...where had all that fury come from? Part of her was afraid to find out.

Her stare turned back to Heather just in time to see...

Oh. Oh, damn. Yep. That would make sense.

Had Dex caught that little chink in Heather's armor? Because in a blink, Heather was back to seeming all calm and cool. Lacey crossed her arms under her breasts, leaned back in her chair, and got ready to see what happened next.

Roman slowly stalked across the room. He stopped on Heather's left side. Crouched next to her. She didn't turn her head toward him.

Like Lacey, Dex was also just watching. She knew he'd told Roman to give them a few moments before he came inside. She'd been right beside Dex when he made that announcement when they'd all gathered outside of the interrogation room. Grudgingly, Roman had agreed.

Now it was show time.

"Aren't you going to look at me?" Roman asked quietly.

Heather licked her lips before turning her head toward him. "It wasn't personal." She seemed to like saying those words.

"Liar." Roman's response sounded like a caress.

Oh, yes. There is definitely something going on here. Or there was.

Heather sighed. "I didn't kill you, did I?"

"No, you just tried to kill someone you thought was important to me."

Heather tossed a glare at Lacey. "So what's your deal, lady? You screwing them both?"

Dex immediately moved to Lacey's side. "Lacey is with me. No one else. I don't know what you think is happening between her and Roman, but you're dead wrong."

Wait, wait, wait. Heather believed Lacey was romantically involved with Roman? "Dead wrong," Lacey echoed. But now everything was making sense. "You're in love with him."

Heather's glare became even darker. "Shut up. You don't know me. You don't—"

"You didn't kill him. You left him alive. Probably because you just couldn't bring yourself to do the deed, hmm?"

"You know *nothing*."

"I think I know a lot. Like...I know the look in a woman's eyes when she stares at the man she wants. You had that look when Roman walked into the room. It was only there a moment, but I saw it." Now her stare slid to Roman. "During the big ball, Dex told me that you and Heather only pretended to be lovers, that she was really your bodyguard." She thought of her own arrangement with Dex. "Sometimes, it's easy for a pretend relationship to become real, isn't it? It's easy for those lines to get all blurred." And the next thing you knew, you were losing your heart when the whole thing was all a lie.

"I didn't blur anything with you, Heather." Roman's voice was low. "We never crossed a damn line."

"You..." Heather's head snapped back toward Roman. "I was right there! In front of you every single day! But you didn't see me!" Her words tumbled out in a furious rush. "Then *I* saw that picture you kept of her. You kept it hidden, but I found it."

Not of me. Of my mom. Her stare darted to Roman. *Their* mom?

"I was supposed to get close to you," Heather added. "I did. I fucking did."

"Very close," Roman agreed.

"No!" She jumped to her feet. Her cuffed hands lifted before her.

Roman rose to face her.

"You wouldn't let me in! You rejected me. I told you that I'd give you everything, but you didn't want it." A low snarl escaped her. One that was a mix of pain and rage. "You didn't want me."

He didn't look away from Heather. "You were paid to hurt me."

"I was paid to kill you." Then she gasped, as if she'd realized she'd said too much.

"Don't stop now," Dex ordered into the stark silence that stretched in the small room. "Do tell us who paid you. I can't stand the suspense."

Heather grabbed Roman's shirt. "Help me."

A muscle flexed along his jaw. "Why did you go after Lacey?"

"Get me a deal. We both know you and Dex work deals together. Get me out of custody. Get me a new identity. Let me walk away, and I-I'll tell you everything."

So this chick had shot several agents, assaulted Roman...*and tried to kill me*, yet the woman thought she was going to get to head merrily into the sunset? "I don't think so," Lacey informed her briskly. "This isn't the time for deals. This is the time for you to talk. If I were you, I'd talk fast. Because from where I'm sitting..."

Heather's head whipped toward her.

"It seems to me you were hired to do a job. You didn't kill Roman, though, and I'm still breathing, too. I'd call that a double fail. If I were your boss, I'd be pretty furious. Especially seeing as how you are now a loose end. And you do know what happens to loose ends, don't you?" She smiled. "They get cut."

Heather's lower lip trembled once more. "Protection," she demanded. "I want it."

Oh, now it was about protection? Not heading into the sunset? "Protection comes for a price." Lacey tossed that part out casually, as if she had some magic power to give the other woman protection. She figured Dex did so... "Why did you shoot me? Considering it wasn't, ah, personal, I believe you said, then that must mean someone else wanted me dead."

Heather seemed to reach some decision. "I was hired to get close to Roman. To find his weakness. When I relayed the information about his obsession with you, my boss told me to aim for your heart. Because you seemed to be the only damn thing that mattered to Roman," she finished bitterly.

A would-be lover scorned. Lacey couldn't feel a whole lot of sympathy for the woman. Considering, you know, the whole shot-to-the-heart bit.

"He was going to find your body. Then I was supposed to kill Roman." Heather heaved out a breath. "But I wasn't. I wasn't going to kill him. I—"

"We know you were running away after you took the shot at Lacey," Dex interrupted to say with a rather bored air. "My agent already told us that part. Just to make certain I have all of this straight, let's recap, shall we?"

Roman's stare was on Heather. Heather was looking miserably at Dex. And Dex...

His eyes glittered as he told Heather, "You were paid to get close to Roman, so you took the job as his bodyguard. I warned you against hiring her, by the way, Roman—which makes this yet another time when I was right."

"Fuck you, Dex."

Dex rolled on. "You tried to find his weakness. While doing that, you fell for your target. He didn't return your feelings and that pissed the hell out of you." His fingers curled over Lacey's shoulder. "Then you found her. You told your boss that Roman was obsessed. That he was looking for her and—wham—she'd just turned up at the same lodge Roman was visiting. I'm guessing you then received the order to take her out. To make that big, bloody statement to Roman, huh? Right before you killed him."

"I told you, I wasn't going to kill—"

"You were going to kill my fiancée. Mine." Dex's voice was different now, definitely not bored. She'd never heard him sound quite so lethal. "That means no deals," Dex continued in a deep, dangerous voice. "That means if you want to keep living past this room, this minute, you talk now. I want the name of the bastard who was your real boss. I want to know where he is. I want to know every single thing about him."

Fear flashed on Heather's face. Her head jerked toward Roman. "You...you won't let him hurt me?"

Roman spun away from her. He stalked for the door.

"No!" Heather lunged after him.

Dex jumped into her path and caught her shoulders. "I want the name. I want everything."

"Roman! Don't leave me!" Heather pleaded.

He was opening the door.

"I don't have a name!" Heather all but screamed. "I never met him in person! We met on the Dark Web, and he paid me—he kept paying me. Wired the money to my account in the Cayman Islands. I'd email him info and—*stop! Roman, don't leave me—*"

He opened the door and walked out.

"Did you use your computer for the emails?" Dex asked in the voice that sent a shiver down Lacey's spine. "The one we confiscated already?"

A miserable nod was Heather's response. Her attention was still on the closed door. Except, now the brown-haired agent from before was strolling back in. His posture was just as perfect as before.

"Thanks for the cooperation, Heather. That wasn't too painful, was it?" Dex inclined his head toward Lacey. "Ready, love?"

More than ready. She stood up and took the arm he offered toward her.

Heather let out a guttural cry and rushed at them. Her cuffs were lifted high as she prepared to strike—

But the agent grabbed her. "Ma'am, you'll be needing to sit down..."

"Why are you so important to him?" Heather yelled at Lacey. "Why you?"

Because he thinks I'm his sister.

Then Heather gave a keening laugh. "I might not have gotten you, but he will!"

He?

"You're with a monster, the worst of the worst, and you don't even know it! Ask him! Ask your precious Dex how many people he's killed, how many lives he's destroyed, how many—"

Dex pulled Lacey outside. The door closed behind them. "That was getting ugly," he said, his voice now ever so casual. As if a woman hadn't just shouted he was a monster and a killer.

Lacey shook her head. She saw another agent close by. A female agent with a gun holstered at her side.

"No one else enters this room, Diana," Dex ordered.

"Absolutely."

Dex led Lacey down the hallway. It turned to the left, and there was Roman. His head was bowed. He had the posture of a man who'd just gotten the hell knocked out of him during a boxing match. *Maybe he had.*

"I didn't know." His voice was wooden. "You won't believe that. You'll think I'm a fool for not realizing she was working for someone else, but...I didn't know. I swear it." He glared at Dex. "Don't fucking say I told you so again."

"I have a man who'll be coming to work on Heather's laptop. He'll be arriving within the hour. When it comes to tech, there is nothing he can't discover."

Lacey wondered if this was the same man who'd already dug up so much information on her for Dex. Hadn't he told her the fellow's name had been Antony?

"You know that you don't get to leave the lodge, right, Roman?"

"Yeah, figured as much."

"Good. You'll be staying with—well, why don't you just consider them new bodyguards for the time being?"

Bodyguards. Lacey figured they were really just *guards*. Dex motioned vaguely with his hand and two men stepped from the shadows. They each grabbed one of Roman's arms. The guy on the left was huge, with a carefully shaved, bald head and hard, angry eyes. The man on right was smaller, still obviously strong, but with thick, dark hair that he'd styled back from his high brow.

"Thanks so much for your cooperation," Dex continued carefully. "Much appreciated." He focused on Lacey. "I think we should get some brunch. Lunch." He frowned at his watch. "Whatever. You haven't eaten, and you've had a long day already."

"*I want a DNA test.*"

Lacey flinched at Roman's demand.

Dex stared into her eyes. "What do you want, Lacey?"

The truth. Wasn't that what she'd always wanted? "The test."

"Then consider it done."

Didn't he need a sample from her? From Roman and—

Hell, he already had samples. He just hadn't run the test. Hold on. Or *had* he already done it? Her eyes narrowed on him.

Dex sighed and led the way toward the elevator. He'd had to use a special key card—and code—in order to reach the basement. Once she'd seen this whole hidden lair part of the place herself, she'd realized the whole lodge was just some kind of front. Sure, plenty of the guests were real. But a supposed retreat for the rich and famous was actually a location for Dex and his spies to keep tabs on everyone.

When she thought of all the things that went on behind the scenes of the world, stuff most people would never imagine, her stomach knotted.

The elevator doors closed, and they began to rise.

"No." Dex's voice was oddly tender. "I don't have the results, and I didn't run the test already. I told you that taking the test without your permission was something I didn't feel right doing."

"One line you didn't cross?"

"With you, it seems there are more lines than you'd expect."

The elevator felt awfully small. "How many of the staff members at this place work for you?"

"A lot less than you're thinking. If they all worked for me, it would be too easy for others to spot them. Plenty of real staff members and guests come and go as they please."

She reached out her hand and stopped the elevator.

Dex merely lifted a brow.

"Who are you?" Lacey asked.

"I'm Dexter Ryan, but you know that."

"That's not what I mean." She crept toward him. Why did she always feel almost as if she was being pulled closer to him? "Heather called you a monster."

"Um, yes, but considering she tried to shoot you in the heart, do we want to take what she says as gospel?"

"Are you a monster, Dex?"

His eyelids didn't so much as flicker. "What do you think?"

CHAPTER FOURTEEN

She couldn't stand this close to him, couldn't smell so good, couldn't look like the best dream of his whole life and think he was a monster.

Dex's muscles ached from tension as he stood before Lacey and waited for her reply.

"You play with people's lives."

Guilty.

"And I think you have more power than most people can imagine."

He did. He knew where a lot of bodies were buried. Mostly because, he'd buried many of them.

But I'm not a monster. I'm a man. Don't look at me and think—

"What matters to you, Dex? Why do you do this job?"

He wanted to touch her so badly. He didn't. *You. I do it for people like you.* For the people in the world who were good. Because the world wasn't all shit storms and nightmares. There were people out there worth fighting for. Things out there that mattered. "You ever see four-year-olds play soccer? They run around the field, trip over each other, and laugh like hitting the ground is the best thing that ever happened to them."

A faint furrow appeared between her eyebrows.

"You ever seen a sixteen-year-old boy take his first girlfriend to the prom? He's nervous as hell, his fingers shake so badly he almost crushes her corsage, but when he drives away with the girl in his truck with him, his smile is so big you'd think he won the lottery."

The furrow grew deeper.

"And have you ever watched an eighty-nine-year-old grandmother wipe away tears when she sees her granddaughter walk down the aisle while wearing the dress she wore so many years ago?"

"Dex..."

"Those are good moments, Lacey. Good people. That's why I do the job." He was talking about moments he'd seen from other people's lives. Because it was those people who mattered. "Someone has to fight. Someone has to do the dirty work and make sure that the world stays safe. And no, it's not pretty. And, no, it's not a job that lets me keep my hands clean." His hands were covered in so much blood that he'd never be able to wipe it all away. He'd stopped trying long ago. He looked down at his hands. The hands that had touched every single inch of her body, and he had to ask her, "Do you think I'm a monster?"

There was a quick beep of sound, and then a voice blasted over the intercom, "Sir, are you all right? Is there a threat?"

Dex's gaze lifted to sweep over Lacey's beautiful face. "Yes, there's a threat all right," he muttered. The biggest threat he'd ever faced.

Her eyes widened.

Hell. "Everything is fine," he said, making his voice louder so that he'd be heard.

"Then we will restart the elevator, sir," the voice responded quickly.

There was a hum and the elevator jerked a little. Lacey's stare darted to the upper left corner of the elevator. "You've got eyes watching us, hmm?"

He didn't bother glancing toward the video camera. "They're being extra vigilant now. Considering what happened, they have to be."

Her attention returned to him. "Whoever is watching obviously saw that I was the person in here with you. Do those agents think I'm some kind of threat to you?"

You are, baby.

The elevator dinged.

The basement level had been buried deep. They'd needed to pass a few storage floors before reaching the lobby level. The doors slid open, and Lacey turned away.

He followed her and reached for her arm. "You didn't answer my question." He pulled her closer to him. They were back in the main heart of the lodge. Staff members bustled around. Fresh flowers had been placed throughout the area. A fire crackled from the massive fireplace. Everything seemed so normal.

If only.

Lacey turned toward him. Put her right hand on his chest and tipped back her head. "You didn't answer mine, either."

Do those agents think I'm some kind of threat to you?

His head lowered toward her mouth. "You're the biggest threat out there," he murmured.

He saw her eyes widen in surprise as he went to take—

"*Lace?*"

Dex stiffened.

"Lace, is that you?"

Very, very slowly, Dex straightened. Several different things occurred to him in that one moment.

First...*Lace?* Who the fuck was calling her *Lace* in that familiar tone? As far as he knew, only Eric called her that, and that voice damn well didn't belong to Eric Wilde.

Second...Shock was on her face. Shock, surprise and...she'd just flushed. Her cheeks had gone pink.

Third...Dex turned his head to see the man who spoke way too casually—with way too much familiarity—to Lacey. A man with long hair that had obviously been carefully styled to appear tousled. Tall and lean, wearing jeans that looked old and ragged but were no doubt from a stupid expensive designer because everything *this* guy did was by careful design.

The man had an image to maintain, after all. As soon as Dex had gotten a look at him, Dex had recognized the prick instantly. He was rich. Famous. The drummer for one of the biggest bands in the country.

He was the jackass who'd wanted to marry Lacey.

"Tim?" Lacey's voice wasn't warm and welcoming. It was more hesitant. Careful.

Tim Wraith.

A wide smile split the guy's face. He rushed forward with his arms up, as if he intended to hug Lacey. When his hands lifted, the sleeves of his shirt pulled back a bit, and Dex glimpsed some of the fellow's signature tats.

Lacey stood a bit uncertainly near Dex. The uncertainty was a new thing, coming from her. The drummer was about to pull her into a hug in three, two, and—

Dex stepped into his path. "Who the fuck are you?"

Tim staggered to a stop. Seemed to notice Dex for the first time. *Seemed* being the key point there. No way had he actually missed Dex, considering Dex had been plastered to Lacey when the drummer had called her name. Dex had been about to kiss her.

A necessary act, of course, since they were continuing their cover of being a couple. So a little PDA was a good thing.

Kissing her was also necessary because he just wanted her mouth.

"Uh, sorry, mate," the faint Australian accent slid through the man's voice. "Just saw my girl so I had to give her a big—"

"No." Rage slid into Dex's gut. "You didn't."

Tim laughed and craned around Dex. "I'm seeing her right now. Clear as day. And, damn, Lace, you're sexier now than when—"

"You didn't see your anything. You saw my fiancée."

Tim stopped laughing. His head snapped back toward Dex.

"And I'm still asking..." Even though Dex knew perfectly well who the drummer was. "Who the hell are you?"

Tim straightened. "Don't you recognize me?" His jaw jutted out.

"Should I?" Dex knew he sounded annoyed. That was the point. A million thoughts swirled through his head, but the main one...

Why is this SOB here? In Fortune, at the same time Lacey was there. In Fortune, the day after she'd nearly been killed.

No way that was by chance.

"Don't know music, eh?" A smirk. "I'm Tim Wraith. I play drums for Implosion Night."

Dex lifted his brows. "Good for you."

Tim's mouth tightened. "And who are you?"

Dex reached for Lacey's hand. He threaded his fingers with hers and pulled her to his side. "I'm Dex." A pause. "Lacey's fiancé."

Tim took a surging step forward. Then caught himself. "Thought you said that word a minute ago. Figured I'd misheard." It sounded as if he was choking. His gaze dropped to their joined hands, or, more specifically, to the ring on Lacey's finger. "Fucking fast."

The veneer and warmth that had first been in his voice when he called out, "Lace!" was gone. His nostrils flared. His jaw tightened and then he was jerking his chin toward her as his green gaze locked on her face. "Thought you didn't want commitment. Thought that wasn't your style."

"Tim." Her voice was measured. "I never said it wasn't my style. I told you that I didn't want to move in with you."

Tim's breath heaved out. "I missed you."

What. The. Fuck.

Dex grunted. "Yeah, I hope she hasn't missed you." He'd wanted to draw the other man's attention back to him, and with those words, he got it.

Tim glared.

Dex smiled. "I mean, if my fiancée is missing another man, then I have a real problem on my hands, don't I?" He brought Lacey's hand to his mouth. Pressed a kiss to her knuckles. The move was deliberate. He wanted her diamond to flash again.

"When...did you meet?" Tim choked out.

"If you're trying to ask if I was seeing Dex when we were together, the answer is no." Once again, her voice was very measured. "My relationship with Dex is a recent development."

Tim was staring—or, rather, glaring— at the ring once more. "You got swept away, huh? The controlled Lacey Amari fell?"

The guy was way, way hung up on her. A problem.

"You could say that," Lacey replied. From the corner of her eye, she glanced at Dex.

He almost smiled because he could practically read her thoughts. Swept away. Blackmailed. Whatever. Semantics.

A curved blonde made her way to Tim's side. She slid her arm around his waist. "I was waiting with the bags forever. You just left me there." Her full lips pulled down in a pout. "I don't like to wait."

Tim didn't look her way. "Congratulations," he said to Lacey. And only to Lacey. His stare was fixated completely on her once more. "As you can see, I've moved on, too. This is Fiona."

Fiona gave them a smile. It didn't reach her eyes. Though when her gaze measured Dex, she did lick her lower lip. She ran her long red nails over Tim's shirt. "I'm starving. Let's go. I don't want to eat alone."

"I was just catching up with an old friend." Tim pushed her away. "Go have your meal. I'll join you later."

"But—"

"We're leaving," Dex cut in. This jackass had some serious issues. And the first thing he needed to do...*stop eye-fucking Lacey.* "Lacey and I have plans, so..." *So bye.* "Interesting meeting you, Jim." Not really.

"My name is Tim, not Jim."

"Right. Sure." He shrugged. "Good luck with your boy band."

Tim's eyes glittered. "It's not a fucking—"

Dex didn't bother to listen. He was already walking away with Lacey by his side. He'd put up with enough bullshit already. The last thing he wanted was that dick anywhere near Lacey.

He headed straight for the private elevator that would take them back to their suite. In order to get down to the interrogation area, he'd had to utilize a special, secondary elevator, one equipped with additional security and one accessed only with an agency clearance card. To get back to their suite, they had to go up via the club-level elevator.

Lacey followed him into the elevator. He pressed the button to shut the door, and when he glanced back, he saw Tim watching them.

As the doors closed, Dex lowered his head and took Lacey's mouth. The kiss was hard, hot, and possessive as all hell. He wanted to send a message, and he needed to be certain that message was received.

She's mine. Stay the hell away.

CHAPTER FIFTEEN

"I don't think he can see us anymore." Lacey pushed against Dex's chest. "But thanks for the show." She felt shaky and uncertain—two things she hated with a passion. The elevator was already dinging—a sign, of course, that they'd reached their floor—and she realized that she'd kissed him for far too long.

And he didn't even mean the kiss. It wasn't real. Just for show. Like everything else.

"Screw him." Dex's voice was an angry snarl that she didn't expect. And then he followed it up with... "Wait, guess you already did."

She stiffened. Her eyes lifted to meet his. "Yes," she told him clearly. "I did."

Dex's jaw clenched.

The doors were open. Without another word, she strode away from him. She passed the agents in the hallway and jabbed her keycard over the sensor so she could get in the damn suite. She could feel Dex closing in behind her, and whatever else they had to say to each other—they were going to do that shit in private.

She pressed her lips together to hold herself in check until she heard the click of the door shutting behind Dex. Then she whirled. "How dare you act like some kind of jealous—"

"*I am.*" Guttural.

Also not the response she'd expected. "What?"

His breath heaved out. "I'm fucking jealous."

"Why?"

He stalked toward her. "Because he had you."

"Yes. You knew that before." She threw her hands into the air. "We've had this discussion. What does it matter?"

"You loved him."

The statement had her gaping. Then quickly recovering. "No, I didn't. If I loved him, I'd be married to him right now."

He stopped his stalking. Appeared unsure. Off-balance. Probably a first for him. "But..."

"You need to calm your ass down and get some things straight." Now she was the one to surge toward him. She jabbed her finger into his chest. "I had a life before you."

"I know that," he rumbled.

"Do you, really? Because—newsflash—I had lovers before you."

"Not really in the mood to talk about—"

"I don't care about your mood! In case you missed it, I'm having the day from hell! Someone tried to kill me, and now my ex is suddenly popping up in my face. That is crazy. That is the worst kind of coincidence, and I don't think—"

"I don't think it's a coincidence at all." His hands had clenched into fists. "There's no way it can be."

"What?"

"I think Tim is obsessed with you. I think he's been watching you. I think he followed you here."

She didn't speak. A cold chill swept over her skin.

"Right." A nod from Dex. "You thought the same thing when you saw him, didn't you?"

Yes, she had thought that because just last month, when she'd been working another case, she'd turned around and Tim had been there. He'd said that he was scouting locations for a music video shoot. That could have been the reason but...

"Is that why you didn't love him?" Dex pressed. "Because you could see the darkness slipping through with him? Slipping through those cracks when he tried so hard to pretend everything was perfect?"

"Nothing is perfect," she whispered. "Not with anyone or anything."

"I don't know about that. I think you're pretty damn close to perfect."

She sucked in a breath. "Is that a compliment from you?"

"Yes."

"So one minute you're snarling at me and saying you're jealous—when, by the way, we are *not* engaged, in case you forgot, so you don't actually have a reason to be jealous—and then in a big, one-eighty, you're throwing random compliments at me." She was still jabbing him with her finger. She started to yank back her hand.

Too late. His fingers closed around her wrist. "I haven't forgotten that we're not engaged. I also haven't forgotten that I had the best sex of my life with you last night."

"There you go," she said shakily. "Tossing out those compliments—"

"I had you, and I don't like to think of you with anyone else. I'm jealous. I'm possessive. And I...don't like him being close to you." The confession seemed torn from Dex. "I don't trust him. Don't trust the way he looks at you."

"How does he look at me?" she asked softly. Curiously.

"Like he can't look anywhere else."

She swallowed.

"I'm sorry that I snapped at you," Dex added, his voice all rough and gruff.

"Snapped? Is that what we're calling it?"

His fingers stroked over her racing pulse. "Fine. I can do a better apology."

"Good. I would love to hear it."

Another careful caress over her pulse. "I'm sorry that I was an asshole who upset you. I was way out of line. You didn't deserve that shit from me. I'll get my jealousy in check. I'm sure most of the men who see you fantasize about having you in bed, so I'll deal with that—why are you laughing?"

"Because that doesn't happen when strangers meet me." Said with certainty. "Why in the world would you think it did?"

He brought her wrist to his mouth. Pressed a kiss to the pulse that jumped even faster now. "Because you're the sexiest woman I've ever seen."

She highly doubted that. She knew the circles he wandered in, and she was sure super models and celebrities were plentiful there. "Tim liked me because I was different. Because I didn't immediately fall at his feet like everyone else. I was a challenge. To him, I'm still a challenge because I left."

"Oh, baby, you are so much more than that." Once more, he kissed her wrist. This time, she could have sworn she felt the lick of his tongue. "But you know what?" Dex murmured. "Don't worry about Tim. I'll handle him."

Now she was extra worried. She was also sidling closer, as if she couldn't help the movement when she knew she should be backing up. "Handle him," Lacey repeated. "Does that mean you're going to throw him in some secret CIA cell some place?" Because, apparently, those cells were hidden everywhere. Even in swanky lodges.

"Don't tempt me," Dex groused. Then he let her go. He turned away. "I have to go do some recon work. You should stay here and—"

"What if I want to tempt you?" *No, no, no.* She hadn't meant to say that. She'd meant to say something a million times different from that. She also had not meant for her voice to come out all husky and sexy.

Dex whirled toward her. "Excuse me?"

Tell him that you can help with recon. Tell him that you can handle Tim. Tell him— "You're jealous. You say you want me." She needed some clarity. "I just don't get—" She stopped.

"What? What is it that you don't get?"

Fine. Cards on the table. "Where do I stand with you?"

His eyes widened. "Where do you want to stand?"

Her arms wrapped around her stomach. This was so hard. "I feel like I'm barely holding things together right now."

"Baby..."

"You know, I should hate that endearment. You don't mean it. You just toss it out."

"The hell I do. I don't call anyone else—"

"But I like it," she told him with a roll of one shoulder. "And I don't know why." An exhale. "Just like I don't know why I feel better when you're close. You've lied to me and used me, and I should be running as far from you as I can, but I'm in this suite with you, and I..." Once more, she stopped.

Dex waited. Waited a little more. "Do not leave me hanging." His voice sounded strangled. "What do you want?"

You. But if she confessed that, would she be the one using him? "Forget it." She walked away. "Do your recon work at the cabin. I'll do recon at the lodge. I want to talk to some staff members and guests and see what I can turn up today—"

"What do you want?"

She wasn't looking at him. She'd almost made it to the bedroom. "I want to feel like I did last night." An absolute truth. "Like I've never experienced so much pleasure and like nothing else matters. I know it wasn't real—what was between us last night. I know it wasn't meant to last, but..." She swallowed the lump in her throat and admitted, "I hurt today."

"If I could, I would take away all of your pain."

Funny. He sounded as if he meant those words. *I want to believe him.* She looked over her shoulder at him. "What do you want, Dex? What is it that you want most in the world?"

"I'm looking at her."

She could see the desire in his eyes. Had he been hiding it all along? Because it was suddenly blazing in his gaze and etched onto his face. He stared at her as if he wanted to pounce, and she didn't move. If they were doing this again, if they were going down this path, there had to be... "Rules," she gasped out.

He gave her a slow, wicked smile even as he began to close the distance between them. "Oh, sweetheart, do you have safe words you want me to use? Absolutely. You tell me, and I will gladly burn them into my memory."

Her breathing hitched. "Chocolate truffles, but no..."

"No?" His hands had gone to the front of his shirt. He was slowly undoing the buttons. "No to what?"

"I didn't plan to use safe words."

"Because nothing is off-limits?" His sexy smile flashed again. "I am down." He dropped the shirt. Kept closing in on her.

She put her hand on his chest. That hot, hard, muscled chest. "I really need rules," she whispered. "This is important to me."

"You're important to me."

Her gaze collided with his.

"Tell me," Dex invited.

"You don't lie to me. You don't use me again. I get that this isn't real. It's just sex and not some kind of actual relationship—"

A muscle flexed along his jaw.

"But I expect honesty from you. In return, you'll get honesty from me." There. Good. Her fingers were stroking his chest. Naughty fingers. They were sliding down his chest. Moving to the top of his pants. Then slip, slip, slipping down a few more inches. Cupping the long, hot length of his cock that she could feel shoving against the fabric. He was definitely ready. *So am I.* Lacey began undoing his belt. Releasing the button on his pants. Easing down the zipper. "Do you...ah..." She licked her lips and leaned forward. Her lips feathered over the strong column of his throat. "Have any rules for me?"

"Just one."

One. She could handle one. Sure. Why not? Her hands were in his pants, and he wasn't wearing boxers or briefs and she was touching his dick. Thick. Long. "Wh-what's your rule?" She pressed another kiss to his throat.

He shuddered against her. "Trust me."

That was...hard.

"The world can think I'm a bastard. Everyone else can call me a monster, but I want you to trust me. I want you to believe I'm different. Just give me that, would you?"

Her head lifted. She stared into his eyes. Saw the swirl of emotion and for one crazy moment, Lacey had the urge to say...

I would give you just about everything.

No. No. She shook her head at the thought.

"Right." His Adam's apple clicked as he swallowed. "Well, I'd like to act like I have some control and pride and that I am going to back away from you now since you're not down with my rule, but we both know that's not fucking happening. Just like before, I want you more than my next breath and nothing will stop me from—"

She shot onto her tiptoes. "Kiss me."

His mouth took hers. The kiss was ravenous and hot. Consuming and demanding. She kissed him back with a need that couldn't be denied. Her hand was still stroking his cock, and he was big and strong, and she wanted him buried inside of her. "Fuck me," she urged against his mouth.

A shudder worked over him. In the next moment, he had her in his arms. She rather loved the way he lifted her so easily. Her legs curled around his hips, and she arched against his cock. She still had her clothes on and they were absolutely in the way, but she rubbed her sex against him, loving the friction and wanting so much more.

He carried her into the bedroom. Light poured through the window, but she didn't care. He lowered her onto the bed, and he started hauling off her boots. The damn boots! They were taking forever and—

Gone. Next, he reached for her jeans. Had those and her panties yanked off in a blink. She tossed away her sweater and her bra and when she was naked—

He already had the condom on. She nodded quickly because she didn't want to slow down. She wanted him in her. Fast. She wanted body-melting release. She didn't want uncertainty. Or fear. Or—

He pushed her legs apart.

"Come in," she demanded.

"Not yet."

Why not? "Dex?"

He took her nipple into his mouth. Licked. Sucked. Her eyes wanted to roll back in her head because it felt so good. Her hands curled on either side of his body as she held on tight. He was between her spread legs, and she arched up because she wanted him *inside*.

One of his hands slid between her legs. In the next breath, he'd pushed two fingers into her. Withdrew. Thrust. He was working her clit with his thumb in the super skilled way that he did. Long strokes, short, fast, hard presses and—

He was licking her other breast. She was probably clawing his sides. When Dex started touching her, control was a distant memory. She wanted him. So badly.

"You know I'll give you whatever you need." He'd pushed up on one arm and was staring down at her. "Don't you?"

What she needed? She needed him. Lacey's head bobbed a frantic nod.

"You want to forget everything else that's going on? Want to have the pain stop and only feel pleasure?"

"Yes!"

"Trust me, and I'll give you pleasure."

Wait...

But he was moving down her body. His hand was gone from between her legs and his mouth took its place. There was no more thinking after that. Only feeling. Her hips surged toward him and his wicked tongue as her hands fisted the bedding. She came quickly, a shattering eruption that had her choking out his name.

"See?" His deep voice rumbled against her. Sent off after-shocks of pleasure. "That's what happens when you trust me."

Her lashes swept up just in time for her to see him rising over her.

"Want more?" Dex asked her.

She wanted everything.

He kissed her. "Then trust me."

She—

He drove into her. Filled her completely. Her legs locked around him. Her hips surged against him over and over. This wasn't slow and tender. There weren't any other careful caresses or sweet promises. This was sex. Desire at its basest. Their bodies heaved together. Their hearts raced and pounded, and it seemed like they couldn't get close enough to each other.

She was urging him on. Chanting his name. He was driving ever harder and deeper into her. The intensity should have frightened her. The whole atmosphere had changed. The temperature in the room seemed to have heated.

Savage. Primal. Desperate.

But she never thought of stopping. Didn't even consider the safe words she'd tossed out to him. She held him tighter. She bit his shoulder and left her mark on him. He was leaving his on her, beneath the skin, where no one else could see but she'd always feel.

She'd compare him to others. They wouldn't hold up. Nothing had ever been like this before. Nothing would be again. Not with anyone else. She knew it, feared it, and—

The orgasm blew everything else away. Her body bucked beneath him as the powerful release hit her.

He came right after her. Came as she was still trembling and riding that high and struggling to catch her breath. His hips shoved toward her once more even as his body stiffened, and he growled her name. She was staring up at him, and she saw his eyes flare with pleasure—saw it sweep across his face.

Then he bent his head. Kissed her.

The pleasure rolled through her and she lost all track of time. Awareness came back slowly.

Her throat was dry. Her legs still locked around him, but with an effort, she managed to make her legs flop to the bed. He was buried in her. He heaved up so that he was braced on his elbows, and he could stare down at her. He seemed to be searching her gaze but she had no idea what he could possibly be looking for as he stared so long and so deeply into her eyes—

His focus shifted to her chest. His head lowered, and he kissed the bruise that was darkening over her heart. The bruise from the bullet. A tender kiss, when there had been no tenderness before. Careful.

At the touch of his mouth on her bruise, she had to blink quickly, and she didn't even know why.

By the time he looked back at her, Lacey had herself under control. Hopefully, anyway. For the life of her, she could not read his expression. She wished that she could, but he'd shut down on her. Hot sex one moment and then—

"I'll be right back." He withdrew from her. She barely resisted the urge to lift her legs and hold him tight.

He padded to the bathroom. She grabbed the sheets and hauled them over her body even as she heard the sound of running water and then...

He was back. He'd wrapped a towel around his hips. "I thought you might enjoy a soak. I started a bath for you."

That was thoughtful. She pushed back the sheets—

He scooped her into his arms. Automatically, she looped an arm around his neck. "You seem to have a particular fondness for carrying me." She was trying to tease. When they'd had sex, something had shifted between them. Gotten dark and basic and...consuming.

She needed to get back to a lighter footing. ASAP.

Back to feeling as if she hadn't just given him a large piece of her soul.

There was no holding back. There was no retreat.

"I like holding you," he said simply. As if it were an easy confession. As if he'd said...*I like long walks. I like crime shows.*

I like holding you.

A basic Dex fact.

When they entered the bathroom, she saw that he'd even put bubbles in the giant, claw-footed tub for her. The gesture surprised her, and she laughed. The laugh felt good after the intense moments before. As he lowered her into the tub, she teased, "Be careful or I'll start to think you're secretly a romantic."

"Is that what you want?"

I want you.

The water sloshed around her. The bubbles tickled her skin. He knelt near the outside of the tub as he studied her. "I'm sorry if I was too rough." His voice was stilted. "I don't keep my normal control with you."

She eased down deeper beneath the water. The back of her head rested against the tub's edge. "That seems fair. I don't seem to keep my normal control with you, either."

His head tilted. "Are we being honest with each other?"

A nod.

"Then how about a little more honesty?"

Her fingers slid through the bubbles. "Go ahead."

"I want to fuck you endlessly."

Her fingers stilled.

"I don't think that I can ever get enough of you. Each time I have you, I want more." His gaze held hers. She saw the truth in his stare. Dangerous and dark.

"Each time..." Her voice was low and husky. "I have you, I want more, too."

He leaned closer. "You bit me."

Her attention darted to the small wound she'd left. It hadn't faded, and wouldn't, not for a few days. "That's gonna leave a mark."

"Good." His fingers had curled around the edge of the tub. He rose and turned away. He still had the towel around his hips. "Maybe next time, I'll leave my own mark."

"You already have."

He glanced over his shoulder. "What did you say?"

Nothing she wanted to repeat, thank you very much. "You're going to do recon work."

"Yes. What I want is to slide in the tub—one that was obviously built for two—and fuck you until we both nearly drown because we're too exhausted to crawl out of the water."

Oh, that was certainly an—

"But someone ordered a hit on you. And I have a job to do. I need to make sure Heather's transport goes off without a hitch, and I have to check out the cabin. I want to be certain no clues were overlooked out there."

"I can come with you." She started to push out of the tub. The water sloshed around her.

"No." Gruff. A little fast. "You should do like you said before...talk to the staff. Do some recon here. I have a...a close friend who'll be arriving soon. Antony will get every bit of intel he can from Heather's laptop and then we'll close in on the bastard we're after."

"A close friend, you say?" She sounded doubting because she was. "The same way that Eric is supposedly your best friend?"

He appeared taken back. "Who told you that?"

"You did. I heard you call him that on more than one occasion. But I got the impression you didn't mean it." Another mask, another ruse. She slipped back down into the warm water because she suddenly felt chilled. "Do you ever mean what you say?"

"With you, yes." A fast response.

"Why should I believe that?"

"Because you're different."

No, she wasn't. She was the same as everyone else, and part of her feared that Dex was playing her the same way he played others. He'd already kept secrets from her. "What bothers me the most," she told him, "is just how much I want to believe you."

His jaw was tight. "Trust me."

Then...

He was gone.

CHAPTER SIXTEEN

Trust wasn't exactly easy for her. Never had been. Never would be. She needed facts. Evidence. Intel. And she really wasn't the type to sit holed up in some fancy suite. If Dex was doing recon work, then she intended to do the exact same thing.

Lacey dressed quickly and made her way to the main lobby. It was easy enough to chat up the check-in staff and discover that ten different guests had checked out immediately after the incident in the ballroom the previous night. Made sense that some had fled—this was supposed to be a safe place to escape from the real world. The elites there would hardly want to stick around if gunfire was erupting.

But she didn't think the person she was after *had* vanished last night. After all, Heather's partner—whoever she'd used to help transport Roman—must have remained close.

"All of those guests have been researched." A quiet, male voice announced from her left. "I assure you, Ms. Amari, you don't have to worry about them."

Her head turned. The ever-so-helpful concierge guy, Charles, had made his way to her side. She'd seen him coming, though, from the corner of her eye.

Charles waved away the check-in staff. Then he propped an elbow on the counter and smiled at her. "You don't have to worry." A nod. "Dex has already followed up on them."

It would have been helpful if Dex had shared that news with her. She leaned toward Charles. "You're on his payroll."

A shrug. "Aren't you?"

Her lips parted. She—

"I knew he was bringing someone here as a cover, but when I first saw the two of you together," Charles added with another shrug, "I actually thought it might be more than just business."

It is more. Only she didn't quite understand what the "more" was, not just yet.

"Walk with me," Charles invited.

She didn't particularly feel like walking with him, but when he inclined his head toward the watchful clerks, she realized that a little distance would be a good thing. Their discussion had been conducted quietly so she knew the others hadn't overheard, but if Charles wanted to share more info with her, she was certainly ready to listen.

They slipped into a cozy nook on the right. Charles kept a congenial smile on his face. To outsiders, it probably looked as if they were conducting a friendly conversation about the lodge. He even gestured around, as if pointing out the artwork and amenities to her.

"Where is our illustrious boss?" Charles asked.

"Doing recon. Same as me."

"Um. I heard it was quite the commotion this morning. I'm surprised he agreed to let you out of his sight."

Her shoulders stiffened. "Just what the hell is that supposed to mean?" Then, before he could respond, she told him, "I don't need a babysitter. This is hardly my first case." *Let me out of his sight, my ass.*

"But you're not CIA."

Her gaze raked him. "And you are?" She'd originally thought he was an agent, but now she wasn't so sure. He just didn't have that edge about him.

"No. I'm not."

Suspicion confirmed. "Then what are you?"

"I'm someone Dex put in place to do a job. That's what he does, you see. He moves pieces around on his board, and he gets everyone to do what he wants." A pause. "What does he want you to do?"

Draw out the perp.

"It's strange that he left you unattended," Charles added.

Now she was offended. "Unattended? What am I? A child? A pet?"

"Dex's pet." He smiled. It was a tight, hard smile and she didn't like it one bit.

Lacey stepped toward him. "You need to watch the tone with me." Her voice was low and mean because she had zero fucks to give at this point. "I'm not anyone's pet. This isn't my first case, and I don't need some CIA wanna-be throwing shade at me. I didn't see you jumping in to save Dex's ass last night in the ballroom. I didn't see you in on the action at the cabin today. All I see is you standing in my way, right now, and making snide comments that I don't need."

He swallowed. A line of sweat appeared over his upper lip.

"I'll be sure to tell Dex how incredibly helpful you've been," she added just to twist her knife. "I know he'll be thrilled by the news." She turned on her heel and marched away—

I'm being watched. The awareness didn't come as some prickle on the back of her neck. It hit her with the force of a sledgehammer and froze her steps. Her gaze jerked up to the next level. She caught movement near the side of the balcony. A figure slid back toward...

Hell, the Whisper Floor.

Charles curled his fingers around her shoulders. "There's no need to tell Dex anything like that." Tension had entered his voice. "I apologize if my words offended you."

She slanted a glance down at his hand.

"I'm not used to this level of danger." Gruff. Rougher. "I know who comes here. For the most part, it's just bored celebs and annoying rich assholes. My job is to watch and report on their activities, but we have never had incidents like this before. Never kept a would-be killer locked up. Guests are fleeing, and I-I wonder just how safe it is here for us all."

Now she looked back at him. "You're definitely *not* CIA." The fear reeked from him.

A quick, negative shake of his head.

She mulled over his words and his obvious anger at Dex. "Let me guess, Dex didn't so much as put you in place here...as he *forced* you to work with him. He's got something on you, doesn't he?"

More sweat poured from Charles.

Jeez. Did Dex blackmail everyone he met? She was starting to think he just might. Sighing, she pulled away. She needed to get up to that second level and find out who had been watching—

"He saved my life, so I knew that I owed him. Hell, it wasn't just me he saved. He saved my entire family. So, no, I wasn't going to refuse him. I *won't* refuse him, no matter how scared I get."

Lacey threw an assessing glance over at him. Charles had straightened his thin shoulders. He suddenly seemed all determined. Interesting. So to Charles, Dex was both savior and sinner.

What is he to me?

She didn't know.

What she *did* know was that someone was upstairs watching her, and she was about to find out exactly who that person was. "Excuse me. I have work to do."

"But—"

She didn't have time to lose. If she didn't move, fast, her watcher might vanish. Lacey bounded up the stairs. She wore a long, flowing tan coat, one that was perfectly designed to hide her weapon. And considering her old jacket now sported a bullet hole, she'd been rather grateful to find the tan coat waiting on the bed after her bath.

She'd made sure to grab her new knife before leaving the suite. Not strapped to her thigh this time, but her knife was still close and ready. When she reached the next level, the Whisper Floor, her gaze swept to the left, then the right. *No one there.* She edged closer to be sure. Her body was tight with tension. She began a slow search of the floor. There were plenty of places to hide on that level, especially if a person ducked back beneath the heavy architecture and the arches that jutted so far out—

Movement.

Slight. Furtive.

Lacey surged forward.

And almost slammed into Elizabeth Radcliff. The other woman's eyes widened with surprise. "Lacey!" She sounded thrilled. Elizabeth pulled Lacey in for a tight hug. "After last night, I was hoping to see you!"

Lacey discreetly hid the knife she'd palmed.

"That scene in the ballroom was absolutely terrifying." A shudder worked over Elizabeth's body. "The lights went out and the gunshot boomed like fireworks." She released Lacey but stared at her with wide eyes. "Last night, Jonathan and I just wanted to escape the ballroom as quickly as we could."

"I think a lot of people wanted to escape." Wasn't that a normal response to danger? To flee?

"This morning, though, when I started thinking about the horrible scene again, I realized everything might not have been as it seemed. You're involved." Elizabeth bit her lower lip. "What I meant is...you...you're here undercover, aren't you?" Her gaze darted to Lacey's hand. And the ring there. A tinge of sadness entered her voice as she said, "You're not really engaged."

Keep up the cover. "My engagement is quite real, but, yes, I'm afraid I am involved." Truth and lies. Crap. She was becoming just like Dex and not in a good way. "I think the shot was aimed at me or at my fiancé."

Elizabeth sucked in a breath as she studied Lacey's expression. "OhmyGod. Do you have a suspect?"

"Someone is in custody, but the investigation is ongoing." That was all she felt comfortable sharing. "What are you doing up here, Liz?"

"Jonathan asked me to meet him here. Said he had a surprise for me." Her left hand waved vaguely around the alcove. "The staff kept assuring us everything was safe, but I've been nervous up here by myself. I keep looking down for Jonathan, but I can't find him anywhere." A despondent sigh. "He should have been here fifteen minutes ago. Wherever could he be?"

Lacey frowned, wondering the same thing and then—

A fire alarm started shrieking.

***

They'd left her alone. Heather Madding twisted her hands in the cuffs and tried to figure out what the hell she should do next. The guard who'd been inside the room with her had been called away moments before. No doubt, he'd be back soon. Or maybe Dex would be striding into the room. Making more of his threats.

Except she knew Dex didn't just threaten. He promised. And if he said he'd toss her into some godforsaken government prison and the rest of the world would forget about her...

I can't let that happen.

She might have to make a deal. As the minutes had ticked by and she'd considered her options, Heather had realized that there wasn't going to be an easy way out of here. She'd been told that her boss would have her back. After all, he'd supplied help when she'd needed it with moving Roman the night before.

Damn Dex! Leaving her alone this way was one of his manipulative tricks. He wanted her to think and worry and spin in her own mind.

The door opened. She tensed. "Look, I want to—"

Keys were thrown on the table. "Get the cuffs off. Put on this coat." He lifted the puffy, black coat in his hand.

She frowned at that coat. It was familiar to her. She was certain that...wait, Lacey Amari had been wearing that coat when Heather had shot at her. Fumbling, she unlocked the cuffs and then grabbed for the coat. Sure enough, there was a freaking bullet hole in the front of the thing. "I don't get it."

"You wear her coat. You pull this hat down over your head as much as you can. Your hair is similar to hers, and you've got a similar build. Just keep your head down and you follow my orders."

There was a scarf inside the coat.

"Pull that up over the lower part of your face. If we're lucky, no one will even notice you, and if someone *does*..."

She was already sliding on the coat. "They'll think I'm Lacey."

A nod. He turned back to the door. Peeked outside.

"Where are all the agents?" she asked.

"Distracted. Don't worry. They're plenty busy. And the ones who aren't—I've got them covered."

"Then let's get the hell out of here." She was more than ready to go. *You won't make me disappear, Dex.* No one was going to shove her into some deep, dark hole of a prison.

No one.

***

Why the hell was the lodge's alarm system going off? Dex received the alert on his phone just as he was rushing back toward the main building. *Lacey.* He'd finished his recon work at the cabin—turned up nothing—and now—

"Sir!" One of the doormen stepped into his path. "Sir, we have a report of a fire, so I will need you to stay outside the building. All guests are being led to the—"

Screw that shit. He had to find Lacey. Dex jerked away from the doorman.

"No, no, you can't go in—"

"My fiancée is in there. I'm going in and no one is stopping me." Dex didn't slow down as he headed into the chaos of the lobby. And it *was* chaos. The guests were rushing for the doors. People were running. Panicking. He spun around as he searched the scene, and then his phone started ringing. *Lacey?* Was she calling him? But, no, dammit. It was his agent in charge. Larry was on the line. Dex shoved the phone to his ear. "What the fuck is happening?" Dex demanded. He looked up.

And saw Lacey peering over the balcony on the Whisper Floor. The vise that had clenched around his heart immediately eased.

She's okay. She's right there. I see her.

"False alarm," Larry snapped back. "Or, shit, I guess it's not false. There's some small fire in the kitchen. Everything is under control, so don't worry. We've put out the flames and the—"

"How many agents are with our suspect?" He didn't take his eyes off Lacey. *She's okay. I see her. She's okay.*

"Two are with Heather. I'm going back down now. Don't worry, like I said, everything is under—"

Fuck control. "I'm checking in on Heather myself." Because he didn't like this scene. Didn't believe in chaos. Hell, he'd used chaos himself too many times. Create a distraction, and it was easy to slip in and out of a location. "I want our people at every exit."

"But—"

Dex was already running for the elevator.

One of the bellmen began, "Wait, sir, you're not supposed to use those in the event of a fire—"

Dex ignored him. He needed to make sure Heather was secure.

***

"What's happening?" Elizabeth asked as she raised her voice. "Should we—ohmygosh, do we need to flee, too?"

The blaring alarm died away. The sudden silence was almost as jarring as the shrieks had been.

Lacey peered over the balcony one more time. Dex had just rushed toward the special access elevator. Obviously, he was worried something was happening down below with Heather.

So am I.

This whole scene reeked of being a setup.

"Oh, wait, I think I see Jonathan." Elizabeth squeezed her arm. "I have to make sure he's all right." She scampered away.

And I need to make sure someone is watching Dex's back. But just as she started to hurry toward the stairs, Lacey caught another flash of movement in the corner. She stopped.

Someone else is up here.

Lacey palmed her knife once more. Kept her body relaxed and casual as she tiptoed toward the corner.

***

The two agents in the narrow basement hallway were unconscious. *Fuck.* They were breathing, but out cold. After checking on them, Dex raced toward the holding room. He kicked open the door.

Handcuffs were on the table. His perp? *Gone.*

Dex yanked out his phone as he turned and double-timed it back for the elevator. Larry answered his call instantly. "Heather's gone!" Dex snarled. "We've got two men down. How the hell did this happen?"

But he already knew the answer to that question. *Heather's partner came to help her.* Whoever had moved Roman last night had helped Heather or—

Or maybe even Roman had helped. Who the fuck knew?

Dex shot a glance toward the security camera in the elevator. Someone should have seen what happened. He had *his* team monitoring security for the special, lower area of the lodge. There was no way that Heather should have just waltzed out of there.

And now she's going to try to escape.

Or...she'd go after Lacey again.

"Get to Lacey," Dex fired into his phone. "She's on the Whisper Floor. *Get her.* Protect her at all costs."

***

The target was right there. Heather could see her. Her breath came in quick, excited little pants. Oh, wouldn't it be perfect if she was able to finish this job? She'd teach Dex Ryan. She'd show Roman. They'd both pay.

Lacey is right there.

Smiling, Heather darted for her prey.

***

The body fell. Just tumbled down right in front of him as Dex ran forward. He'd been trying to get Lacey on her phone, but she hadn't answered him.

Then the body hurtled down. He had a quick flash of dark hair. A woman's body flew from the second floor. Then a terrible, bone-breaking thud.

For an instant, he froze.

She fell from the second level. The Whisper Floor. *Dark hair.* And...that was Lacey's puffy coat. She'd worn it that morning when she'd been shot by Heather.

Blood bloomed beneath the figure on the floor. There were screams and shouts from all around him. The woman—she'd been tossed right in front of him.

Don't be...Can't be...

Dark hair. Lacey's coat. *Lacey was on the Whisper Floor.*

He didn't remember falling to his knees beside the woman. Didn't remember roaring her name. Her right arm was twisted, broken. Dark hair and a loose cap covered her face. A scarf was getting soaked in her blood.

"Baby?" Dex breathed the endearment as he reached out with fingers that shook. Everything in the world had slowed down. Almost stopped. He was focused entirely on the woman before him.

She wasn't moving. Didn't appear to be breathing. Her neck...*God, no. No.*

He brushed back the hair. Slid back the cap.

And stared at Heather Madding's still face.

It took a long moment for her identity to register for him. The lodge's doctor raced to Dex's side as Dex crouched beside the fallen woman. Unfortunately, there wasn't going to be anything that the doc could do. Not with the way she'd landed and...

Why is there so much blood?

His hand slid under the thick coat. *Lacey's coat.* His fingers touched Heather's back.

Lacey's coat, but not Lacey. Not Lacey.

As he touched Heather's back, he felt the wet warmth of blood. Shit. Dex yanked up the coat so he could see her body.

"I need you to step back," the doctor ordered.

She'd been shot in the back. He hadn't heard the shot, so he knew the shooter must have used a silencer on his weapon. For the first time, Dex looked up now. He *should* have looked up at that second floor sooner, but he'd been out of control. Fixated and *lost.*

Because he'd thought Lacey was before him. Because he'd thought it was Lacey's blood. Because he'd thought she was dead.

Now he looked up and caught sight of Roman staring down with wide, horrified eyes.

Fucking Roman.

"Dex?" Lacey's voice. Lacey's shaking, beautiful voice. He lurched to his feet. Saw her near the stairs. Dex ran to her, shoving people out of his way because he *had* to get to Lacey.

Fear flashed on her face. "What's happening? Dex—"

He dragged her into his arms. Held her in a grip that he knew was too tight and too fierce. A grip that he knew might hurt because he was holding her too hard, but he couldn't let go.

I can never let her go.

"Dex, I can't breathe. Ease up!"

He lifted his head. Eased his hold. And kissed her. Deep. Wild. Desperate.

She's alive. It wasn't Lacey. She's alive.

In that moment, as the fear settled in his very bones, he understood a truth he hadn't wanted to face. A truth that would change everything.

Her hands pressed against his shoulders. She pulled her mouth from his. "Dex?" Her breath heaved out. "What happened? What's going on?"

He stared down at her. Her beautiful face. Her dark eyes. "You aren't leaving my side," he swore.

Her eyelids flickered. *"What is happening?"* She stood on her toes and tried to look over his shoulder.

He turned with her and saw that a crowd had gathered around the body.

"Dex." Now her voice was lower. "What happened here?"

He curled his arm around her body. *Can't let her go. Won't lose her.* "Heather Madding is dead."

"What?"

"Roman was on the second floor. Come on." He took off, but he made sure he didn't let her go. They raced together for the stairs. The hotel's security was scrambling, and Dex saw Larry rushing toward him, too. Dex motioned with a curt jerk of his head for Larry to meet them on the second floor.

When they reached that level, Roman was standing next to the railing. He had his hands up and a gun—equipped with a silencer—was on the floor near him.

Dex whipped out his own weapon. "Turn around. *Slowly.*"

"I know this looks really bad..." Roman began as he turned. "But I *didn't* fucking do it."

Dex glanced at the gun. "Are you fingerprints going to be on the weapon?"

"Yes," Roman bit off. "*Because it's my gun.* But I think Heather stole it when she attacked me last night. I couldn't find it when I went back to the room today."

A good story. One Dex wasn't ready to believe. "I don't care what connections you have, Roman. We're taking you into custody."

"Dex." Fury seethed in his voice. "I'm being set up! I didn't do this!"

Dex studied the scene. Roman was near the balcony. The gun was at his feet.

"I thought it was Lacey," Roman gritted out. His desperate gaze was on her. "When I saw the coat...the hair..." A shudder worked over his body. He took a lurching step toward her. "God, I thought it was you."

"Maybe that's why you put a bullet in Heather's back before you shoved her over the balcony," Dex snarled. "Because you thought you were getting rid of Lacey." Rage nearly choked him. "All this time, I thought you wanted her back. But the truth is...and I damn well saw it in your eyes this morning...*you hate your sister, don't you?*"

CHAPTER SEVENTEEN

"We're getting the hell out of here." Dex's voice was ice cold. His expression was locked into deadly lines of rage, and when he moved, waves of lethal fury seemed to pour from him.

They were back in their suite, and he was grabbing her bag. "Good thing you already packed."

"The black coat was in the luggage." The comment slipped from her.

Dex stilled. "What?"

She sucked in a sharp breath. "This tan coat I'm wearing—when I came out of the bath, it was waiting for me on the bed. I thought you'd left it for me."

A slow, hard shake of his head.

Oh, shit.

"I'd packed the other coat in my luggage earlier. When I was planning to, you know, get the hell out of here." But it was obvious someone had taken that coat. Left her another one in exchange? Maybe left the tan coat so she would never look for the puffy coat?

"You're telling me that someone *came* into this suite after I left you? While you were in the tub, naked and unarmed, some bastard was in here?" Cold. Low. Deadly.

She didn't think that she'd ever seen Dex out of control. When they had sex, yes, he went wild. So did she. But this was different. The mask that Dex usually wore was cracking before her eyes, and beneath that cold exterior...

So much rage.

"Yes." She licked her lips. "I think that's what is happening. But I didn't hear a sound. And if the intruder wanted me dead, don't you think I would be dead right now?"

He cursed. Low and extremely inventively.

"I'll take that as a yes," she responded. "The other coat should have been in the bag you're holding. Whoever helped to get Heather out of that holding room downstairs must have taken it. We have similar builds and hair, so maybe the coat was part of some disguise to help her escape. But then the person who shot Heather saw her from the back, saw her in my coat and thought—"

"She was you." He looked down at the luggage he gripped so fiercely.

"This is all bad. Exceedingly bad. But whoever broke into this suite has to be on a security camera." Another question...just how had the person gotten past the agents Dex had ordered stationed outside the room? Not like the intruder was a ghost.

His eyes glittered as he glanced back at her. Then, low and rough, "No."

"No?" No to what?

She knew he'd talked to his team downstairs. *After* Roman had been taken away. The conversation with the team had been quick and angry.

"All the security in the lodge went offline right before the convenient fire in the kitchen. It just came back up, thanks to Antony."

"Antony? The tech guy who dug up all the info on me?"

A quick knock sounded at the door. She stiffened, and her gaze swung toward—

"Right. Him. Antony is on the other side of the door. I told him to haul ass up here as soon as he checked out security." Dex let go of the luggage and strode for the door. He glanced through the peephole, then wrenched open the door. "About time."

The man on the threshold blinked at him. Tall, blond, and wearing glasses that shielded intelligent eyes. The fellow held up the laptop in his hands. "Perfection takes time, you know that."

"Get your ass in here." Dex hauled him across the threshold. "You'd better have something we can use."

The newcomer rolled back his shoulders. "It's certainly nice to see you again, too, Dex. I'm good. Yes, very good. Thanks for asking. It was a bit of a rough flight. You know, because someone had me flying through a *snowstorm,* but hey, I made it. No big deal. Happy to be of service to you."

Dex growled. "I am not in the mood for your shit."

"You are never in the mood for shit." The stranger's gaze darted toward Lacey. Lingered. "Hello." The faintest edge of curiosity was in the one word. "I don't think we've met."

She studied him and something niggled at the back of her mind. She didn't think they'd met, either, but Lacey was sure she'd seen him somewhere before.

"Stay here. I need to talk to the guards outside." Dex strode out.

Okay. Lacey looked at Antony. He looked back at her.

Antony cleared his throat. "I'm assuming—since you are here with Dex and he's actually allowing the two of us to meet—that you have high enough clearance that you won't blow my cover."

Clearance, huh? "Working on that," she replied.

The door flew open. "Sonofabitch!"

Lacey sighed. "Let me guess. You asked the guards if anyone came in this room, and they told you no?"

"They swear no one came through this door." The door he slammed closed and locked. "Not like our perp can freaking walk through walls! If I find out those jerks went on a break..."

"Did they *say* that they left?" Lacey asked.

"They're swearing on their lives that they never moved and that *no one* got past them."

Then how had the coat gotten inside?

Dex strode toward her. His hand lifted and the back of his knuckles slid over her cheek in a careful caress. The care seemed at odds with the blazing fury in his eyes. "Nothing like that will happen again. I will *not* lose you."

Lose her?

Once more, Antony cleared his throat. "You know, I can go work in another suite. If the two of you want alone time or something."

Dex's hand dropped.

"By the way, she *does* have clearance?" Antony pushed. "Because I don't exactly want the world to know about this side job of mine."

Dex crossed his arms over his chest. "We don't need alone time. What we need is intel. I want you to give it to me."

"But the clearance—"

"I trust Lacey completely."

He did? Her stomach dipped at Dex's rough confession.

"And I trust you, Antony," he continued, "or else you would never be near her."

Antony cocked his head. "I caught the kiss downstairs. Figured it was just for show. You *do* enjoy putting on a good show, Dex. But then I remembered how obsessed you were with discovering everything about—"

"What's on the laptop?" Dex snapped, cutting through Antony's words.

Hmm. She wished Antony had been able to finish telling her just what had obsessed Dex.

"Right. Laptop." Antony lifted it and then headed toward the table near the window. "Nice to meet you, Lacey," he tossed over his shoulder. "I take it that you are Dex's partner on this case?"

"She's my fiancée," Dex responded before Lacey could say anything.

Antony stumbled. Then whirled around. "Bullshit."

Lacey lifted her hand. Wiggled her fingers. The ring flashed.

"I thought Dex was punking me. Didn't think you would actually agree to marry him." Antony shook his head. "You poor, poor woman."

"*Lap...top.*" Dex's voice snapped.

Antony put it down and popped open the screen. "Just so we're all updated, the security hack on the lodge was an inside job. Someone manually uploaded a virus into the system. Clever bug. Took down every camera and sent the fire alarms blaring."

"What about the kitchen fire?" Dex demanded. "I thought that was real."

"It was real, but I'm sure it was set deliberately. All the kitchen staff are swearing they didn't do it. They just found the grills burning."

She edged closer to the laptop. "Is that Heather's?"

Antony's fingers flew over the keyboard. "Yep. And she was telling the truth. She *has* been talking to some mystery perp. A perp who wanted her to take out Roman. She must have sure hated the guy to turn on him so badly." He glanced over at Dex. "You know how it is, right? When your boss is a total asshat?"

"Don't push me now."

Antony narrowed his eyes. He finally seemed to *see* Dex. Antony tensed. "What's wrong?" Just like that, the mocking veneer he'd worn since he entered the suite seemed to fall away. "You're worried. You never worry."

Dex didn't worry? Lacey thought he did. She thought he just might worry all the time, about everyone.

"Has hell frozen over?" Antony's growing concern deepened his voice. "What. Went. Down?"

"This shit is personal," Dex said.

Antony nodded. "I see." He pulled off his glasses. Polished them on his shirt. Swept Lacey an assessing stare. "I see," he repeated.

"I doubt it," Dex muttered. "You don't even have your damn glasses on."

Antony slipped the glasses back into place. "Happy now?"

"I'm not going to be happy until I know who Heather was working with. Tell me his name."

Antony went back to typing on the laptop. "It's not that easy. I don't just wave my hand or something and everything is revealed. I'm not a magician." He kept typing. "This is the posting she was using on the Dark Web. If you look at it, you'll see it's full of mercenaries looking for jobs."

Lacey leaned in closer so that she could view the screen.

"It's all in code. Look...right here, where this guy is offering pest control services? He means he's a hitman."

Lacey's eyebrows rose.

"And this one here?" He waved toward the screen. "Where it says the poster is looking for someone to do renovation work? It means he wants a building destroyed."

"How do you know this?" She crept even closer to him.

"You smell really, really nice," Antony murmured. "Like roses. I bet you like to buy that Midnight in the Rose Garden bath gel, don't you?"

That was awfully specific. "Yes, I do."

He went back to typing.

"What else do you know about me?" Lacey asked him quietly.

"You're a great dancer." He was frowning at the screen. Typing faster and faster. More boxes kept popping up. "You don't drink coffee. You like hot chocolate. You dated that drummer Tim Wraith, but haven't seen anyone else seriously since then so your surprise engagement to Dex here is—"

She'd been right about him. "You're the one who investigated me." Dex *had* mentioned Antony before. With everything that had happened in the last twenty-four hours, she'd let that important detail slip too far from her mind.

Antony's fingers stopped typing.

Dex swore. "Antony, how many times do I have to tell you, you can't multitask for shit?"

Antony glanced back at her. "I don't like to think of it as me investigating you. I prefer to view it as recon work. Normal, you know, for when you're checking out an operative."

"Learning that I like hot chocolate is normal? Learning what kind of bath gel I use?" She doubted that was on the typical background check.

Antony coughed. A fake sound. "Dex wanted to know everything about you." A pause. "Now I see why."

Her attention lasered toward Dex. She glared. "You know everything about me. But I know nothing about you."

"Absolutely not true."

"Oh, really?" She advanced on him. Their bodies brushed. "Tell me what I know. Because I feel like—"

"You know I lost my mind when I thought you were the one lying broken on the floor. If you don't know it, you should." His voice vibrated with his rage. "You should know that in that moment, I couldn't see anyone else. Couldn't even breathe, not until I moved back the hair and realized it wasn't you. In that moment, *nothing* mattered. When I thought you were gone, that someone had taken you from me, the whole world went dark. I couldn't breathe. Couldn't move. I was on the floor next to the body, and if that had been you, I—"

"Stop. Just stop right there!" Antony directed. Or, maybe he pleaded. "This seems like an extremely personal conversation, and, fun fact about me, I don't like being involved in other people's personal conversations. I especially don't like being involved in *your* personal conversations, Dex. Knowing info about you will only come back to bite me in the ass."

"Probably," Dex agreed without even hesitating.

Lacey didn't look at the other man. She couldn't take her eyes off Dex. The confession he's just given had sounded so real. So honest. Almost as if... "Watch it, Dex," she heard herself chide, "or I'll start to think you care."

His gaze swirled with intensity. "I. Fucking. Do."

Her lips parted.

"I should leave." Antony leapt up. "I can work on this in another room. You two obviously need to hash out some private stuff here—"

Dex locked a hand around Antony's shoulder and pushed him back down. "Lacey's safety is my number one priority. I need you to find out who was working with Heather. She's dead so it's not like she can talk to me now. I thought Heather was about to roll and give me usable intel. But her partner—her boss, whatever the hell he is—got to her first."

Lacey sucked in a breath. "Wait. Do you think the perp *intended* to kill Heather? Or did he think she was me?" Because she'd been under the impression that—

A muscle jerked along Dex's jaw. "I'm sorry, Lacey."

Oh, no. "When you apologize, it makes me exceedingly nervous."

"I know you think I've kept you in the dark, but the truth of the matter is that this whole time, I didn't know who we were up against. So I couldn't very well tell you when I didn't know myself."

"But—but Roman—"

"*I should not be hearing this.*" Antony hunched his shoulders.

"Antony, you know I would take a bullet for you, just like you'd take one for me. I trust you. So just get the job done, will you?"

Antony. Antony. Her head turned toward him. The name and face clicked in her mind. "Antony Kyle," she realized as she connected his face with the flash in her mind. "You're the famous gaming designer. A little bit of a recluse. You usually let your partner take the spotlight." His partner's name was... "The bad boy of tech," Lacey murmured. "Sebastian Ridgeway."

"He *hates* that nickname," Antony told her. "With a passion."

"I read an article about the two of you a few months back. You own that big gaming company—

"Shark Gaming and Design." His shoulders stiffened a bit. "I'd appreciate it if you would not tell the world about my involvement with Dex. I do try to keep that part of my life on the down low."

"You're a spy?"

His head inclined toward her. "I prefer the term seasoned technical operative."

"Okay." She squeezed her eyes shut. "Did Dex blackmail you into the job?"

"No." Spoken softly. "Dex is my friend, even though some days I want to strangle the guy."

Her eyes opened. *I can relate to that feeling.*

"Dex has my back, and I have his. His methods might not be ones that others can understand and they might fall on the dangerous side, but Dex is one of the good guys."

Dex swore. "Are you seriously trying to talk me up right now? Is that what you're doing? Being a wingman or some shit? Trying to make me look—"

"Like less of an asshole?" Antony hurried back to typing. "Indeed, I am. I figured you needed as much help as you could get. See, that's Dex's deal. He doesn't let people close. If people get close to him, then *those* people are vulnerable. It's why he was apologizing to you, in case you didn't know. I bet Dex never intended for you to be in danger. Hell, I'd imagine he thought the safest place for you was at his side. That's probably the whole reason he got you to come to this lodge with him in the first place."

He was wrong. "No. He wanted me to be his partner on this case. You know that. You even asked me when you came into the suite—" But Lacey stopped because...

Dex.

"You're always three steps ahead," she recalled. He'd told her that before.

Dex's eyelids flickered.

"You didn't want me to help you bring anyone down, did you?" And suddenly, she was seeing everything differently in her head. "You...wait..." She held up her hand. The diamond caught the light and glittered. "You proposed to me as soon as we arrived at the lodge. I thought you did it with everyone around because you were setting up our cover story. But the ring—it was protection, wasn't it? You wanted me to use my real name. You were adamant that I do that. You—"

"I found you," Dex said simply. "I knew who you were. I knew why you'd matter to Roman. I also know that Roman has plenty of enemies. Enemies who would love to use a long-lost sister against him. I thought that by giving you my ring—and, yes, my protection—and by setting up a meeting between you and Roman—a meeting here at the lodge, where I could watch over you, then your safety would be assured."

"All of the agents here...they're to keep me safe?"

"Doing a shitty job of it." Dex raked a hand over his face. "*I'm* doing a shitty job of it. You were almost shot at the cabin, and then I just had a hard message delivered to me—loud and clear in the lobby."

Her temples were throbbing. "Spell things out for me. *Now.*"

Antony was quiet. Just typing away on the keyboard.

"*I* thought Heather was you when she fell. Because she was wearing your coat. Because her hair looked like yours. Because the scarf and cap were even yours."

Wait, they had been? She hadn't noticed them.

"But, no, I don't believe the killer thought she was you, baby. I suspect the killer is the one who *gave* her the coat, the hat, and the scarf. He's the one who broke her out of holding downstairs. She probably thought he was there to help her, but he wasn't. Instead, he dressed her up like you, and then he killed her right in front of me."

"That's one damn brutal message," Antony noted.

A shiver slid over her body.

Dex never took his attention from her. "I thought you could be used against Roman, so I gave you my protection. The problem is...you can also be used against me. That's what the perp knows."

"Roman is the perp." She wrapped her arms around her stomach. "You already had your agents take him into custody. He was on the second floor. Right beside the gun. He was—"

"Your brother is many things. Not all of them are good, but I don't think he would kill you. He's looked for you too long."

"But he wasn't killing me. He was killing Heather. And making you think it was me." All so messed up and crazy. Yet she could see in Dex's eyes, he truly didn't think Roman was guilty. "How can you be so certain of him?"

"We were partners once."

They had been?

"He was a double agent who worked secretly with the CIA. A mission went to hell." Dex lifted his right hand. The sleeve fell back and he stared down at his wrist. The scars. "Roman's real allegiance was discovered. The people holding him used Roman to get to me. Said if I didn't turn myself over, he'd be sent back to the CIA in pieces."

Her throat had gone dry.

Antony had stopped typing.

"I turned myself over. They cuffed me. Anchored the cuffs to a weight and shoved me in a fucking river."

OhmyGod.

"They thought I was dead. But you should never try to take a former SEAL out by throwing him in the water."

He'd been a SEAL? That was news.

"I got out, but I needed backup to free Roman. I was hurt because they'd shot me before dumping me in the water. You know, more fun that way."

Nausea rolled in her stomach. "Fun?"

"Roman didn't know that I'd turned myself over for him. He was told that I never showed for the exchange. That I deserted him when he needed me." A slow exhale as his hand fell back to his side. "They tortured him for hours."

Her skin felt so cold. "But when you and your team came for him..."

"By then, he didn't care anymore. Was convinced that he didn't matter to me or anyone at the agency. In fact, since that day, I don't think he has cared about much at all. At least, not until the night when he came to me and called in the debt he said I owed to him."

Why was it so cold in there? Goose bumps seemed to cover her. "I was the debt."

"He wanted you found. In the years since he worked with me, Roman has slipped deeper and deeper into the shadows. If you were out there, I knew you'd be the key."

"The key to bringing Roman back to your agency?"

"Lacey, you are the key to everything for me." His hand lifted and the back of his knuckles brushed over her cheek.

She realized what he was doing. She'd said that she didn't know anything about him, and he was giving her pieces of himself. Telling her how he'd known Roman before. Revealing his past as a SEAL. He was trying to give her what she wanted, Lacey could see it in his eyes. And she kept hearing his voice in her mind, telling her...*I. Fucking. Care.*

She cared, too. So much. Far more than she'd ever believed she could about a man who tangled her up in twisted knots.

"He's here." Antony cleared his throat. "Not talking about whoever took Roman all those years ago. Talking about the mystery perp we are after now. The bad guy is at the lodge. Bad guy, boss, super perp. Whatever you want to call him. I just sent out some bait, he took it, and I can tell you that he is using a computer owned by the lodge. I'm tracking him, and the guy is downstairs, lobby level. He's online right now—"

Dex whipped his head toward Antony. "*You can see him?*"

Antony kept typing. "I can lead you straight to the bastard, right now."

***

Dex and his team went in with guns blazing. Because how else would they do anything? They followed the trail Antony had set up and when the agents surged into the back office on the first floor...

They found Charles Hatch hunched over his computer.

Lacey was there for the takedown. Dex had insisted she come with him. Part of his strategy to protect her? She figured it was. He didn't want to let her out of his sight because he thought he was her bodyguard. Or something.

"Put your hands up," Dex shouted at Charles.

Charles squeaked, and his hands immediately flew into the air.

"Did you think we wouldn't find you?" Dex demanded. Two agents closed in on Charles. One of the agents was Larry—no last name. Just Larry. That was how he'd been introduced to Lacey moments before. An intimidating fellow, he immediately did a rough pat-down on Charles before he yanked Charles's hands behind his back.

"What is happening here?" Charles asked. "What are you doing? *I'm on your side.*"

"No matter how hard you try, you can't find good help these days." Dex headed toward the computer. Flipped the screen around. "Hire any mercenaries lately, Charles?"

"This is not what it looks like! I swear it! I'm doing research for a book and a friend told me how to access—"

Larry slapped cuffs around his wrists.

Charles let out a high-pitched cry. "This isn't what you think! I haven't done anything. *I am on your side.*"

Dex didn't appear to believe the other man. Lacey's gaze darted around the office. Her stare lingered on the framed photos. Charles and his wife on their wedding day. Charles and a little boy with a wide grin and two missing teeth wading into dark water as they went fishing.

She picked up the fishing photo from where it rested on his desk.

"I swear, I was just on this site because I'm doing research! You know...you know I always wanted to write a spy book!" Charles was frantic.

Larry was leading him away.

"*Dex, please!*" Charles cried.

"You'll have plenty of time to tell me your story while you're in custody." No emotion was in Dex's voice.

No emotion.

But he'd shown her plenty of emotion only moments before.

This feels wrong. No, worse than wrong. It felt too easy. Taking the photo, she stepped into Charles's path. "You told me that Dex saved you and your family."

Charles looked as if he were about to cry.

"How did he do that?" Lacey pushed. She was missing something here. Dex was acting off. *And I can tell it. I can tell when something is different with him now.* And Charles—he'd seemed so sincere when they'd previously spoken.

"He...there was a bomb at my wife's work. She's a medical researcher. I was going there to have lunch with her. She—she was pregnant with my son. Dex found out about the attack. Got us out...right before..." He licked his lips. His head swiveled back toward Dex. "I don't know what you think is happening here, but I swear, I didn't do anything against you! I wouldn't."

She didn't believe that he would. "Who was the friend who told you about the site you were just on?"

"Ah...it was Roman." A quick nod. "Roman Valentino. He even gave me his username and code and everything to use. Said I should get on today around this time because that's when the real players are on, and I could get the best intel—"

Roman. Why wasn't she surprised to hear his name?

"Dex?" Charles shuddered. "I don't know what's happening here, but I haven't made any move against you or anyone you care about. I would never do that."

Dex sidled closer. Stared at Charles with expressionless eyes.

Lacey caught Dex's hand. She pushed the framed photo against his palm. "I believe him."

"We just caught him red-handed—"

"Look what you gave him, Dex. *Look.*" She forced him to hold the photo. "You think he'd turn on you? It's not blackmail keeping him loyal. I don't think it's blackmail keeping any of your people in line, not really. You might believe that. You might think that you're controlling people but maybe people are on your side because they've seen the real you."

"You...you wouldn't leave that building without me and my Sarah," Charles whispered. "We were the last ones inside. I heard the others shouting for you to get out. You wouldn't. You *carried* Sarah out of there."

Because Dex wasn't the bastard that he wanted the world to believe he was. Lacey was realizing that he was so much more.

"Where is Roman right now?" Lacey asked.

Dex stared at the photo.

"I think we need to talk to him." *Because I'm worried it might be too late for the brother I never knew. I think he may be trying to destroy us both.*

"Talk to him!" Charles urged. "Yes, yes, do it! He can tell you the truth! He had his girlfriend Heather come to me yesterday. She wrote down all of the info that I would need. She gave me everything!"

Well, damn. Heather, huh?

An absolutely dead end.

CHAPTER EIGHTEEN

The Whisper Floor. He was really starting to hate this damn place. Dex had gone back to the scene of Heather's killing because he knew there was more evidence to be found.

"You're not going to arrest Charles, are you? Because I truly don't think he's turned against you." Lacey's voice was halting as she stood a few feet away.

He didn't want her out of his sight so wherever he went, Dex was dragging her with him. Probably not a rational response, but he wasn't exactly feeling rational. Not where she was concerned.

He glanced over the edge of the balcony. Saw the roped off area below. The blood had been cleared away. The body removed...

Not Lacey. It wasn't my Lacey.

But he'd never forget the fear that had filled him. The absolute terror and the soul-jarring realization that...

I can't lose Lacey. I love her.

Love. The worst of the four-letter words. A word he'd *never* used with another woman in his life. Well, okay, fine. He'd loved his mom. Absolutely, he had. She'd been amazing. Strong and determined as she battled cancer until the very end. He'd loved her with the complete love that a son feels for his mother.

When he'd lost her, the world had been darker. He'd been darker.

His father had been in and out of his life as a kid, before he'd disappeared entirely when Dex was ten. A few years ago, Dex had, uh, used his resources to find the man.

Resources...AKA...Antony.

Dex had realized he'd been far better off without the fellow. What he'd learned from Antony—and what he'd seen first-hand himself when he made the mistake of getting up-close for some surveillance—had been enough to shut that door.

"To me," Lacey continued, "it sounds like Heather might have been setting up Charles. But we should still question Roman and see what he knows."

Dex turned away from the balcony and tried to block the memory of the falling body. Of the thud when the body had hit the floor. His gaze zeroed in on the alcove on the right. Roman had hidden in that spot the first time he'd warned Lacey to stay away from Dex. Now, Dex marched into those arches.

"Are you listening to me?" Lacey's whisper drifted to him.

He stiffened.

"Because I could swear you're not. In fact, it feels like you are shutting me out."

Dex whirled and marched to Lacey. He found her in the other set of arches. "I am not shutting you out. I have let you into my life, I've opened myself more to you than I have to anyone else in years."

Her head tilted back. "Then why aren't you talking to me? Something has changed. I swear, I almost feel like you are barely looking at me."

"Because...*I keep seeing you on the floor.*" He threw his hand out toward the balcony. "I know it was Heather, but I keep seeing you, and that is what the SOB who killed her wanted me to do! He wanted to get in my head, and he did. Now I can't think straight. I can't figure out my next move. He has me tearing apart on the inside and I can't—"

Her hands curled around his jaw. She shot onto her tiptoes even as she pulled him toward her. And Lacey kissed him.

A soft, gentle touch of her lips.

Fuck that. He was way past the gentle point.

His arms curled around her in a too-tight grip. He hauled her against him, making sure their bodies were pressed intimately together. His mouth opened, so did hers, and his tongue thrust past her lips. He kissed her with a ravenous hunger. With the desperate need that clawed at him.

He kept thinking of her dying. He couldn't have that. He didn't want a world without Lacey in it.

Maybe because she was becoming his world.

Her soft fingers were still pressed to his jaw. Her mouth and tongue met his eagerly. He wanted to strip her. Wanted to take her. Wanted to wipe away the fear and know nothing but her. Yet...

"*Not here,*" he rumbled against her mouth. Then he had to kiss her once more. Twice more. Dammit, three times. "Can't...my control isn't strong enough. Others will see." He finally managed to lift his head.

Her lips were plump. Her cheeks flushed. He could read the desire clearly in her eyes. The desire and—

"See," Lacey repeated. Her eyebrows scrunched. "See," she said again.

Um, yes. "I want you. But I don't want anyone else watching us." *Watching you.* "The floor looks empty, but with the way things are going, shit, it's not a chance I can take. My control doesn't last with you." A soul-true confession as he backed away. "If I don't keep my hands off you, there will be no stopping." Because the adrenaline that fueled him was making him even weaker.

He wanted to claim her. To thrust deep and hard into her as she wrapped her arms and legs around him. Only then, when he had her that close, when they were that close, would the fear he felt ease.

She's not dead. I didn't lose her. She's right here.

"See," Lacey said yet again.

"Uh, sweetheart? You okay?"

But her hands dropped to her hips. "I was right up here. Moments before Heather fell. I didn't see her."

"There was a lot of confusion," he pointed out. "The alarms were blaring. People were running."

"I was the only one up here. Well, me and Elizabeth. But she left when she saw Jonathan down below. Then it was just me. I didn't see anyone else." She began to slowly walk toward the nearest set of arches. "The first night I was here, I didn't see Roman, either. I was sure I'd searched the area, but I didn't know he was close by, not until I heard his whisper."

"There are lots of nooks and crannies up here. It would be easy enough for someone to hide."

A nod as she kept poking around. "But I learned my lesson after Roman. I *checked.* Thoroughly. I didn't see anyone."

"Heather probably came up here after you left. That's why you didn't notice her—"

"I was near the stairs. You'd seen me on the second floor—I know you did."

He had seen her. Right before he'd raced down to the basement level to discover Heather was gone.

"So I stayed close by to wait for you. I never saw Heather go up the stairs."

"She was disguised, remember, wearing your clothes?"

Lacey didn't answer. She was in the corner, under the thick arch. Her fingers slid over the ornate wood carvings. "Do you know what my favorite show was, back when I was a kid?"

"*Scooby Doo,*" Dex answered immediately.

Lacey gave a little jerk. "Ohmygosh." Her head angled toward him. "Antony found out that for you, too?"

Actually, no. "When I was at your place, I saw the Scooby Doo cookie jar you had in your kitchen."

A fleeting smile came and went on her lips. "Do you know what was often in those cartoons?"

Other than a talking dog and some sleuthing kids?

She went back to pressing on the wood. "Secret passages."

He'd been approaching her, but at those words, Dex stopped.

She slid her fingers over the carving of an owl. "This building is old. Historic, right? Huge and sprawling. I'm sure it holds lots of secrets, you know, like a secret underground CIA lair."

He had actually wanted to use the lodge because of the array of rooms but... "I've seen the design plans for this place. There isn't any secret passage on this level."

Lacey glanced back at him. "*Historic* building. Maybe you saw some of the plans, but did you see them all? I read the plaque in the lobby. This place has been here since the early 1900s. Perhaps there are a few things about it that even you don't know." Her eyes widened. "Our suite."

"What about it?"

"You said you questioned the agents and they didn't see anyone get in our room. You probably thought they were lying or that they'd left their post, and you are planning some sort of horrible interrogation or grilling for them—"

Already occurring, actually. He'd given that task to Larry. Larry excelled in those situations.

"But what if another secret passage was up there? Maybe a little corridor that connected one suite to another? Or, hell, it could just be a large air vent running along the suites on that level, and someone flexible enough was able to slip inside. I don't know, but I think I am on to something." She turned back to the wood. Kept pressing. "I really do."

He watched her. Considered possibilities.

"Not like a ghost walked through walls," she said. "Our perp is real. Flesh and blood. A secret passage makes sense."

His eyes raked the area. If there was a secret passage, they weren't going to find it easily. "We need to talk to experts."

"What experts? Who?"

"Charles." He knew the lodge inside and out. And... "Roman."

She spun back toward him.

He took her hand. Curled his fingers around hers. "Come on. We can push on the wood for hours and still turn up jack. Let's talk to them. I'll also get Antony to dig up everything he can find on the lodge."

"Oh, that's good." Her steps kept perfect time with his. "He's good at finding secrets, isn't he?"

Most days, yes.

They hurried down the stairs—

"*Lacey!*"

Sonofabitch. It was not Dex's day.

Just as they reached the end of the steps, Tim Wraith scurried across the marble floor. His arms were up as he ran straight for Lacey. The man's obvious intent was to hug her.

I am not in the mood for this shit.

At the last minute, Dex moved into Tim's path. The drummer barreled into him. The jerk's arms even wrapped around Dex's shoulders.

Dex sighed. "I do not know you well enough for this." He shoved Tim back. "And I don't want to, jackass."

Tim blinked. Recovered. His face mottled even as he told Lacey, "I was so worried! I heard about the woman's body...even heard some people saying your...ah, fiancé here, thought it was you at first!" He shook his head. "My Lacey, I was scared. I was—"

"*Not* your Lacey," Dex snapped. He was beyond not in the mood for this crap. He needed to have a come-to-Jesus-meeting with this fool ASAP. "Back off, Tom."

"Tim. My name is Tim."

"Do I look like I care?" When he'd moved into Tim's path, Dex had let go of Lacey's hand. Now he reached for it again. Twined his fingers with hers. Lifted her delicate hand *just* enough for the diamond ring to sparkle.

The flash of fury on Tim's face was easy to see. Too easy.

"Why are you here?" Dex wanted to know. But he knew the reason. The SOB had tracked Lacey to the lodge. "There's no boy band convention so—"

Tim took a swing at him. It was the attack Dex had been hoping to provoke. He even let the other man's fist hit his face as Dex released Lacey's hand. Such a weak-ass blow.

Lacey gasped behind him. "Tim! What are you doing?"

Exactly what I wanted him to do.

Tim stood there, fists clenched at his sides, breath heaving. "I'm not in a boy band. I am the drummer for Implosion Night! I am a fucking rock star, which means I'm a million times better than some lame-ass prick like you. And if you don't believe me, why don't you just ask Lace? She can tell you exactly how good I am."

Dex smiled at him. "Know what you are, Timmy?"

"It's Tim!"

"You're out of your league." He'd just caught sight of Antony hurrying toward them. Dex motioned toward Lacey. "Antony, would you be a buddy and keep my fiancée company for a moment? She has a theory she needs to run by you, and...well, I have a swing that I'm due. It's my turn to punch the rock star."

Antony stopped. Behind the lenses of his glasses, his eyes widened.

Lacey grabbed Dex's arm. "What are you doing?"

He turned his face toward her. "He hit me. You saw that. He took the first swing. Don't I have the right to hit back? I believe I do. I think that's a thing."

"That is not a thing." Her voice was low. "You know it's not. You also know he has no shot against you."

He did know that. But it was nice of her to notice.

"You telling him how good I am, Lace?" Tim demanded, voice all aggressive. "Telling him to hit the road because you want to be back with a real man?"

What the hell was that BS line supposed to mean? That Dex was a pretend man? *Such. A. Dumbass.*

Lacey didn't even look at Tim. "We have work to do."

Yes, they did. And even though it looked like he was just about to have fun by punching Tim, Dex was also doing his job. Knocking out two birds at once and all that. "I don't believe in coincidences." They'd already talked once about Tim's arrival being way too convenient. "I want to make sure no one is pulling his strings."

Her brow furrowed. "You think Tim could be involved?" A whisper.

Dex thought he didn't trust the jerk. And it was time for answers. "Stay with Antony." Antony was a damn lethal agent. *So is Lacey.* "I just need five minutes alone with the drummer. Just five."

Five minutes was all he'd need to break the bastard. Five—

"No," Lacey said clearly.

"What?"

"You don't want me to see what you'll do to him. You think I can't handle it when you go dark?"

It wasn't even going to be a whole lot of darkness involved. He was just gonna flex a little. Dex was counting on the fact that guys like Tim always crumpled quickly. All arrogance. No substance.

"I can fight my own battles, Dex, and it seems like he is stalking *me*. Not you. You won't shut me out. Deal with it." A brisk nod. Then she took a step back. Focused on Antony. "We want to know if there are any secret passages on the Whisper Floor."

"Secret what?" He squinted.

"I know you heard me," Lacey retorted. "See if you can dig up any proof of a passageway on the Whisper Floor. One there *and* a way that someone could have accessed the suite Dex and I have without going past the guards who were stationed outside our door."

"Yes, ma'am. Secret passage." Antony turned away. "Always liked Velma the best."

Lacey's gaze darted around the lobby. Landed on a small room to the right. "What's in there?"

"It's a privacy room," Dex told her. "The concierge team will often meet with guests when they have—"

"Tim, I want to talk to you in there, now."

Tim smirked at Dex. "Damn straight you do. Told you, asshole..." He followed Lacey into the room. "Once you have a rock star, you never settle for second—"

Dex strode inside, too, then closed the door. Only he, Lacey, and Tim were in the privacy room.

"Are you stalking me, Tim?" Lacey asked.

"You want me. You want me back. I know you do. Why are you playing these games?" He grabbed for her hand. Held on tight. "Why are you dicking around with him? *You told me* to come for you. *You told me* that you missed me. *You told me* that you loved me."

"No, I didn't. Now let go."

If anything, he moved closer. Held her tighter.

Yeah, enough of this shit.

Dex lunged forward, grabbed the bastard, and shoved him against the nearest wall. Then Dex took the SOB's right hand and clenched his fingers around it. "Do you think you'll still be a badass drummer with a broken hand?" He squeezed.

"What are you doing?" Alarm—fear—flashed in Tim's eyes. "Let go!"

"Actually, you know what? Why stop with one? Let's make it two broken hands."

Tim tried to get away. Fucking useless. Dex effortlessly held him in place.

"Stop it! Let me go!"

"I don't think I'll just settle for a few breaks. I'll make sure the damage is severe and long term. With the right therapy, maybe you'll be able to play again. Maybe not. That rock star life of yours might be over."

"Don't! Oh, fucking hell, please, don't! I am begging you! Let me—"

"Dex, stop playing with him," Lacey ordered with a sigh.

Dex stared into Tim's eyes. He wanted this message received. "I'm not playing."

Tim whimpered. "My hands, man, my hands!"

"When it comes to my fiancée, I don't play. Ever."

Frantic nods. "I-I get it! I'll stay away, I swear! I wouldn't have even come here if she hadn't contacted me and said—"

"I most certainly did not contact you!" Lacey words whipped out. "Are you crazy? Why would you say that? I broke up with you. And when I saw you a few weeks ago on another case, and you asked me out, I told you yet again that we were done."

"But...but then you sent me that text..."

Dex released the fellow. Stepped back. "You believe what you're saying."

Tim reached into his pocket.

Dex immediately tensed.

"I am not going for a weapon! Calm down." He fumbled and his shaking fingers pulled out a phone. His finger slid over the screen and then he turned the phone toward Dex. "Look! Look! See, she texted me! Lacey is lying to you. If you want to be mad at someone, be mad at her." He sniffed. "I'm mad at you, Lace. You hooked up with this psycho, and he was gonna break my hands for you! That shit is not cool! What did you want, for him to be jealous? For me to be jealous? Are you playing some kind of game with us—"

"Dumbass, Lacey doesn't play jealousy games." Dex scrolled back through the messages that had come from "Lacey" on Tim's phone.

Sure enough, some of them seemed legit. They probably were, going by the dates. There were several texts from Lacey saying...

"It's over."

"No, I don't want to meet you for dinner."

"Don't call me again."

"I wish you luck in your life, but it's not working. Stop contacting me."

"Tommy, you need to get a fucking clue," Dex growled.

"It's...Tim."

The most recent texts from Lacey, though, were different...

"I miss you. Didn't realize how much you mattered until you were gone."

"No one can take your place. Other men can't compare."

"Come find me. I need you."

The last text had been sent the same day that Lacey and Dex arrived at the lodge. The text even included the lodge's name, saying that she was close by, just a small distance away from Tim's winter home in Aspen.

"Be mad at her," Tim urged him. "Not me. She screwed us both."

A snarl built in Dex's throat.

"Oh, fuck, that was the wrong thing to say, wasn't it?" Tim's voice rose. "Don't break my hands, don't—"

"Lacey didn't send those texts. You were set up. Someone wanted you here, probably so that you could distract us from what was really happening. Or maybe someone wanted you to be the fall guy. Don't really know what the end game is where you are concerned."

Tim gaped at him. "Say what?"

"Lacey isn't interested in you," he enunciated slowly. "She didn't send those texts."

"But, they came from her number—"

"Someone set you up." He glanced over at a silent Lacey. "Someone set her up, too."

A rough laugh tumbled from Tim. "Man, why would you say that? It's clear to see the number is hers. All of those texts are from her, even the break-up ones. Look, I get it, you don't want to believe that she was double-timing you and—"

"I trust her," Dex said simply. "Even if I didn't trust Lacey, I'd still know how ridiculously easy it is for the right people to clone numbers and send false texts. You wouldn't know that, though, and since you wanted Lacey back so desperately, you were more than ready to believe anything."

"She texted me—"

"No," Lacey said, voice quiet. "I didn't. Someone pulled you into a very dangerous situation. You should leave the lodge. Take your blonde friend with you and go."

"Hey, don't be jealous, Lace! She just—you know, she was with me in Aspen, and so I brought her along because it would have been rude to leave her, but I swear, I was going to ditch her as soon as I saw how things with you and me—"

"Take your friend with you," Lacey repeated. "And get the hell out before more bullets start flying."

His Adam's apple bobbed. "Bullets?"

"I'm keeping your phone." Dex pocketed the device. "I'll get a buddy to see if he can track down the real sender of the texts."

"But..." Tim's lips pulled down. "Lace, you don't want me back?"

Her fingers curled around Dex's shoulder. "I have a fiancé. He's the only man I want."

If only she meant those words. Dex's heart surged hard into his chest.

Tim slowly nodded.

"Lacey..." Dex murmured her name carefully. "Will you please give me one moment alone with Tim?" He angled his head toward her. "Just one?"

Suspicion had her eyes narrowing. "What are you going to do?"

"*Don't break my hands!*" Tim pleaded.

He glanced heavenward. *Deliver me from dumbasses.* Then he looked at Lacey. "I'm going to give him a quick word of advice. I think it will have more meaning if we can talk privately."

Her eyebrows lifted. "Do not kill him."

Tim whimpered. "Who is this guy, Lace? Why do you even have to tell him shit like that? You know that's not normal, don't you?"

"Do not hurt him," Lacey continued.

"*OhmyGod. Are you involved with like...a mobster or some shit?*"

Without answering Tim, she strode for the door.

"Lacey!" Dex called out.

She paused.

"Stay close," he urged her. *I want her where I can keep an eye on her.* "Sixty seconds is all I need."

A nod. Then she slipped out.

Sixty, fifty-nine...

"She texted me," Tim insisted.

"Thompson, you were used."

"Tim. Name's Tim, and you know that. I've corrected you like fifty—"

"Lacey didn't text you. Someone else did. Someone threw you into my path probably because that person didn't care if I kicked your ass or simply made you vanish from the face of the planet."

Another whimper. The dude whimpered a lot. "Can you...do that?"

"You don't want to find out." He held Tim's gaze. "Take this message and let it burn into your brain. Lacey isn't interested. She's marrying me. You come near her again, and you will not be living that rock star life you love so much, I can guarantee that."

"Y-you'll break my hands..."

"Think bigger. You see, I can break your entire world. I can take away every contract you've got. I can make your money vanish. I can have your fame crumble around you. All it will take are a few well-placed words from me, and you're done."

"Nah. Nah, you don't have that kind of power—"

"That is exactly the kind of power I possess." He didn't even blink. "Lacey is mine. I protect what's mine. Understand?"

CHAPTER NINTEEN

I didn't send the text.

No way would she have texted Tim. But someone had sure wanted it to look as if she had.

"I trust Lacey completely." Dex had sounded as if he meant those words.

Her back pressed to the closed door. She couldn't hear anything from inside that little space, but she knew Dex was probably scaring the ever-living-hell out of Tim. She should go back in there. She needed to—

"Lacey!" Elizabeth darted toward her.

Lacey pushed away from the door.

"Thank God!" Tears streamed down Elizabeth's cheeks. "You can help me. Please, please..." She grabbed Lacey's hand and held on tight. "You'll help me, won't you?"

What in the world?

"Come with me," Elizabeth begged. "You can help me to find him. I know you can! You work for Wilde. You can do anything!"

Hardly anything. "Elizabeth, slow down. Tell me what's happening."

"Everyone is leaving this place. People are *dying,"* Elizabeth whispered. "And...Jonathan was supposed to meet me, but he never showed up and it's getting later and later...*help me."* She pulled on Lacey's arms.

The door opened behind Lacey.

Tim hurried past her. "I'll be gone in the hour."

Elizabeth frowned at him. "Is that...isn't he in Implosion Night?"

Dex's arm brushed against Lacey. "Darling, we have that appointment that we must keep," he said smoothly. "You know we have those last few questions that need answering and—"

"Jonathan is missing," Elizabeth blurted. "I can't find him, and I need Lacey's help." Tears dripped down her cheeks. "It's not like him to vanish. He's the one who planned this whole trip, and it was supposed to be so special, but he's missing."

Lacey focused on Dex. "You go handle those last questions. I need to talk with Elizabeth."

"I am sure her husband will turn up," Dex muttered. Then, louder, "Elizabeth, did he perhaps go out skiing? Maybe he was delayed on the slopes."

"He—I don't know. He just isn't answering his phone and with that poor woman dying...I have to find him." She still held onto Lacey. "You're my friend. You're the only person here that I can trust. Please, please help me."

"We kind of have some situations of our own here, Elizabeth," Dex retorted. "So I'll get lodge security to help you, but—"

"I'll help, too," Lacey said. "Excuse us for a moment first, will you, Elizabeth?"

A slightly confused nod was Elizabeth's response as she finally let go of Lacey.

"You." Lacey pointed to the luggage guy who was working undercover for Dex. She'd only recently learned about him. "Keep her safe until I come out." Lacey put her hand on Dex's chest and shoved him back into that little privacy room. The door closed behind them.

Dex glanced at her hand, then up at her face. "Sweetheart, what in the hell are you doing? I told you, I wanted you close. I want to—"

"You want to protect me. Yes, I get that. Here's the thing, though. I want to protect my friends, too." Her heart was about to jump out of her chest. "You and Roman were both at the lodge during the same time—I'm assuming that was deliberate. But Tim was lured here. How do we know that Elizabeth and Jonathan weren't somehow lured to this location, too? I worked with them before. They are my friends. I was so surprised to see them when we crossed paths in the ballroom, and now, if Jonathan is missing—"

"Guy could just be off drinking somewhere."

Lacey snorted. "Really? With everything else that's happening, you actually think that?"

His expression softened. "Why do I find that little snort so sexy?"

"What are you talking about?" Her chin notched up. "I don't snort. Never have. Never will."

A grin stretched across his face. "My God, I love—"

He isn't saying, he can't be saying...Dex, are you saying—

"—the way you can make me smile even when the world is shit around me. Only you can do that, Lacey. Only you."

Bam. Bam. Bam. Her heart was racing even faster now. "Glad I can amuse you," she managed to say. *Why did you think he was about to make some epic confession?*

And a follow-up question to herself...*Why are you so disappointed that he didn't?*

Dex's brows lowered. "That's not what I meant."

"Lacey?" Elizabeth's worried voice rang out. She gave a small, uncertain knock on the door. "Should I go start searching for him? And why is the bellboy watching me?"

"Just wait. Give me a minute!" She blew out a long breath. *Get your focus, woman. Dex wasn't making some big confession and saying he loves you. It's pretend. Why can't you keep remembering that?* "Dex, go and talk to Roman. You know him far better than I do. If he's lying, you'll see through him. I won't." She backed up.

Dex followed her. "You know I want you close."

"I know you've been protecting me. Doing your usual manipulation. Pawns on your chess board—"

Dex's jaw hardened. "How many times do I have to remind you?" He brought her hand to his mouth. Pressed a kiss to her knuckles. "You are the queen. Not a pawn. You never sacrifice the queen. You protect her at all costs."

Fine. "The queen protects the other pieces on the board. That's *her* job. Elizabeth and Jonathan

are my friends. So I am going to protect them."
And it sure seemed that perhaps Jonathan had
been taken. If he *had* been taken, would Elizabeth
be the next target? *If she's searching the lodge for
her husband, she's vulnerable because she's in the
open. I need to get her to a secure location.* "You
get your agents to help in the hunt for Jonathan.
I'll go back upstairs and stay with Elizabeth. I'll
question her and find out exactly what's been
happening during her stay here in the lodge."

His lips parted—

"You can send a guard to stand outside of our
door. Or to stay in the room with us, whatever.
But I'm not helpless. I can defend myself. I can
protect her. You need to trust me to do that."

"I do trust you, Lacey."

"Really? Then tell me the truth about Charles
and Roman. Right now."

His eyes narrowed. "The truth?"

"You don't buy that Charles turned on you, do
you? I don't think you really ever believed it, not
knowing his past as you do."

His eyelashes lowered.

"But you still had him taken into custody. You
did that..." *I'm starting to really figure you out,
Dex. It took some time, but I see you now.* "You
did it to protect him, didn't you? Because maybe
even your pawns are valuable."

"Do you know the name of his son?"

She shook her head. "No, I just saw the photo.
He never told me—"

"Charles named his son Nathaniel Dexter
Hatch." His gaze held hers. "So, no, I didn't
think—even when the evidence was right in front

of me—that Charles had turned on me. I believed him when he said that Heather gave him the access to that site. I also believed that he could be in danger, so I removed him from the equation."

"Dex, you have got to stop keeping things from me! You need to tell me the truth. If this is going to work between us—"

"This?" Dex pounced. "You mean our pretend engagement? If it's going to keep working?"

Don't say it. Don't say it. Don't—ah, screw it. "I'm not talking about pretend anything. I'm talking about the way I feel about you and the way I think you might feel about me." She pulled her hand free of his grip. "Here's the problem, though. You're so secretive. You won't let anyone inside. You won't let me know how you really feel about me. You want this to work? You want *us* to work? Then you tell me. You let me in." Once she'd started talking, her words just wouldn't stop. "You keep the rest of the world out, fine. Do it. Tell them they don't have clearance to learn your secrets. Keep fighting the dark and keeping everyone safe from the shadows. Someone has to do that shit, after all. But when it comes to me, *to us,* you share with me." She blinked quickly because her eyes had gone a wee bit blurry with what could have been tears. "You let me in those shadows with you because that's where I want to be. I want to be right with you."

He didn't speak.

She hadn't been able to stop talking, and he wasn't saying a word.

That seemed right.

She tipped back her head and stared up at the ceiling. "I don't hear Elizabeth. I asked your undercover guy to watch her because I was afraid she'd go off on her own, and that woman's survival skills—speaking from our last time together—are not the best. She may also be walking straight into a trap that's been set by the bad guy. I have to go to her." She side-stepped. "Excuse me—"

"I don't truly think that Roman killed Heather. I ordered him taken into custody because I wanted to protect him, too."

The moisture in her mouth seemed to dry up. "Are you sharing with me right now?" *Finally?*

"Roman matters to you, so I wanted him safe."

"He—wait. I just met him. He seems to hate me so—"

"Family matters to you. That was obvious from the beginning. Roman kept being targeted, so I wasn't going to wait and see what happened to him next." A quick exhale. "I also wanted to see what would happen if he was in holding downstairs. I figure he'll make an attempt to escape, but he won't actually flee the property. He'll stick around because he wants to make certain you're safe. You matter to him, too, and I wanted him to know that shit. I wanted Roman to stop glaring at you and *appreciate* you. To fucking love you. You deserve love. You deserve to have a family around you who loves you and wants to do everything possible to make you happy. Everything, even if it involves twisting or damn well obliterating some rules out there."

Now he'd been the one to talk too much. Only, it hadn't seemed like too much. Not really.

"Lacey?" A soft knock. "I'm scared," Elizabeth cried. "The bellman won't let me move. So many people have left the lodge already. It's like a ghost hotel or something. Like that Stephen King book with—"

"I'm coming! I'll help you!" Lacey promised. She lowered her voice. "I have to go. Look, I have the new phone you gave me after we arrived at the lodge. I'll keep it with me. You call me as soon as you have news. I'll go to her suite, and we'll figure everything out."

"I don't like this plan."

"Yes, well, it's not exactly sunshine and rainbows, but Jonathan is missing and Roman is waiting, so we have to split up." Once more, she side-stepped. Lacey grabbed for the doorknob.

"I think I might love you."

There was no way—no way—that Dex had just said those words to her. Lacey shook her head because she knew she was wrong.

"You're right."

A fist squeezed her heart. Her breath froze in her lungs. Her head turned—ever so slowly—toward him.

Dex nodded. "I said the wrong thing."

Yes, yes, he had, damn him, and for one incredible moment, she'd hoped—

"I don't *think* that I love you. And there is no *might* involved." His shoulders straightened. They'd already been straight, but they squared up even more. "I love you. There. No secrets. No lies. No manipulations. I've been an extra asshole because I knew I was falling fast, and with you, there was no holding back. There was no keeping my emotions separate. There just...there just was you." He seemed to flounder at the end.

He wasn't the floundering type.

"I don't expect you to say the words back or anything. That's not what this is about. I'm trying...*I want you to know that I did let you in.*"

She swallowed. "You've been my pretend fiancé for a few days. Is that really long enough to fall in love with me?"

"Sweetheart, I fell in love with you the first time we met." His grin lit his gray eyes.

Impossible. Wasn't it? But... "I pulled a knife on you the first time we met."

"The knife was unnecessary. You were already holding my heart."

Now he was being poetic? In his way, at least.

Elizabeth pounded on the door. "*I need you!*"

Lacey nodded. She started to open the door. Stopped. Then she whirled and launched at Dex. Her arms wrapped around him. His head lowered toward hers. And she kissed him with hot, frantic passion. "You are going to tell me that again," she breathed against his mouth. "When this mess is over, when we are alone..." Another kiss. "You are going to tell me all of that again."

But for now, she let him go. Once more, her fingers reached for the door.

"I'll send one of my best agents with you. And I'll get people to search for Jonathan. I'll talk to Roman, then I'll come join you."

She nodded and pulled the door open.

Elizabeth stood on the other side of the threshold. When she saw Lacey, relief flashed on her face. "Finally."

Lacey stepped forward.

The bellman slipped away.

"*Lacey.*"

She looked over her shoulder at Dex's deep voice.

"You stay safe, my love. Remember that you matter to me more than anything else. If you get so much as a bruise on you, I will be very, very pissed off."

Lacey licked her lips. Tasted him. "And you stay safe. You matter more than I ever imagined." So much that it scared her. "If you get so much as a bruise on you, not only will I be very pissed off, but I will kick the ass of the person who bruised you."

His white teeth flashed. "How could I not love you?"

Her body trembled. She'd always known that Dex was a dangerous man. She just hadn't always known...

How much I'd care about him.

Elizabeth grabbed her. "This is great and all, but the man *I* love is missing! Come on, Lacey! Come on!"

***

She hadn't said she loved him. Dex hadn't expected a confession from Lacey. One would have been nice, certainly, but he knew he still had to build more trust with her.

When it came to Lacey, he wanted no secrets. He wanted to let down the wall, as she'd said, and let her in. No one else had ever been as close to him as Lacey. When he thought of his life without her, a brutal cold seemed to sweep around him.

Because she brings warmth. Life. All of the things that he'd told her he fought for at the CIA? The kids on the soccer field? The teens going to prom and the proud grandmothers? All of that had been true. But...

He also fought for people like Lacey. People who lit up the world simply by being in it.

She'd certainly lit up his life.

He watched as she made her way to the elevator with Elizabeth. One of his undercover operatives was nearby. A man who'd earned Dex's respect with his skills and intelligence. Dex approached Cornell Tait and quietly ordered, "Go up on that elevator with Lacey. Show her your ID. Tell her that I want you near her and Elizabeth at all times. Stay with them until I personally come and relieve you of duty. I cannot stress how important it is for you to be with Lacey every moment."

Cornell nodded and immediately headed for the elevator. "Hold the ride!"

Lacey threw out her hand to stop the door. Her gaze darted from Cornell to Dex.

Dex gave a slow nod.

Cornell entered the elevator, and when the doors closed, Dex drew in a deep breath. Time to confront Roman. He'd let the guy stew long enough. Lacey had been right—as she was often proving to be—he could tell when the other man tried to bullshit him.

He called some of his agents. Got them to begin searching the area for Jonathan Radcliff. Dex made his way down to the holding area. The elevator ride was brief, and when the doors opened—

Antony was standing right there. "Lacey was right." He gripped a laptop in his hands. Not the same laptop he'd held before. This one was a dark silver. Probably the fellow's own machine which meant it would be decked out to the extreme.

"What is she right about this time?" Dex nodded as he passed two other agents and marched to holding. He'd have to close this CIA location as soon as the case ended. Definitely compromised. Pity. The lodge had been convenient, and he'd enjoyed the whole underground lair aspect of the facility.

"There are spaces that don't make sense in this lodge. I pulled up some architectural plans, and when I look at them and compare them to the rooms and floors that I've actually walked in myself, the dimensions are off. Probably not enough to be noticed by the average person, but you know, I don't always think like—"

"I know your mind often goes off on its own, fun, interesting tangents," Dex allowed carefully. He paused in front of the holding room door. "I'm in a bit of a hurry here, so could you get to the point?"

"The dimensions are wrong on the plans. They don't match up. That means there is space in some areas—like on the Whisper Floor—for there

281

to be tunnels. Small passageways." His eyebrows wiggled. "Secret passages, do you get what I'm saying?"

"Jinkies," Dex replied.

Antony pushed up his glasses. "Is that supposed to be funny right now? Because I knew I made a mistake when I told you about Velma."

"I was always a Daphne fan myself, but you do you, my friend." He needed to be in the interrogation room. "Did you find some of those empty spaces in the suite I share with Lacey?"

"No. Everything seems to measure up in that area. The upper floors are newer, and the designs clearly show the architects were trying to use every available space. But..." Antony trailed away.

"Do you know how badly I want to get in this room?"

Antony glanced at the door.

"How about you don't leave me hanging with a dramatic 'but' and you simply tell me what you're thinking."

"Fine. No secret passageways, but I think someone could have used the air ducts. The person would have to be small. Petite. Probably around Lacey's size, no bigger. The perp would have needed to gain access to the ducts from another room on that floor."

"Figure out which rooms would have provided the best access. Then come find me." He curled his fingers around the doorknob. "And by the way, I've got a search team on the property, hunting for Jonathan Radcliff. His wife can't find him, and since she and Jonathan are both friends of Lacey's, the worry is that he might have been targeted by our perp."

"Radcliff," Antony repeated. He seemed to mull the name.

"He's a duke. Related to the Queen of England and all that stuff." Dex opened the door. "Used to be in the press pretty regularly—some kind of royal Romeo bit—until he fell hard for his lady."

As the door swung fully open, Roman lunged to his feet.

The ever-reliable Larry slapped both of his hands on Roman's shoulders and shoved him right back down in his chair.

"Take this, too." Dex tossed Antony Tim Wraith's phone. "Lacey didn't send those texts. Find out who did."

Roman glared at him.

"Come in if you get news I need," Dex directed Antony. Then he shut the door. Propped his shoulders back against the wood.

Cuffs were around Roman's wrists. Dex couldn't help but glance down at his own wrists and the scars that marked him.

"I can't believe you took me into custody!" Roman snarled.

Dex lifted his gaze. "And I can't believe you haven't escaped yet. So disappointed. Are you losing your touch?"

Roman's lips thinned. "If I run, I'd look guilty."

Larry still had his hands wrapped around Roman's shoulders. "That's because you are guilty."

"And you're an idiot," Roman threw back. "Another flunky who lives to do Dex's bidding. Never realizing that you've tied yourself to a sadistic asshole."

"Words hurt, you know. They wound." Dex sighed as he sauntered forward. He pulled out a chair, flipped it around, then straddled it as he took a seat and stared at Roman. He could see that Larry's hands had tightened on Roman's shoulders. Dex could only imagine the pressure that Larry was applying.

"Larry doesn't like it when people talk shit about me," Dex noted. "Doing that in front of him is a bad mistake."

"Why?" Roman laughed. "Because you have him convinced you're some secret hero? Bullshit. You're a user, a manipulator—"

"True and true." Dex cocked his head. "But who says users and manipulators can't also do a little good here and there? Not like the stuff is mutually exclusive."

"You don't even know the meaning of the word good."

"That's just insulting. Sure I do." He sniffed. "Lacey Amari."

"What the hell does that mean?"

"She's my something good. I look at her, and I know the world is worth saving. I know that happiness is real. And I know that even cold-blooded bastards like me can have a shot at a normal life." He motioned with a flick of his hand. "Thanks, Larry. You can ease back. If he gets twitchy, though, feel free to reengage."

"Will do." Larry backed away.

Roman leaned forward. "You seriously think you have a shot with my sister?"

"What? You think I don't?"

"You're using her. The same way you use everyone else. The same way—"

"I can tell you a thousand ways how you're wrong. But I won't bother. Simply put, I don't care to bother. Believe whatever the hell you want about me." He tugged down the sleeve of his shirt, making sure the scars were hidden. "You always have."

"*You left me. You didn't come until those bastards had taken their time giving me a taste of hell—and you think I will let you near my only family?*"

"Lots of rage. Lots and lots of it." Dex glanced up. "Is that why you killed Heather? Why you dressed her up in Lacey's coat and hat and scarf and shot her in the back? You wanted to send a message to me? You wanted me to see that if I didn't stay away from Lacey, she would be the next to die? That you'd rather see her dead than to ever see her with me? Is that what you were trying to say?"

"Hell, no!" A fierce shout of denial.

Larry inched forward.

"Not yet, Larry," Dex murmured. "I don't think that counts as a full twitch yet."

"Are you sure?" Larry didn't look convinced. A bit disappointed, but not convinced.

Dex nodded.

"*I did not kill Heather!*" Roman thundered. "I was pissed at her. Felt used and betrayed. But I didn't hurt her. I wanted to know who she was working for. I wanted to know who put out the hit on Lacey—and on me."

"Well, you have screwed over lots of bad people during your time as a double agent. I mean, you screwed me over, too, when you went rogue after the rescue mission. When you wouldn't listen to reason and you went dark."

"Rescue mission?" Roman's face reddened. "Are you insane? There was no rescue."

Yes, there was.

"You honestly think I could ever trust you again?"

Now they were getting to the good stuff. "You trusted me to find Lacey."

Roman's stare cut away.

"I've been thinking a whole lot about that. About just why you turned to me—a man you purportedly hate with every fiber of your being."

"Screw yourself."

Dex ignored that—uh, offer?—and continued, "Maybe...maybe you asked for my help because you were worried. Worried that when you were all pissed at the CIA and selling your secrets to the highest bidder, you made some bad enemies. Enemies that you knew would use a sweet, innocent sister against you. A sister who didn't grow up in your world, so she'd have no way to handle the danger you brought to her."

Roman wasn't meeting his stare. "She doesn't seem so sweet and innocent, not if she's falling for you."

"She is a fucking sweet perfect rainbow, and don't you ever say any different."

Roman's gaze whipped back to him. "Are you serious right now?"

"As a heart attack, I believe the saying is." He rolled back his shoulders. "So, you didn't deny any of the things I said. That means they're all true."

"You knew that stuff was true," Roman muttered. "You always know, don't you? You don't enter a room with a suspect unless you've got the winning hand."

"I want to know who it is that you fear the most. Who is here at the lodge? What enemy? Who am I missing?"

"I don't *know*," Roman gritted out. "If I knew, I would have killed him by now!"

So they were all chasing their tails in the dark. Wonderful. "Then make me a list. Give me the top ten names of the worst badasses that you screwed over. I can get my tech super star to find out exactly where those people are."

A bitter laugh. "You know these people have multiple identities, right? Just like you? Like me? It's not as easy as tapping on a computer in order to find—"

The door swung open. Antony stood there, holding tightly to his laptop. "I found something. Something you need to know."

Dex leaned back. "See? Sometimes, it is that damn easy."

"Dex." Antony's voice was tense. "It's about Lacey..."

Dex lunged off the chair.

CHAPTER TWENTY

"Does he have to stay in here?" Elizabeth whispered as she cast a quick glance over at Cornell's silent form. "I-I need to discuss something private with you."

They were in Elizabeth's suite, and a warm fire crackled nearby. Cornell had taken up a position near the fireplace. "Cornell stays. He's here for our protection." Lacey raised her voice and said, "Besides, I'm thinking he can keep a secret or two, can't you, Cornell?"

"Kept plenty of them." His deep voice rumbled as he never changed his stoic expression.

She gave him a smile. "Thanks." She sat down on the couch next to Elizabeth. "See? You can talk in front of him. Your safety is paramount right now."

"I'm not the one missing." Elizabeth grabbed her hand in a claw-like grip. "It's Jonathan. I...I didn't tell you everything downstairs."

"What is it?"

"We've been having some trouble."

Lacey didn't let her surprise show.

"The media...the press...they paint us as this perfect couple..."

When Lacey had been working the protection detail for them, they *had* seemed perfect together.

"But no one is perfect," Elizabeth continued with a voice that shook. "When he told me that we should get away, that we should come here, I thought—this is our chance. He wants to put us first. He'd been working so much, shutting me out, and he seemed so different from the man I'd fallen for...but here, here everything could go back to the way it had been."

"We'll find him," Lacey assured her. "You two will have the chance to work out whatever is happening."

Elizabeth nodded. "I-I thought he was cheating on me."

Cornell gave a low whistle.

Lacey frowned at him.

"Sorry, but if he's cheating on you, he's a fool." Cornell shrugged.

Elizabeth straightened a little. Even managed a brief smile. But then the smile wobbled. "I found texts. He left me in the middle of the night. I thought—I thought he went to her." She rose. Paced across the suite. She put her hands flat on the desk that waited in the corner.

The flames danced in the fireplace. Darkness had fallen outside. Lacey couldn't see the mountains or the snowfall that had been predicted.

"I didn't trust him." Elizabeth reached for the desk drawer. "Would you like to see why?"

Damn straight, she would.

***

"Who the hell is this one?" Roman demanded to know. "Another blindly-following lackey?"

Antony didn't even glance at Roman. "I don't have time for him." He put the laptop down on the table. Pointed to the screen. "Do you see this?"

Dex leaned forward. Narrowed his eyes.

"The name in the bottom of the corner. One of the original designers of this lodge. Looks familiar, doesn't it?" Antony pushed.

"Thaddeus Radcliff," Dex read. Then his head snapped up.

"You're the one who has always told me, there are no coincidences in this world." Antony pulled off his glasses. Began to polish them on his shirt. "Did a little digging. Back in the early 1900s, it seems that Thaddeus Radcliff—the second son of a duke—came to the US seeking fortune. Like, literally, as in the name of this town. Fortune, Colorado. He was one of the first to settle here. He even helped to build the lodge. It was originally the home for one of his friends but—"

Dex was already whipping out his phone and whirling for the door.

"But if he was one of the builders, then he would have known where the tunnels were located. That's why the name Radcliff nagged at me when you said it. Because I'd seen his name on the old images I pulled up and—"

"Somebody get me a comm links, now! I want to be connected to every agent on this property!" Dex was already rushing down the hallway. He heard Roman shouting behind him, but he didn't stop.

The phone he gripped to his ear rang once. Twice. Three—

Lacey, pick up.

***

Her phone rang, vibrating in her pocket. Lacey pulled it out and frowned at the screen. "It's Dex." Lacey swiped her finger over the screen and put the phone to her ear. "Did you locate Jonathan?"

"Lacey," Dex growled, "I want you to come to me right now."

Elizabeth's fingers fluttered near the drawer.

"Why?" *Oh, God.* "Jonathan?" Had Dex found Jonathan, or rather, his body?

"You were right about the passages on the Whisper Floor, and I think Jonathan knew about them, too."

But, wait, if Jonathan knew—

"Can you help me?" Elizabeth suddenly asked Cornell. "I think the drawer is stuck."

He hurried to her side.

"Jonathan's ancestor freaking built this lodge. You know I don't believe in coincidences," Dex snarled.

Neither did she. And hadn't Elizabeth just told her that Jonathan had gotten mystery texts? That he'd disappeared in the middle of the night?

Elizabeth's husband could be the killer we are after. Elizabeth had been worried the man might be a cheater. This was worse. He was a murderer—

Elizabeth's hand came up in a fast blur. Her fingers were curled around something. What was that?

"Lacey? Lacey, are you listening to me?" Dex demanded.

Lacey jumped to her feet.

Elizabeth had just shoved a syringe into Cornell's throat. He was trying to pull out his gun.

"*Cornell!*" Lacey yelled as she surged toward him.

He fell. Elizabeth grabbed his gun. She aimed it at Lacey. "Hang up the phone." The gun was shaking in her grasp.

Cornell wasn't moving.

"He's not dead. Just unconscious. And I don't want to kill him. But if you don't hang up the phone, I will. I will shoot you and him."

Lacey had the phone gripped in one hand. She hadn't been given the chance to grab her own weapon. *Because I didn't suspect Elizabeth.*

"Lacey!" Dex was shouting in her ear. "What's happening? Baby, are you hurt? *Talk to me.*"

Elizabeth moved the gun. She put it against Cornell's temple. "Hang up right now or I will pull the trigger."

Lacey swiped her finger over the phone's screen. She *didn't* end the call, though. Just acted as if she'd hung up, and then she tossed the phone behind her onto the sofa. "Happy now?"

"No. I haven't been happy for a while." Elizabeth didn't move the gun from Cornell's temple. "You care about other people. I saw that when...when you worked with Jonathan and me before."

"You mean when I saved you both?"

"Appearances are deceiving," Elizabeth replied.

"Yes, I'm getting that." Her hand slowly began to inch toward—

"I know you like knives, Lacey. I learned that about you before, too. I sincerely hope you aren't reaching for a knife right now. I don't want to kill this man. His death would be so unnecessary."

Her hand froze. "I don't think you will kill him. I don't think you're a killer. I don't think—"

The gun fired.

***

"Lacey!" Dex roared. He'd been listening the entire time. Hearing every single word.

Elizabeth Radcliff. She'd seemed so innocent. Acted as if she was a real friend to Lacey.

I guess Lacey and I weren't the only ones pretending at this lodge.

He'd been on the elevator from the basement level, racing up to her, with Antony at his side. Antony had given Dex his comm link. Dex was damn grateful he'd had the link on him. While Dex had tried to reach Lacey, Antony had texted more of the team members. He'd ordered them to swarm on the Radcliff suite.

But at the sound of that gunshot...

The world stopped.

Dex waited for more. There had to be more. Lacey—bless her clever heart—had left the phone on so that he could hear what was happening. There should be more after the gunshot. There should be another sound. Someone talking. Something, something!

There was nothing.

"Lacey, baby, I am coming." If the elevator would just *move*.

The doors opened. He'd made it to the lobby. Now he had to take a fucking second elevator ride in order to get to his destination. Sonofabitch. He ran across the lobby. When someone stepped into his path, Dex didn't even slow down. He shoved the man out of the way. Jumped into the next elevator—the one that would take him to the suite he needed. Antony was right on his heels.

"How small is Elizabeth Radcliff?" Antony asked quietly when Dex jabbed and jabbed the buttons on the elevator. "Do you think she could have fit in the air duct and gotten into your suite?"

Yes, she could have fucking fit.

"Her suite is on the same floor as yours. Figured that out, too, and if she—"

Dex drove his fist into the elevator's control panel. "Why the hell isn't this piece of shit moving faster?" He still gripped the phone to his ear. Still hoped that Lacey would say something but—

"Dex." Antony grabbed his hand. "Dex, man, this isn't you. Take a breath. Get that famous control in place—"

"*There is no control without her!*" Guttural. Didn't Antony get that? Lacey gave him his strength. She kept him grounded. Without her, he was shattering.

She can't be hurt.

Can't be dead. No, no, she's not dead. Not Lacey.

Elizabeth just found the phone. She turned it off. Muted it. Something. That's all. That's—

The elevator dinged. Dex rushed into the hallway just as he saw the stairwell door fly open. Two of his team members ran out.

They all headed for the suite. When Dex got to the door, he didn't even slow down. He just lifted his foot and kicked that door in. First fucking try. The door slammed back against the wall. "*Lacey!*"

"Dex!" Antony barked behind him. "This isn't protocol! This isn't you! This isn't—"

Cornell was on the floor. Sprawled with his arms loose at his sides. Dex stumbled toward him, put his hand on Cornell's throat, and felt the thready pulse. "Get him an ambulance, now!"

There was a hole in the carpet next to Cornell. Dex's eyes narrowed. A bullet hole.

That was the shot I heard.

He surged back to his feet. His agents had been searching the suite.

"It's clear," Harmony Skylar said. "No one else is here."

Where the fuck was Lacey? Dex ran through the suite himself. Searched every-damn-where.

"Does he not believe me?" Dex heard Harmony say.

"Just give him space," Antony advised.

Dex raced back to the couch. Lacey's phone was on the couch. Muted. Rage and fear rose, nearly choking him. *Lacey is gone. I was supposed to protect her. Lacey is gone.*

"Um, Dex?"

His head whipped round at Antony's call.

Antony pointed to a knife that was half-way under the couch. "Looks like we have a weapon." Carefully, he eased it out. His breath released in a rush. "No blood on it."

"That's Lacey's gift."

Antony's brow furrowed. "Her what?"

"She was supposed to keep it on her. I told her to keep it close." He surged toward Antony and grabbed him by the shirtfront. "Where did they go?"

"Dex, ease up—"

"You just had the plans for this building. You know this lodge. Tell me, where did they go? Where *would* they go?" His head turned toward Harmony. "You came up the stairs. Did you see anyone in the stairwell?"

"No. But we came from the third floor. If they were going up, not down, then we wouldn't have passed them."

Up. He looked up. The roof. The roof could be an escape route. *But you'd need a chopper.* You'd need someone to fly up and meet you if you were planning to escape via the roof.

Or...

Or you could just go to the roof if you wanted to toss a person over the side. You could let the body crash into the ground if you wanted to send a message.

The way that Heather had been a message when she'd been tossed below.

His gaze flew around the suite. One agent— Ken Rathers—was at Cornell's side. "You stay with him. Don't leave his side for a moment." His stare whipped to Harmony. "I want this whole lodge searched. Every room, every nook. We're looking for Lacey Amari, Elizabeth Radcliff, and Jonathan Radcliff. Elizabeth and Jonathan should be considered extreme threats. Pass the damn word." He stormed for the door. "Antony, on my six. I need you to reach out and contact every—"

Roman appeared in the doorway. A broken cuff dangled from his wrist and blood trickled from a wound near his mouth. "Where...where is my sister?" Roman panted.

Antony gasped. "How the hell did you get up here?"

"Get out of my fucking way so I can find her," Dex blasted at Roman. Then he didn't wait for Roman to get out of his way. He shoved the bastard back. He didn't have time to waste on Roman, and, unlike Antony, he knew exactly how the guy had gotten up there. Roman had fought— and won—a battle against Larry. Not an easy task, and Dex was sure that when Larry regained consciousness, he'd be ready for a rematch. Right then, though, Dex didn't have time to deal with Roman's shit.

Lacey. She was all that mattered.

His feet pounded across the floor as he raced toward the stairwell.

Baby, please hold on. I'm coming.

CHAPTER TWENTY-ONE

"So what's the plan?" Lacey kept her arms at her sides even as her teeth began to chatter. "You're going to make us both freeze to death?"

"*Shut up!*" Elizabeth yelled. She still had the gun in her hand—the gun she'd had shoved into Lacey's back the entire time they climbed the stairs to the roof. In time with her yell, she jabbed the muzzle of the gun deeper into Lacey's back.

The snow was falling on them. Lacey knew that the longer they were out in the cold, the more uncoordinated she'd become. She was going to have to make her move soon. Otherwise...

What does she intend? To shoot me in the back, like Heather? Then to toss me over the edge? Except... "You couldn't have shot Heather. I saw you leave the Whisper Floor." Lacey had been with the other woman. Then Elizabeth had spotted Jonathan—or she'd said she'd spotted Jonathan—and she'd hurried down the steps. Lacey had even seen her in the crowd.

But I never saw Jonathan.

Lacey glanced over her shoulder at Elizabeth. Tears were on Elizabeth's cheeks. "He's the killer. Not you."

"You...you fell for a killer, too, didn't you?" Elizabeth sniffed. "One day, you think your man is perfect. A real-life prince charming. You have this idea that your life will be great. Then you find out the truth."

"Dex isn't a killer!"

"Yes, he is! Jonathan told me he was! You fell for a killer. I fell for one. But we can't change them. No matter how hard we try, you can't touch the darkness inside of them."

Lacey turned slowly toward Elizabeth.

Elizabeth didn't lower her gun. When Lacey turned, the gun pressed right in the middle of her chest. *Okay, not the best position.* "When did you realize that Jonathan was dangerous?"

"I...I..." Then she shook her head. "Where do you think he gets the money? You really believe after all these years there was any *family* money left? The business and estate are a joke. A front. He's been trading secrets that he got from the House of Lords, working deals with people who terrify me. But once you're in, there is no getting out."

"I can help you get out. I have connections. Dex. Eric Wilde. I can—"

The gun jabbed into her. *"You don't understand! I don't want to leave him!"*

"You're hurting me. Why don't you put down the g-gun..." Okay, the cold was starting to get to her. "So we can talk?"

"I like you." Elizabeth nodded. "I do. You're my friend."

Friends don't put guns to the chests of other friends. It should be understood. A given.

"But I love Jonathan. He told me that he needs for you to be a lesson."

She had to make her move. Lacey glanced over Elizabeth's shoulder. Focused in the spot to the right. "Is that what I am, Jonathan?" Lacey called out. "A lesson? Some sort of warning to Dex? Or maybe even to my brother Roman?"

"Jonathan?" Elizabeth turned her head and looked to the right. "You're going to have to kill her because I—" She moved the gun, just a bit, as she realized that Jonathan wasn't actually there.

That small movement was all that Lacey needed. She grabbed Elizabeth's wrist and shoved hard to the left, forcing the gun away from her body in one fast move.

The gun blasted.

But the bullet missed her.

Elizabeth screamed and tried to bring the gun back around. *Not happening. I am way stronger and better trained.* Lacey twisted Elizabeth's wrist, and the gun fell from Elizabeth's hand. Then Lacey head-butted the other woman, sending Elizabeth stumbling back. Elizabeth slipped in the snow and crashed down onto her ass.

Lacey dove for the gun. Grabbed it and came up with it pointed at Elizabeth. "What was in the syringe that you gave Cornell?"

Elizabeth shoved hair out of her face. Her gaze locked on Lacey, and she did not look away as she said, "A sedative. I don't know what exactly. Jonathan gave it to me."

"Let me guess...were you supposed to use the sedative on me? Were you going to knock me out when I came up to your suite with you? Only I didn't come alone. I brought Cornell with me, so you had to—"

"Yes," a deep voice rang out from behind Lacey.

Dammit. Her shoulders stiffened.

"My beautiful bride was supposed to use the syringe on you, but it looks like we had a change of plans."

Lacey stared down at Elizabeth. "Nice job keeping your eyes focused on me. Bet it was hard not to glance his way when you saw him closing in."

Elizabeth scrambled to her feet. "He has a gun pointed at you."

"And I have a gun pointed at *you*." Lacey licked her lips. "So that puts us in a stand-off, doesn't it, Jonathan?" Lacey shouted to Jonathan. "But of course, I have an advantage here."

She could hear the crunch of his footsteps on the snow. "What advantage might that be?"

"My fiancé is coming for me. He'll be bursting onto this roof any moment. Then he'll kick your ass." Yes, she said the last part a little smugly, but she had faith in Dex.

I have faith in Dex. Wow. The full implications of that hit her just as—

Jonathan laughed. "There's no way he can burst onto the roof. Sorry. I took the liberty of securing the door. Putting a little trap in place while you and Elizabeth were having your chat. He tries, and he'll get his ass blown to hell. A small device, but necessary."

Lacey whirled toward him. Her gun pointed at him. His pointed at her. "If you put a bomb on the door," Lacey said, "you won't be able to get off this roof, either."

"Sure, I will." He smiled at her. "I have another means of transport coming."

Of course. The roof. A helicopter had to be on the way.

"The snow fall isn't hard enough to stop my pilot," he assured her. "Hell, with the money I'm paying him, nothing will stop my guy."

Her breath sawed in and out. She didn't even feel the cold any longer. Dex would be coming after her. She knew it. Dex would be rushing up those stairs. Frantic, her gaze flew to the left. *I have to stop him.* Lacey sprang for the door.

And she heard the sound of an explosion.

"*Dex!*" In that instant, he was the only thing she could think about. She hurtled toward him as—

"Got you!" Elizabeth cried out. She grabbed Lacey and drove something sharp into the side of her neck.

Another needle? That...bitch...

Lacey tried to bring up her gun so she could hit Elizabeth in the face but instead of rising, the gun fell from her fingers.

Elizabeth let her go. She yanked the needle and syringe away from Lacey. Tossed them onto the roof.

As she sank to her knees, Lacey stared at the needle. Snowflakes landed on top of it.

"There wasn't a lot in that dosage," Elizabeth was explaining to Jonathan. Her voice sounded distant. Far away. "It was the back-up. Had to use the other dose on some agent with her. But this will knock her out for a few minutes. I couldn't risk her shooting you!'

"You did a great job, Liz. Brilliant."

Brilliant, my ass. You turned the woman into a killer!

Her body slumped onto the roof. She could hear something. A thumping sound. Lacey struggled to keep her eyes open. It was so freaking hard.

Elizabeth's face appeared in front of her. "I'm really sorry things are ending like this for you. At least this way, it won't hurt so much when we kill you." Her hand curled around the gun Lacey had dropped.

Inside, Lacey was screaming. Over and over again, she was calling out Dex's name. But on the outside...

She didn't make a sound.

***

"I thought you were disarming the damn thing!" Roman roared as he swatted the flames on his shirt.

"I did. I bought us five seconds before the explosion so that we could get our asses away from the door. You're the one who didn't move fast enough when I ordered, 'Haul ass!' Antony didn't get so much as a sputter of a flame on him because he moved." The explosion had been designed to kill the person who opened the door to the roof. Controlled impact. Brutal death.

Dex had seen a device like it more than a time or two, and he'd known that waiting for bomb techs to arrive wasn't an option. So he'd decided to trigger the blast.

Only now, there was shit in his way. Sputtering flames. Chunks of the wall and the door that were burning. He kicked those pieces out of the way even as he heard the distant beat of—

"A helicopter," Dex breathed.

When he'd realized that Lacey must be on the roof, Dex had figured Jonathan would be trying to escape via a chopper.

The hell you are.

Dex glared at the flames, then he dove through the wreckage. He barely felt the bite of the fire on his skin as he leapt through the remains of the doorway. He surged forward. "Lacey!"

The chopper was closing in. The wind from its blades sent the snow hurtling toward Dex. He could see Elizabeth and Jonathan—they were standing near the right edge of the roof. And Jonathan...

He's holding Lacey. A Lacey who wasn't moving. Her head slumped back, and her body hung limply in his arms.

"Let her go!" Dex bellowed.

The chopper was growing closer and closer. Soon it would start to descend.

Jonathan laughed and then the twisted fuck jumped onto the edge of the roof. *With Lacey still in his arms.* "Got through the bomb, did you? Guess someone was feeling motivated."

The chopper sent snowflakes swirling around them. The whir of the blades was so loud.

"Get your ass off the roof, Dex," Jonathan commanded. "You, Roman, and whoever that other prick is—get off now or I will drop Lacey to the ground right in front of you."

Roman and Antony had closed in on either side of Dex.

"I will give you whatever you want!" Roman shouted. "Just let her go. *Let her go!*"

Elizabeth was holding a gun. A gun she kept swinging between Roman and Dex. She was shaking, and Dex figured that gun would go off at any moment. "Antony," he said curtly.

"On it," Antony murmured back. He slipped away.

"You're still here, Dex!" Jonathan twisted his body and shoved his arms out—so that Lacey was now beyond the edge. He was holding her over the side of the building. "I don't know how good my grip is." He had to shout over the noise from the approaching helicopter. "You know, what with the helicopter blowing so much wind and snow at me, I might just *drop* her accidentally. So you'd better get the hell out of here."

"The helicopter is a problem," Dex agreed. He lifted his left hand. Tapped his comm link. "Get the chopper out of here."

The chopper immediately started to rise. To angle back to the left. *Away* from the lodge.

Jonathan yanked Lacey closer. "*What?*" His shoes slid over the icy ledge on the roof. "What the fuck?"

The chopper was higher now. Definitely going left.

Elizabeth watched it even as she edged back a few, careful steps.

"Sorry," Dex said, and he wasn't, not even a little bit. "Did you think that was *your* guy piloting the chopper? It wasn't. Mine. Plan B for me. This lodge is pretty remote, so I figured anyone here who wanted to make a quick getaway would try using a chopper. That meant I reached out to every pilot service within a three-hundred-mile radius. Let it be known that I would pay *triple* to take control of any bird that went in the sky and was directed to fly to this location." He still had his weapon aimed at Jonathan even though there was no shot. No shot at all because if he hit Jonathan, the bastard would drop Lacey.

Why is she so limp? Why isn't she moving?

"I was told about this chopper on my way to the roof. One of my agents gave me his comm link so I could talk to my team. So I could get shit done..." Antony had been that agent. Sneaky Antony—he'd almost made his way to Elizabeth's side, and she hadn't even noticed him. She was too intent on gaping as her means of escape vanished. "Antony even managed to get my team to patch me through to the pilot, and all while I was taking care of that piece of shit bomb you left for me."

"*You think you're so fucking smart!*" Jonathan screamed. "But I outsmarted you! I found her first! *Me.* I was the one!"

Dex nodded. "That's why you hired her from Wilde, wasn't it? Because you'd tracked her down. You wanted to see if she was the real deal."

"I knew Roman had a sister. His mother approached my father once, begging for him to help her. I was there. Watching from the shadows. She was crying and pleading. She wanted Roman to come and live with her and his sister."

"*She wanted what?*" Roman's voice choked out.

"But why the hell would my father help her? He had such a good thing going with Gideon Valentino."

Antony attacked. He sprang forward and grabbed Elizabeth. She screamed and fired, but the bullet just shot off into the dark.

"*Let her go!*" Jonathan demanded.

Dex bounded forward. "No. No, you bastard, you aren't giving *any* orders, you hear me? Your chopper is gone. That means your escape route is gone. Your wife is in custody. Antony, get her off the roof, *now*."

Elizabeth was twisting and fighting, but Antony picked her up and carried her away.

"*Elizabeth!*" Jonathan almost followed her. Almost.

"You want her?" Dex taunted. "Climb your ass down. Give me Lacey. Then you can go after Elizabeth. The two of you can be together forever in a nice cell, I'll make sure of it. Who wants to separate love birds?"

"*I'm not going into a cell!*"

Lacey's head moved a little, as if she was starting to stir. He didn't see any blood on her.

"You think I did all of this...to wind up in a cell?" Jonathan shouted.

"I have no fucking clue why you did all of this. I just know you made the worst mistake of your life when you came after her."

Roman shuffled forward. "He did it because of me. Same reason you went after Lacey."

First, I didn't go after her. I damn well fell in love with her.

Lacey's arm had hung loosely a moment before, but it sure looked as if the fingers on her left hand were flexing. *She's waking up.*

"You knew I was a double agent, didn't you, Jonathan? And you were worried that, since you'd done business with my father, I'd have intel I could use against you. You thought I'd screw up your precious world, so you grabbed Lacey. You were going to kill her as what, some warning? Some message for me to keep my mouth shut?"

"Originally, yes, but then I changed my mind. Decided to kill you both. That would send a real message to every bastard out there who thought I could be controlled." Jonathan's head was covered with snowflakes. "Heather was supposed to shoot Lacey, then you. But she wouldn't kill you. I helped Heather drag your body up to the cabin. I helped her set the scene. I knew Dex would bring Lacey with him out there, it was the perfect chance to attack her. But Heather screwed things to hell!"

"You were the boss she had on the Dark Web," Dex said. Like he hadn't already figured that shit out.

"Yes! I was also the guy in the ski mask who helped her haul Roman's sorry ass. She thought I was some hired muscle. Didn't know I was her real boss. She'd knocked him out, but I dosed him to be sure he wouldn't wake up during the transport."

Dex inched forward a little more. *Need to get close enough to grab her. We have to keep the bastard talking. I need to be closer.*

"Because Heather screwed up..." Roman had also crept closer to the ledge. He now stood right beside Dex. "You killed her."

"Well," Dex said before Jonathan could reply, "not like he could risk having her turn on him."

"Of course, not," Roman said. "How foolish."

Jonathan pulled Lacey closer to him.

Dex risked another small advance. "I don't see a weapon on you," Dex noted. "Probably would have been smarter to hold a gun, not an unconscious woman." He lifted his gun. "From this angle, I can shoot you right between the eyes."

Once more, Jonathan laughed. "I've got the best weapon there is! The only weapon that will hurt *you*. Thought you were just using her at first, the way you use everyone. So I tested things...and saw what happened when Heather fell right in front of you."

"Get off the ledge." Dex could hear the rage burning in his own voice. "Bring Lacey down right now." He still wasn't close enough to touch them. Not yet.

Dex took one more step forward.

"You lost it for a moment, didn't you? The great and deceptive Dex. Yes, I know plenty about you. You've been my enemy for years, and you never knew. It's always hard to spot the enemies hiding in plain sight, isn't it?"

Yes, those were the hardest bastards to find.

"When you saw the body hurtling over the balcony and crashing into the floor. You thought it was your Lacey. This time, it will be."

Fuck. Fuck, no. "Why didn't you kill her sooner?" Dex asked. *Have to keep him talking.* From the corner of his eye, he saw Roman slide forward. "You hired Lacey before. Why not kill her then?"

"Because the woman truly saved my life." He glanced down at her. Frowned. "And Elizabeth's. I...I thought maybe a different solution to my Roman problem could be found. After all, I knew where Lacey was. I could get her anytime. I *looked* for another alternative. But there just wasn't one."

"Well, aren't you a fucking saint." Rage burned ever hotter in Dex. "You *thought* about not killing her because she saved your ass. You—"

"I'm not going in a cell! I'm not going to lose the life I have! Killing her wasn't what I wanted, but it doesn't matter any longer! You think I'll go from reigning in the House of Lords to pissing in some pot in a ten by eight cell? No, I'm not. That isn't me. And if I can't have my wife and my life, I'll make sure that *you* don't get any happy ending, either."

He was going to jump. The sonofabitch was going to—

"*No!*" The bellow was torn from Dex's soul. "I'm putting down the gun." He immediately slapped it down near his foot. And crept forward. *I think I'm close enough. I think I can grab her hand.* "I can have your chopper back here in minutes. You let Lacey go, and you fly away. I'll even have Antony bring Elizabeth back to you."

Lacey's fingers fluttered. Did Jonathan see that small movement?

"*I can make this work!*" Dex yelled. He wanted the bastard's attention to stay on him.

Jonathan shook his head. "You'll just hunt me. Because of what I planned to do to her. You won't ever let anyone go who wants to do something bad to Lacey, will you?"

Yes, you prick. I will hunt you. I will kill you. I will make you scream before I send you to hell. "I will let you go," he lied. Lies were easy for him. They always had been. "I won't hunt you. You can disappear. Hell, give me Lacey, and I don't care where you go or what you do."

"Dex…" Roman grated. "What are you doing?"

Jonathan's head jerked toward him. "The same way you didn't care about the people behind the attack on *him?*"

Fucking fuck.

"Because while Roman may not know what happened to those men—to those bastards who broke the agreement and didn't let Roman go even when you traded yourself for him—I know. I know you and your team killed all of the enemies you found on site. Then you tracked down everyone associated to them. You eliminated them all." Jonathan shook his head. "You will promise me anything for her, but we both know that if I give her back to you, you will not stop until I'm dead."

Time seemed to slow down. Dex tried to figure out his options.

Three steps ahead.

He was supposed to be three steps ahead. He'd always been so cocky. So confident. So sure he could manipulate and control everyone and everything.

But Lacey was in Jonathan's arms. Jonathan was on the ledge. If he shot the bastard, Lacey would fall. If he didn't shoot the bastard, *Lacey would fall.*

He'd wanted to protect her. By loving her, he'd put her at even greater risk. "She is my world," he said simply. No lies. Only truth. "I want her back."

"Then come and get her," Jonathan taunted.

Then the bastard stepped off the edge of the roof.

CHAPTER TWENTY-TWO

"She is my world. I want her back."

Lacey heard those wonderful, perfect words right before...

She felt movement. Jonathan—asshole bastard—was going to step off the roof. She knew it. Awareness had come back slowly for her. She'd heard distorted voices. Felt wind and snow blowing against her, then become aware of the tight grip on her body.

By listening to the conversation, she'd realized that Jonathan must have her near the edge of the roof.

And he was threatening to jump. To kill them both.

What can I do? Her body had been so heavy. She'd tried to move and jerk away from him, but all she'd managed was to wiggle a few fingers. All she'd managed—

"Then come and get her," Jonathan said.

Oh, no. No. She knew he was jumping.

Her eyes flew open and she shoved her right hand into his throat, a fast, hard hit designed to close his air way.

He gasped, choked, and his hold on her eased as—

He fell. He was falling. She was falling. They were going over. Her hands flew out as she tried to find—

"Got you."

A hard, powerful hand closed around her wrist. Her left wrist. Then her right. Her body was dangling over the side of the lodge, her feet kicking weakly because she didn't have all of her strength back. When she looked down, she saw—

Jonathan.

No, no, she didn't want to look down at his broken body. Her head whipped up.

Dex. Dex was there.

She wanted to look at him.

He was holding tightly to her left wrist. He'd caught her as she fell. And...

Roman was clinging to her right wrist.

"Pull up," Lacey gasped out because both men seemed frozen. "Pull up now, please."

They yanked her up. As soon as she was over that ledge, Lacey tore free of Roman and locked her arms around Dex. "I knew you were coming."

His arms closed around her. His body was shaking, but she didn't think it was from the cold.

"You went over," he gasped out. "Baby, you were falling."

She shook her head against him. "You caught me."

"Ahem." From Roman. "I helped, too. I hope we can all remember that."

Dex's hold tightened on her. "I fucking love you, Lacey."

She felt her lips curving. She was freezing and terrified, but one thing was clear… "I love you, too, Dex."

He jerked against her. Jolted as if electricity had hit him. He eased back. Tilted her chin up so that he could see her face.

More agents were spilling on the roof. She could see them all from the corner of her eye. They were watching. Waiting.

Dex was staring down at her as if he was having some kind of dream. Or nightmare. She wasn't sure which one.

"You didn't go over the edge. I-I didn't lose you."

"No, I didn't." Or, she had, but he'd brought her back.

"I didn't lose my mind. This is real. You're alive. You're safe. *You are safe with me?*"

He was breaking her heart with the pain in his voice. She caught his head. Brought his mouth down to hers. She was freezing cold and there were snowflakes on her lips, but she kissed him. "I'm real." Another kiss. "And I love you."

His arms flew around her again. An unbreakable grip.

She held him back just as fiercely. *Unbreakable.* Damn straight they were.

***

"You probably want to get the hell out of here as fast as you can," Roman murmured as he shifted nervously in the lodge's suite.

Not the suite that Lacey and Dex had used before. Dex had gotten them moved to another location. She thought it might be the presidential suite or something. And, yes, Dex had assured her that they were getting the hell out of there ASAP. But first...

First, he'd arranged for her to talk privately with her brother.

Several hours had already passed since the madness on the roof. She had no idea what time it was. Didn't care. The drugs were finally gone from her system, and she felt normal again.

Jonathan's body had been taken away. Elizabeth was in custody. The case was over.

"I can't believe he let you out of his sight," Roman added. "I mean, with that death grip he had on you upstairs, I figured he'd be glued to your side."

Death grip. "Let's try to avoid the death references for the moment, shall we?" Because whenever she lowered her guard, the image of Jonathan's twisted body hurtled through her mind. Lacey walked toward the fireplace and extended her shaking fingers toward the flames. "And Dex isn't far away, I can promise you that." Her head turned toward Roman. "That's a new bruise under your eye." She knew Larry had been stationed at the door of her current suite. Dex had already told her about *how* Roman had come to be on the roof in time for the takedown and rescue scene. "Guess you got a payback hit, hmm?"

Roman rubbed his hand over his jaw. "It was worth it. Getting up there to you—it would have been worth anything." His hand fell. "Despite what you may believe, I'm not a total bastard. I've done plenty of things that I'm not proud of. But I've also done some good. I've—"

"I would like to get to know you. Dex told me that you were a person worth knowing."

"He did? When?"

"Five minutes ago. Right before he asked if I wanted to see you or if I wanted to make you vanish from the face of the planet." An absolute truth. So very Dex.

Roman blinked. "And you went for option A?"

"Yes."

"Thanks for that."

"You did grab my wrist on the roof."

"I wasn't going to let my sister die."

Sister. She paced toward him. Studied him. "I'm guessing that isn't your natural hair color?"

"Or my eye color. Contacts. Not my native accent, either. With the right tricks, I've been able to become dozens of different people. I'm a walking, talking chameleon."

Her head tilted back.

"Our father was evil to his core. Our mom...she was right to leave him. To keep you away. I just..." He stopped.

But she knew what he'd been going to say.

I just wish she'd taken me with her.

Lacey didn't know why her mom had made the decisions that she had. But she was sure she would learn more. And she'd use her family to help her with that discovery.

Her family...*Eric Wilde. Ben Wilde.* She wasn't going to sneak around and use their resources. She'd tell them everything.

Her family...*Dex*. Dex was family. He held her heart. Their engagement had started out as only pretend, and they'd only been together for such a short time, but she couldn't imagine her life without him. He would have her back. She knew it. He would also tear the world apart to find the intel that she needed. That was just her Dex.

Her family...*Roman*. Staring down at her with so much desperate hope and longing on his face. "You can come with me," Lacey heard herself say.

He swallowed.

"Come into my world," she invited him, and she meant the invitation. "Step away from the shadows. Leave whatever life you lived before— leave it behind. Everyone can have a fresh start. Including us."

"I've got so many enemies out there. I brought Jonathan to you. I did this." He shook his head. "You need to stay far, far away from me. I will just—"

"I thought you were a chameleon. That you could become anyone." She wasn't going to give up on him. "Become someone new. Come into my life." It was time for him to leave the darkness behind. It clung to him so heavily.

"What will I do if I'm not working in the shadows? I'm not really cut out for much else."

"Well, as to that..." She offered him a smile. "Turns out, you have more family than you probably know. We have a cousin who owns a protection business, and I bet he can find just the right job for you."

"Provided your fiancé doesn't throw me into one of his deep, dark holes somewhere."

The door opened behind him. Dex strode inside.

"Speak of the devil," Roman muttered.

"I gave you five whole minutes," Dex snapped back. "Five minutes alone. I've been going out of my mind while I waited for you. Lacey was hanging over the edge of a freaking building tonight. Do you know what that does to a man's self-control?" His gaze flew to Lacey. Warmed. He released a slow breath. "I just needed to see you again. If you want five more minutes, I can go back outside."

"I'll be damned." Roman turned toward him. "That wasn't some BS up on the roof. You weren't just playing Jonathan in order to distract him so that I could get close."

Dex stalked toward Lacey. "Is that what you thought I was doing?"

"It's what I thought *we* were doing," Roman replied. "We've played that game before. One distracts, the other acts. Especially when you put down your gun and offered him anything." Disbelief and shock tinged his words. "You were dead serious, weren't you?"

Dex stopped beside Lacey. "Dead serious." He smiled at her. "I would do anything for you."

Her heartbeat quickened.

Dex's smile slipped as he angled his head to see Roman. "And I would do *anything* to protect her. So you try to pull any BS that hurts her, you stray from the line of the straight and narrow for even a second, you look sideways at her and—"

"You didn't leave me with those bastards all those years ago, did you? You really did trade yourself for me?"

Dex didn't reply.

Roman cleared his throat. Focused on Lacey once more. "You should marry him. I mean, for real. He's a good man."

"Did you strangle on those words?" Dex wanted to know. "Because they sounded a little painful."

"He'll protect you. He'll fight for you. And even I can see that he loves you." Roman backed away. "Dex, when you're ready to deal, so am I. Any terms you want. I'll give you all the information I have." He hurried for the door.

"Deep down—like, way deep down—you're a good man, too, Roman." Dex reached for Lacey's hand as he said those words.

Roman stilled.

"To be clear, though, I don't just want information from you. I want my fucking friend back."

Roman glanced over at him.

"I also want Lacey to have her brother. Don't slip off and try to lose yourself in missions that turn deadly anymore. Try living a normal life here in the US."

"Never been real good on normal."

"I can help you," Lacey said. This mattered. He mattered. She'd never forget how he'd looked when he was hanging over the side of the lodge, his eyes frantic as he and Dex hauled her back up. "You pulled me back from the edge. Now it's my turn to help you."

He stared at her a moment. Cleared his throat. "Technically, you were already over the edge."

As crazy as it was, his comment made her want to smile. "I can see why you and Dex were once friends."

His gaze slid to Dex. "We still are."

They were?

"You treat my sister well, Dex, or I will kick your ass." With that, Roman resumed his march for the door.

"Do I look scared?" Dex asked. He seemed curious. "Lacey, do I?"

She stared up at him. "No, love. You don't." In fact, the only time she'd ever seen him look scared...

Was when he was hanging over the edge of the roof, pulling me up.

The door clicked closed behind Roman.

Alone. With Dex.

He slowly exhaled, as if he'd been waiting for the chance to be alone with her. As she stared up at his face, Lacey saw his mask begin to slowly slip away. The cockiness vanished. The cool curve of his lips faded. The gleam in his eyes warmed even more.

And...

"*God, I was fucking terrified.*" He pulled her into his arms and held her tightly. "I kept trying to get closer and closer to the ledge. I needed to get close enough to grab you. I just needed to grab you. And I was right there—" A shudder worked over the length of his body. "Right there when he stepped off the edge."

Her arms wrapped around his waist. "You caught me. I didn't fall."

"I wasn't letting go. I will never let go."

She could feel the frantic beat of his heart. Or maybe that was her heart beating so wildly. Her head tipped back and she gazed up at him. "Neither will I."

His gaze searched hers. "I need you."

"I'm right here."

"It's...I'm shaking apart. I'm scared because I keep imagining that I didn't get to you in time. I want to rip Jonathan apart. I want—"

"He's dead," she said softly. "And guess what I want?" She didn't want rage and fear. "I want you."

His eyelids flickered. "Baby, my control—"

"I don't want control. Because I'm scared and angry, too. Because I want to feel the way that *only* you can make me feel." She bit her lower lip. "How long until that private plane of yours is supposed to be here to get us?" She knew he'd made arrangements for it earlier.

He kissed her. His lips took hers, and his tongue thrust into her mouth, and she took that to mean...

They had enough time. Even if they didn't, she was sure Dex would just make the plane wait.

He scooped her into his arms. She locked her legs around his hips even as her hands gripped his shoulders. The scene on the roof before had been a nightmare, but they'd survived. She'd been absolutely helpless. So weak on that roof.

The EMTs had checked her out after Dex had gotten her back downstairs. The drug had slowly passed from her system, and the doctor who'd arrived had given her the all-clear. But while the drug had been controlling her, she'd been so weak. A doll trapped in Jonathan's arms.

She didn't like being weak. That wasn't who she was. She liked to fight. She liked to battle. She liked to kick ass just as much as Dex did.

But even as she'd come back to consciousness in Jonathan's arms, she'd heard Dex's voice and she'd known...

"I trusted you," Lacey said against his mouth. Then she bit his lip because it was ever so bitable. "I knew you'd save me."

His head lifted even as he walked forward and pinned her against the nearest wall. Her legs stayed locked around him. His hands were tight on her hips. "Baby..."

"Just like I'd save you." She meant that with all her being. "I would do anything to save you."

He kissed her again. A hot brush of his mouth over hers. "You did save me."

No, she hadn't. He'd been—

"You'll probably never realize how much you've done for me. But believe me, Lacey, *you saved me.*"

Those words sounded *almost* as good as when he told her that he loved her. Oh, hell, they *did* sound that good. She kissed him again. Open-mouthed, deep, desperate.

They somehow managed to shove aside most of their clothing. A messy, jerking stripping. And he even got her to a bed. Then he was sliding those warm, strong hands of his all over her body. He was dipping his fingers between her legs. Making her arch up toward him. Making her breath catch and her heart race—*"Dex."*

He looked up at her. Desire had turned his face savage.

Her fingers trailed over his chest. Down, down to his waist. To the thick cock that bobbed toward her.

She wanted to taste him. "Stretch out on the bed for me?"

His eyes narrowed. "Lacey, I will not last. I need you too much."

"You don't have to last. I want you. I want to taste you."

His pupils seemed to swallow the gray of his eyes. He slid his fingers from her—one more stroke that had her gasping—and then he was stretching out on the bed. She straddled him. Caught his hands when they reached for her, and she pushed them back on either side of his head.

Her fingers trailed over his wrists. The faint scars there. He thought that she'd saved him? He was wrong. Dex had been saving the world long before she came along.

But from here on out, she'd be helping him with that job.

She pressed a kiss to his chest, right over his heart. Then she made her way to his nipple. Sucking. Flicking with her tongue.

"Lacey."

She took her time. Forget the plane. They deserved this.

Down, down, she slowly went. His cock shoved toward her, and she blew a soft, sensual breath over that heavy length.

His dick lifted even more, as if begging for her mouth.

And since her mouth wanted *him*...

She parted her lips and took him inside. She sucked and licked and tasted the faint saltiness on her tongue. Lacey loved the way he tasted. Loved the way he felt. She was getting more and more turned on with every stroke of her mouth over him and—

She was on her back. He was between her thighs. His cock pressed at the entrance to her body.

"No...condom..." His eyes blazed. "Give me a second...give me..."

"I'm on birth control. I'm clean."

"So the fuck am I—I mean, shit, I'm not on birth control but—"

His ragged words pulled a laugh from her. She was on the hungry edge of desire, but she was able to laugh and it just felt great. He felt great. Right.

Her hips surged up against him. "What are you waiting for?"

He sank into her. Filled her completely.

There was no more talking. Or laughing. There was just the hard, frantic drive toward release. Faster and faster. Rougher and rougher. Her nails scraped over his side. His thrusts shook the bed.

When she came, the pleasure burst through her. Her body buckled, and she held him even tighter.

And when he came, she could see the pleasure on his face. Flashing in his eyes, slackening his jaw and—

"*Fucking...love you...Always...*"

She could even hear the pleasure in his voice. Hear the pleasure and the love.

Lacey held him tight and knew...*Dex, I will never let you go.*

She'd found what she'd been searching for so long. Not just family, but a place where she belonged. She belonged with Dex. He belonged with her.

Her hand slid down to the bedding. The diamond ring gleamed.

One day, their engagement wouldn't be pretend. Lacey understood this with certainty. One day, it would be real. As real as the love she felt for him.

EPILOGUE

"I can't believe she said yes." Eric Wilde frowned suspiciously at Dex.

Dex adjusted his tie. The tux was a little tight in the shoulders, but it would do. A quick glance in the mirror told him that he looked semi-presentable.

Good enough.

"I mean, I warned her. Told her that there were guys out there a whole lot less shady than you..."

Now he glowered at Eric. "Seriously? You understand that *this* is my wedding day, too? Are you trying to piss me off?"

Eric shrugged. "Are you getting pissed?"

"Look, I get it. You think I'm dangerous and manipulative and that I somehow tricked her into marrying me."

"You *are* dangerous and manipulative. And *didn't* you trick her into marrying you?"

"I may have used some faint trickery in the first engagement, but this last one has been completely real." He and Lacey had dated for six months. *Six months.* He'd been nearly going insane because he wanted her legally tied to him. He wanted permanence with Lacey.

He wanted everything with her.

"She loves you," Eric noted. His voice was very careful. Considering.

Dex adjusted the tie once more, even though it didn't need adjusting. "Good to know. Because I'm insane for her." A quick glance at his watch told him that he needed to get moving. *It's time. Finally, it's time.* He headed for the door.

Eric moved into his path. "We're going to be family."

"Aw, is this your way of welcoming me? Come here, bring it in." He grabbed Eric in a quick bear hug. "Feel better now?" He'd made the guy his best man. What else did Eric want?

"Let go, Dex."

Smothering a smile, he did. "You just can't admit you like me, can you? And it's hurtful since I've thought we were best friends for like...ever." He made his way toward the door.

"Lacey told me to look behind your mask."

Dex exhaled. *He's Lacey's family. You have to play nicely with—*

"I told her that I already had. I know you're a good man, Dex, and I think you'll make my cousin very happy."

Dex spun toward him. "Then what is all this grilling about?"

Eric smiled at him. "Because messing with you is fun?"

What?

Eric winked. "Welcome to the family."

"Between you and Roman, I have the feeling this family will exhaust me." But the exhaustion would be worth it.

Having Lacey? She was worth any price that he had to pay.

***

He could barely breathe as she walked down the aisle. She was wearing some flowing white dress—looked like it was made of silk—and her thick, dark hair tumbled around her shoulders. She smiled as she came toward him. Roman held one of her hands. In the other hand, she gripped a bouquet of red roses.

Eric's wife, Piper, served as Lacey's matron of honor, and Eric—he was standing all tall and proud as Dex's best man.

Eric leaned toward him and whispered, "Breathe before you pass out. That shit will be embarrassing."

So he was able to take a breath. Then Lacey was in front of him. He realized that she'd been staring at him during that whole, endlessly long walk down the aisle.

She pulled her hand from Roman's. Took Dex's. Their fingers twined together.

"Hi," he said. Random. Inane.

Her smile stretched.

And Roman lingered. Why was he lingering? Then, as if on cue, Roman mumbled, "You don't have to do this."

Seriously? What the hell? What was with this family? Dex glowered. *Not cool.*

But Lacey laughed. "It's not like he's blackmailing me."

Dammit. Dex could feel heat stinging his cheeks.

Her fingers tightened around his. "Dex is what I want. Now and always." Then she glanced toward the watchful pastor. "So, not to rush or anything, but when is the part where I get to say..."

"I do," Dex finished.

He bent his head and kissed her.

"I do," Lacey murmured against his mouth. "I definitely do."

***

Dex had dance moves. Who the hell would have thought that? Roman stood in the corner and couldn't help but smile as he saw Dex whirl Lacey around the dance floor. Her laughter rang out—strong and clear and so happy.

She loved Dex.

Roman had no doubt that Dex loved her.

He'd still given Lacey the out option at the altar, though, because wasn't that what brothers were for? A reliable guy who would have an escape plan at the ready?

In the months since the nightmare in Colorado, he'd grown close to Lacey. Dex had helped them both. With Antony Kyle pulling up his tech magic, they'd even managed to locate a long forgotten nanny who'd cared for Roman when he'd been a toddler. A woman who remembered his mother all too well.

And how devastated she'd been when Gideon Valentino had refused to let her have her son. The woman had known that Roman's mother would come back over the years, that the only reason she kept returning to Gideon was so that she could have glimpses of her son. Gideon had never let her talk to him—because, yes, he'd been a fucking twisted prick—but she'd been able to see Roman from a distance.

She'd lied to Gideon. Falsified DNA tests and said that Lacey wasn't his child. Thanks, again, to Dex and Antony, they'd even learned that Jason Amari had been in on the subterfuge He'd met Elora while she was pregnant with Lacey. Had married her. Had fallen in love with her.

And he'd loved Lacey as if she was his own child.

To Lacey, Roman knew Jason Amari *would* always be her father.

There were more pieces to discover in the puzzle that was his life, Roman knew that. But he'd learn everything in time. He had people helping him now. People he could depend upon.

And he even had his friend back. His friend, his enemy. Dex had been both over the years. Now he had a new name.

Brother-in-law.

Yes, he'd be needing a few drinks to deal with that one.

Roman snagged a champagne flute from a passing waiter.

"So..." Eric drawled. "Are you just going to leave me hanging?"

His cousin. More family. More people trying to pull him out of the dark.

"I made the job offer several weeks ago, and you haven't answered me yet," Eric continued as he came to a stop near Roman. "What do you think about joining the team at Wilde?"

He drained the flute. Another crossroad was before him. He knew it. If he took this path, everything would change and...

Lacey was laughing again. So was Dex.

They looked so happy.

Can I ever be that way?

His grip tightened on the stem of the glass. "Screw it. Yes, yes, I'm in."

Eric slapped a hand on his shoulder. "You won't regret this."

"No, but you might."

Eric laughed. "Don't worry. I've got just the partner to train you."

To *train* him?

"You'll absolutely love her."

"Highly doubtful."

Eric just grinned.

THE END

A NOTE FROM THE AUTHOR

Thank you for taking the time to read SAY I DO. I hope you enjoyed reading tricky Dex's story. He's a character who demanded his own HEA, and I had such a fun time bringing him in to the "Wilde" world. As you can tell by the ending of SAY I DO...it appears that Roman might just be brought into that world, too... (And maybe Antony? What do you think?)

If you'd like to stay updated on my releases and sales, please join my newsletter list.

https://cynthiaeden.com/newsletter/

Again, thank you for reading SAY I DO.

Best,
Cynthia Eden
cynthiaeden.com

ABOUT THE AUTHOR

Cynthia Eden is a *New York Times, USA Today, Digital Book World*, and *IndieReader* best-seller.

Cynthia writes sexy tales of contemporary romance, romantic suspense, and paranormal romance. Since she began writing full-time in 2005, Cynthia has written over one hundred novels and novellas.

Cynthia lives along the Alabama Gulf Coast. She loves romance novels, horror movies, and chocolate.

For More Information

- *cynthiaeden.com*
- *facebook.com/cynthiaedenfanpage*

HER OTHER WORKS

Wilde Ways

- Protecting Piper (Book 1)
- Guarding Gwen (Book 2)
- Before Ben (Book 3)
- The Heart You Break (Book 4)
- Fighting For Her (Book 5)
- Ghost Of A Chance (Book 6)
- Crossing The Line (Book 7)
- Counting On Cole (Book 8)
- Chase After Me (Book 9)
- Say I Do (Book 10)

Dark Sins

- Don't Trust A Killer (Book 1)
- Don't Love A Liar (Book 2)

Lazarus Rising

- Never Let Go (Book One)
- Keep Me Close (Book Two)
- Stay With Me (Book Three)
- Run To Me (Book Four)
- Lie Close To Me (Book Five)
- Hold On Tight (Book Six)
- Lazarus Rising Volume One (Books 1 to 3)
- Lazarus Rising Volume Two (Books 4 to 6)

Dark Obsession Series

- Watch Me (Book 1)
- Want Me (Book 2)
- Need Me (Book 3)
- Beware Of Me (Book 4)
- Only For Me (Books 1 to 4)

Mine Series

- Mine To Take (Book 1)
- Mine To Keep (Book 2)
- Mine To Hold (Book 3)
- Mine To Crave (Book 4)
- Mine To Have (Book 5)
- Mine To Protect (Book 6)
- Mine Box Set Volume 1 (Books 1-3)
- Mine Box Set Volume 2 (Books 4-6)

Bad Things

- The Devil In Disguise (Book 1)
- On The Prowl (Book 2)
- Undead Or Alive (Book 3)
- Broken Angel (Book 4)
- Heart Of Stone (Book 5)
- Tempted By Fate (Book 6)
- Wicked And Wild (Book 7)
- Saint Or Sinner (Book 8)
- Bad Things Volume One (Books 1 to 3)
- Bad Things Volume Two (Books 4 to 6)
- Bad Things Deluxe Box Set (Books 1 to 6)

Bite Series

- Forbidden Bite (Bite Book 1)
- Mating Bite (Bite Book 2)

Blood and Moonlight Series

- Bite The Dust (Book 1)
- Better Off Undead (Book 2)
- Bitter Blood (Book 3)
- Blood and Moonlight (The Complete Series)

Purgatory Series

- The Wolf Within (Book 1)
- Marked By The Vampire (Book 2)
- Charming The Beast (Book 3)
- Deal with the Devil (Book 4)
- The Beasts Inside (Books 1 to 4)

Bound Series

- Bound By Blood (Book 1)
- Bound In Darkness (Book 2)
- Bound In Sin (Book 3)
- Bound By The Night (Book 4)
- Bound in Death (Book 5)
- Forever Bound (Books 1 to 4)

Other Romantic Suspense

- Never Gonna Happen
- One Hot Holiday
- Secret Admirer
- First Taste of Darkness
- Sinful Secrets
- Until Death
- Christmas With A Spy

CPSIA information can be obtained
at www.ICGtesting.com
Printed in the USA
FSHW021003191021
85577FS